SUN, RUM, AND STOLEN FUNDS

RAYMOND PATRICK

Copyright © 2025 by Raymond Patrick

All rights reserved.

No part of this book may be reproduced in any form or by any electronic or mechanical means, including information storage and retrieval systems, without written permission from the author, except for the use of brief quotations in a book review.

Ebook: ISBN: 979-8-9936497-0-2

Print book: ISBN: 979-8-9936497-1-9

The characters and stories in this book are entirely fictional—well, mostly. Some tales may sail dangerously close to the truth for a sentence or two before veering off into far more entertaining waters. Any resemblance to real people, places, or events is purely coincidental, circumstantial, or the result of one too many happy hours. A few support characters did not want their names changed – you know who you are.

To my mom, Judith Ann, 1948 – 2024

PROLOGUE

March 2022 - Chicago

Jessica walked up the passerelle onto Antonio Campanelli's yacht, the late afternoon sun glinting off the polished chrome rails. The first warm day of spring had pulled half the city to the lakefront, though the breeze still carried a trace of winter sharp enough to raise goosebumps on her bare legs. She ignored it. A little discomfort was worth the entrance.

She wore a crisp white blouse—tight and deliberately unbuttoned just low enough to draw eyes—and a black skirt that was barely long enough to avoid being called a mini. Each click of her heels on the gangway rang out against the quiet slap of water against the hull, the sound announcing her before she even reached the deck.

In most yachting circles, her full-sleeve tattoo alone would've kept her off the guest list, let alone the crew roster. But Campanelli liked that look. Jessica wore it like armor.

At the top of the gangway, she was met by a large, silent man with no name and no neck—just muscle, sunglasses, and a permanent scowl. She looked around for Campanelli but didn't see him.

Sighing, she already knew what was coming. The pat-down. Always extra. Always unnecessary. Like she could hide anything in an outfit this snug.

"Arms up," the man said flatly.

Jessica raised her arms and rolled her eyes as he began the ritual—hands over the barely-there skirt, fingers trailing a little too slow along her thighs. Then up, across the blouse, methodical and thorough around the cleavage that—sure, fine—could technically conceal a weapon or two.

As he finished, she lowered her arms and said, dry as dust, "I'm not sure who should be tipping who here."

The man cracked a grin and waved her through.

Jessica didn't return it.

She preferred her usual domain: three rows deep at the bar, everybody shouting over the music, ice flying, bottles clinking, pure chaos. But it was *her* chaos. On her side of the bar, things were safe. Organized. Efficient. She wasn't just good—she was fast. Legendary, even.

That's how Campanelli found her.

November 2021 - Downtown Chicago, Friday Afternoon, Campanelli meets Jessica

The bar was slammed. A wall of office workers had descended like a tidal wave, desperate to drink themselves into the weekend. Voices rose in chaotic chorus, orders flying from three rows deep.

Behind the bar, Jessica was in her element—fast, fierce, untouchable. Her hands moved with muscle memory: shaking, pouring, garnishing, flipping bottles like weapons.

A finely dressed man stepped up to the bar. He didn't push—he didn't have to. The crowd seemed to part for him, instinctively.

He stood still, eyes on Jessica. She met his gaze with easy composure, waiting him out. After a beat, she raised her eyebrows and tilted her head slightly, open-mouthed like, *Well?*

Just as she turned her attention to the next customer—done waiting—he finally spoke.

"Manhattan... please."

She spun into action. Rye. Vermouth. Bitters. Stir. Strain. Cherry. She flung a coaster onto the bar like a playing card and set the drink down with flair.

He smiled. "Why don't you smile?"

Jessica paused, then slowed, turning back to him like he was the only man in the room. She leaned in just enough to give him a better view —white blouse, inked arm, full eye contact.

Campanelli looked very pleased with himself.

Jessica smiled, finally. But it was the kind that meant *you think you're clever, don't you?*

"So, what do you do?" she asked, sweetly flirtatious.

He sipped the Manhattan. "Oh, a little of this, a little of that. I'm usually in front of a computer. Spreadsheets. Business dashboards. Meetings. I have a lot of... endeavors."

Jessica batted her lashes once. "So, when you're in front of your computer, checking your spreadsheets and dashboards or whatever..."

She changed tone mid-sentence—dropping the sweetness for full-volume sarcasm. "Do you sit there and *smile* at it like a f*cking idiot all day long?"

Then she turned sharply, already halfway to the next customer.

Campanelli blinked—and then grinned. Nobody talked to him like that. He liked her immediately.

Back to March 2022

As Jessica stepped past the silent muscle at the top of the gangway, Campanelli descended the stairs from the flybridge.

"Ciao, Bella!" he said, greeting her with a single kiss on the cheek.

"Mr. Campanelli, so good to see you," she replied with practiced charm. "It's my understanding we'll be having four guests today, sir?"

"Yes—just the three ladies and little Gorgi."

"Very good, sir." Jessica moved behind the bar and got to work, already slipping into bartender autopilot.

She hated this job. Hated the leering guards, the phony charm, the heavy air of money and danger. But the pay was impossible to walk away from—one afternoon of pouring drinks for Campanelli equaled a full week of hard-earned bar wages and tips back in the city.

Campanelli had always been flirty, but never crossed the line. Jessica had served drinks to his guests, even his wife once or twice. She knew what this was about—it wasn't about cocktails. It was about control. Campanelli liked having beautiful people in his orbit. He *loved* knowing that Jessica, with all her sass and defiance, was only *barely* under his control.

That 'barely' was what thrilled him.

She opened a case of Tito's and started stocking the bar. As she reached in to pull out the last bottle, her fingers brushed something cold and metallic at the bottom of the box.

An earpiece and a thumb drive.

She slipped the earpiece in with a subtle brush of her hair.

"I don't want to do this," she mumbled under her breath, checking glassware and scanning her liquor lineup like nothing was out of place.

"You're doing great," said the voice in her ear. Calm. Rehearsed. "It's going to be easy. You've got this."

"Got the thumb drive," she whispered.

"Okay, great. You know what to do. Just wait for your opening. Just like we practiced a hundred times."

Jessica kept moving, efficient and fluid. She loaded cabinets, stocked mixers, and arranged the bottles perfectly in the well. She mixed up a Manhattan and brought it to Campanelli, who was now lounging on the aft deck couch, laptop balanced on his knees, feet on the footstool.

As she leaned in to set the drink on the coaster, Campanelli glanced up from the screen—just long enough to enjoy the view.

"Anything else, Mr. Campanelli?" she asked sweetly.

"Not right now," he replied, taking the glass. "I think I'll take this down with me. Guests should be here any minute."

He stood and moved toward the staircase, laptop still open on the footstool.

Jessica walked behind the bar, grabbed a bar rag, and turned abruptly, hustling back to the spot where his drink had left a wet ring on the end table. Her heart pounded.

Now.

She moved quickly, glancing around—no one in sight.

In one smooth motion, she bent and inserted the thumb drive into the laptop.

"I got it before the screen-saver kicked in. I adapted," she muttered, watching the screen.

25%. 56%. 78%. Complete.

She yanked the thumb drive out, slipped it into her apron, and turned—then froze.

She forgot to *actually* wipe the table.

Doubling back, she quickly ran the rag over the surface, just as no-name muscle rounded the corner.

Jessica gave him a casual nod and turned back toward the bar.

"Nice work," the voice in her ear said. "Make sure to ditch the drive, in case they search you again."

CHAPTER ONE

March 2022 - St. Thomas, US Virgin Islands
Happy Hour

In the distance, a long horn blast rumbled through the air, jolting Ray from his brief slumber. He opened one eye, squinting against the radiant Caribbean afternoon sun, its brilliance accentuating the tranquility around him. He exhaled slowly, savoring the feeling of waking up on the water, far from the chaos he had once called life, traded for a new kind of chaos. As he raised his head, trying to get his bearings, three quick horn blasts followed, signaling the departure of the three o'clock ferry to St. John.

He stretched his arms and took a moment to absorb the beauty of Vessup Bay. A satisfied grin spread across his face as he realized he was alone. A turtle popped its head above the water, taking three breaths before vanishing again to the grassy bottom. "Must be nice," he muttered. No bills, no emails, no broken promises to clean up. Just instinct and the rhythm of the ocean. Maybe in another life, he'd come back as a turtle. That wouldn't be so bad.

The turquoise waters blended seamlessly with the deeper blues that stretched towards St. John on the horizon. He inhaled deeply, tasting the salt air and rain's humid promise. The earthy hues of the rocky point, and the blue water crashing against the rocks in a gentle explosion of white mist, rising up to the lush green fauna clinging to the side of the cliff. It was all so familiar, yet never quite the same. Even after all this time, the islands still had the power to catch him off guard, to remind him why he had chosen this life in the first place.

Above St. Thomas, the sky remained a tranquil blue, while darker clouds loomed ominously over St. John, creeping ever closer. A shift in the weather was inevitable.

St. John lies three miles from St. Thomas, separated by Pillsbury Sound. Despite the locals with 'St John Tunnel Pass' stickers on their island cars, no bridge, no tunnel. Only options -- a human ferry or a car ferry, or Kenny Chesney's private yellow helicopter, or a private charter boat like Ray's catamaran. Ray looked toward St. John, studying the clouds forming. When St. John is covered in a gray veil, the rain will soon make its way west to Red Hook. Ray looked to the north, checking the other visible land. From his mooring in the bay, he could see the top of Thatch Cay to the northwest, then Grass and Mingo and Lovango Cays. Past Lovango, farther north, was Jost Van Dyke, part of the British Virgin Islands. Jost was getting some rain, but that had little bearing on St. Thomas weather with the dominant Easterly trade winds.

Happy Hour in the Virgin Islands starts at three o'clock and runs until six. He hoped to reach land before the impending rain swept across the Sound. Despite the looming weather, Ray was determined to honor his commitment to meet a friend... unless it pours, then a change of plans is expected. Adaptability was a hallmark of island life, where unexpected occurrences like sudden rain showers, power outages, or traffic snarls caused by visiting cruise ships were all just normal parts of island time. As St. John gradually disappeared from view behind a gray veil, Ray hesitated, contemplating whether to proceed. *Maybe I should bail,* he thought, but then shook his head. *Bob would give me so much shit. No respectable sailor would let a little rain prevent the dinghy ride to shore.* His sense of obligation to his friend prevailed, reinforced by the amount of harassment he would take.

Ray hastily changed into a white linen button-down shirt, his customary attire for the island heat. Still trying to beat the rain, he quickly descended the aft stairs of his catamaran, hopped into his dinghy floating off the stern of *Purrfection*. Ray pulled the engine starter cord and darted toward shore, a quick downwind ride with the waves.

He dipped his hand in the ocean and ran some salt water through his hair and splashed it on his face to freshen up, sailor-style, struggling to remember the last time he had a fresh water shower. He smirked at the thought, shaking the water from his fingers. *Maybe I should actually shower*, he mused, then smirked. *Nah, if the ladies don't like a little salt, they aren't for me anyway.*

Just as Ray approached the dock, the rain commenced, a gentle drizzle reminiscent of water sprinkling from a low-flow shower head. He sighed. *Of course.* A good rinse, perhaps overdue. The thought made him chuckle. Perhaps way overdue. With raindrops trickling down his Aviators, he secured his dinghy to the railing, tossed his flip-flops onto the dock, and hopped ashore.

The bar was only a hundred steps away, but already the downpour had begun in earnest. He shook his head, half-laughing. *Guess Mother Nature decided I needed a shower after all.*

Making his way to the bar, Ray met up with his old pal and Happy Hour companion, Bud Light Bob. A legendary figure in Red Hook, Bob was a 72-year-old bachelor and tennis teaching pro from New Hampshire, easily recognizable by his slender frame, diminutive stature, and mostly bald head. With his unassuming appearance, Bob's warmth and charm endeared him to everyone he met, from tourists to locals to the bar staff. Despite battling colon cancer, he maintained his daily tennis regimen and Happy Hour routine, a testament to his resilience.

Bob's Happy Hour ritual never changed—Bud Light in a bottle, every time. He was supposed to catch the 3 o'clock ferry from St. John to Red Hook, which meant an even longer walk through the rain than Ray had. Yet there he was, already perched at the bar, looking suspiciously dry. Ray considered giving him shit about sneaking in under an umbrella, but Bob jumped in anxiously before he could even take a seat.

"Well, is she gone?" Bob inquired, skipping any kind of greeting, his trademark grin accompanying his straightforward New England manner.

"She's gone somewhere, yes. Off my boat at least. Took her to shore this morning. Then I took a very peaceful nap." Ray responded matter-of-factly. The arrival or departure of crew members to or from *Purrfection* was a common occurrence. However, this particular departure had been notably eventful.

The question of new crew was inevitable. Sailing solo was an option, but not a practical one, especially on a boat the size of *Purrfection*. With a 51-foot catamaran—49 feet when paying for a marina—Ray needed an extra set of hands. Finding crew was easy; finding the right crew was nearly impossible. The transient nature of sailors meant people were always looking to hitch a ride, some with experience, others with nothing but enthusiasm. His references were solid, and he had his usual methods of recruitment, from sailing forums to crew networking groups. Still, the right fit was always elusive.

"What's next? Sticking around or sailing off?" Bob fished.

"I have a very interesting potential charter. I'm not 100% sure it's legit yet, but if it is, it's going to be another crazy adventure. Just say 'YES,' Bob, that's my motto."

"Oh yeah, that sounds promising. Make some money and have the adventure. Boy, I sure envy your life, Ray." Bob said in his playful, snarky New England tone. He leaned in with curiosity. "So what's this project?"

"I've always wanted to use this line.... It's top-secret, Bob. I could tell you, but I'd have to kill you." Ray replied in all seriousness. After an appropriate pause, he continued, "... or in reality, somebody else probably would do it. It wouldn't be ME doing the killing. I'm a lover, not a fighter. Now that I think of it, not sure why they'd kill you.... They'd probably kill me. I'm not even sure who 'they' are yet, but 'they' said keep it quiet. I better shut up." They both laughed at the absurdity of the statements, but given the crazy things that happen in the islands, Bob knew it was probably partially true. Probably.

Ray tended to over-share, particularly when under the influence. But in this instance, his first drink hadn't even hit the bar yet. Suddenly, magically, a tequila and water with lime showed up in front of him. The lime had been squeezed in and discarded. Ray looked up and gave Izzy a nod. She had poured his drink without even asking, both a blessing and a curse that Ray enjoyed all around Red Hook. He could never order anything else. His drink, basically a watered-down tequila shot that he sips, was HIS drink. Everybody knew it, every bartender poured it, usually without consent. Typical sailors are famously known to drink rum... Ray was anything but a typical sailor.

Ray took a sip of his tequila, choked back a bit, and looked up to find Izzy. She was hiding behind the order pad, giggling. The islands are famous for what is commonly referred to as the 'island pour'. It's a bit heavy-handed and has knocked many mainlanders on their asses. But Izzy's pour for Ray was beyond heavy. She enjoyed seeing Ray's face the first time he sipped her drink, before the ice melted a bit to help water it down. Izzy took great pride in getting Ray to stumble out of the bar. Small but fierce, Izzy was a tattooed brunette whose giggle had a way of disarming even the most guarded souls. She radiated boldness, charm, and a kind of unpredictable joy.

Bob, as always, was fascinated by Ray's ability to find new crew. The idea that strangers willingly flew to his boat to work as crew was something Bob struggled to wrap his head around. But in the sailing world, it was standard practice. Captains needed crew, and crew needed boats. Some were experienced sailors, some were wanderers looking for adventure, and some had been influenced by that damn reality TV show and thought it was all cocktails and sunsets and shenanigans below deck.

Crew came and went, but the right person was rare. Ray had been lucky before, especially with Miranda. She had been a perfect mate—organized, hardworking, and fiercely professional. Their working relationship had been clear from day one, and she had whipped *Purrfection* into shape, preparing her for the first season of day charters. She had even sailed with him to Grenada during hurricane season. It was a lucky break for both of them, and it led to bigger opportunities for her. Now, she was on a private yacht, a dream job with a small crew and no charters. From what he'd seen on her Instagram, she was in Italy. That was the kind of trajectory he could offer to crew—experience that led to better gigs on bigger boats.

Bob shifted the subject back to Ray's next project. "When will you hear about this next top-secret project?" Bob asked somewhat seriously. Bob had a habit of quickly pivoting subjects.

"Oh, Bob, it's not that top-secret. I don't think anything will come of it, but I'm meeting the guy tomorrow at Salty Siren." In the islands, so many outlandish stories end up being somewhat true. Bob wasn't sure if Ray was serious or joking. Just around the corner, two miles away, lies Little St James Island. Epstein's Island. All the terrible things the general public later found out about had been the stories on St. Thomas for many years prior. Everyone here knew something was going on. Outrageous stories that can't possibly be true – those stories occur as often as the morning rain down here in the islands. The motto of St. Thomas is "Can't make this shit up".

While they talked, two young women at the bar had noticed the Sail Purrfection logo on Ray's phone case. The playful orange cat, wearing a turquoise sailor hat with an anchor emblem and matching sunglasses, a nod to the old superstition that orange cats were lucky aboard ships. Even the cat's ears in the design were asymmetrical, a subtle reflection of the quirky, offbeat nature of sailors themselves.

"That's a cute cat on your phone. Do you have a cat?" one of the ladies said.

"Thank you. That's the logo for my boat. I run day charters. And yes, she is a cat."

"Wait, so what's the name of your cat?"

"The boat, she's a catamaran. Her name is *Purrfection*."

"Oh, I get it." They claimed. Ray wasn't sure the ladies understood, but the blonde seemed to suddenly connect the dots, "So you have a boat? We've been looking to go out on a boat!"

"Yes, ma'am, I'm moored right out here in the bay."

"Can we come out and see it?! We'll bring drinks!"

Bob shook his head, amused but not surprised. He had seen this scenario play out many times. Ray had an effortless way of attracting attention.

"I'm about to head back out, sure. Run up and grab yourselves some drinkage from the mini-mart and meet me back here in a few minutes." Ray instructed the girls. They scurried away, giggling.

"Bob, you wanna come out? I'm just going to do chores while they drink in their bikinis, but you are more than welcome. Looks like good eye candy at least. You can bartend for them. Help them with their Influencer in the Wild selfies."

"Nah, I don't wanna get myself in trouble. I don't understand how you stay out of it."

"Nothing wrong with letting the girls have their fun, Bob. Even though they have absolutely NO clue, they're always safe on *Purrfection*. Who knows what other boat they might end up on? With my luck, I'd have to rescue them later from some bad captain."

Ray gave Bob a knowing look before heading out. "I'll probably see you at Salty in a few hours for wine," he said with a wink.

Bob chuckled, shaking his head. "Probably."

CHAPTER TWO

March 2022 - St. Thomas
Not So Clandestine Meeting

About noon the next day, Ray gathered up some laundry. His goal was to get two loads in the machines, then get some lunch for the wash cycle, and meet this so-called top-secret guy to hear his proposal. So far, they had only communicated through some text messages. Nothing was clear, other than the meeting location, the Salty Siren Bistro.

Ray tossed the blue mesh laundry bag into the dinghy, grabbed a bag full of quarters, and headed on into the dock. The laundry mat was always hot, and the machines barely worked; chickens often ran around inside. It was run by an 80-year-old gentleman from Guadeloupe, Mr. Max. He spoke some kind of backward ass French when talking with his workers. Two quick loads loaded in the machines, without slamming the door, something that makes Mr. Max overly grumpy. Quarters luckily went in the machines without incident, then Ray headed across the street to Salty Siren.

Entering the establishment, Ray's attention caught on the bartender—a striking young woman with a dancer's grace and naturally blonde hair pulled back in a no-nonsense ponytail. She moved behind the bar with the quiet confidence of someone who knew exactly how much attention she was drawing. After six years on the island, she still managed to keep her Minnesota complexion. A simple dress framed her bare shoulders, where a small peace sign tattoo peeked out—more statement than decoration. Regulars endured her sass like a badge of honor, and newcomers quickly learned she didn't suffer fools. Ray didn't usually go for the type, but something about her mix of dry wit, unapologetic confidence, and nerdy charm made it hard not to notice. He wasn't the only one. Alli had a following.

"Hello, Alli. I didn't realize it was Tuesday. Did you have a good Sunday?" Ray's greeting indicated a common theme in the islands - nobody is ever really sure what day it is, until you see who is tending bar.

Alli responded as she was working the bar, "Oh, hey Ray, yeah, Sunday Funday on the beach. But then I worked later, so couldn't overdo it."

Ray sat down at the first seat on the corner of the U-shaped bar, his seat, giving him a clear view across and down its length. The right side of the bar, a somewhat secluded dead-end, typically remained empty until the rest filled up. It was one of the nicer bars in Red Hook and notably one of the few with air conditioning. Behind the bar, rows of wine bottles lined the wall to the ceiling. Always good fun when one of the ladies had to scale the wall to grab a bottle.

"I'm just waiting for a guy to discuss a potential charter of some kind." Before Ray could finish the sentence, a glass of tequila appeared in front of him, silver tequila with ice, some water, and a lime. Alli had made it in the short time Ray checked his phone for a text from his client. Ray was thinking a beer would be more appropriate for this meeting, but per usual, too late.

In through the door came much of the regular lunch crowd. The Salty Siren was a little higher-end than most places in Red Hook, but still a favorite among the captains. Not that the captains had any more money than anyone else, they just liked to pretend they did. If they needed another reason to show up besides cool air, it was Alli. She was the real draw, the one they came back for.

An unknown face came through the door and pulled up the barstool right next to Ray. He seemed to know exactly who he was looking for. He was a typical larger American, who almost looked like a tourist, but not quite. He had the all-too-familiar look of a middle-class businessman coming to the islands for the first time to explore his dream retirement.

"Hi, I'm Jake."

"Oh, hey, you found me. I'm Ray." Ray never introduced himself as Captain Ray, ever. Although some called him Captain Ray, it was never his lifelong goal. If not for COVID, he might have never studied for his Captain's license. He had been many things before a Captain. Nobody called him Director Ray when he was a software executive. Nobody called him Engineer Ray when he was an engineer. Besides, Captains that insisted on being called Captain Whatever were usually Captain Assholes.

"Captain Ray De Soleil, good to finally meet you," Jake exclaimed.

"Your texts were a little… off, Jake. Not the normal charter questions. What exactly is this 'project' you speak of? We just call them charters around here." Ray asked, arms crossed.

Jake grinned. "Oh, it's gonna be a fun one, Ray. Pays well, too. You're perfect for it."

"At some point, I suppose you'll grace me with the big reveal about this so-called 'project.' Is that today's meeting or …?" He could already feel the old flicker of irritation bubbling up—something he *hadn't* felt much since leaving his former life behind. The trials of owning and sailing a catamaran had taught him patience. Letting go. But Jake was pressing his nerves faster than most.

Jake leaned in slightly, voice dropping just enough to feel conspiratorial. "Well, Captain Ray, I work for a certain federal agency—and we could use your help…"

Ray interrupted, "Oh shit, there it is. What, FBI? I've already had a run-in with you assholes a few months back. Or the IRS, I'm not on the best terms with the IRS either. CIA, I haven't dealt with yet.... At least I don't think so? Maybe that Dominica thing counts? I guess that's the point of the CIA, I'd never know. Huh?" Ray paused to search his memory before snapping out of it, "So which alphabet mess do you come from?"

"Well... Captain Ray, I *am* with the FBI," Jake said, his tone calm but firm.

Ray leaned back and gave a short laugh, his thoughts raced through all the misadventures the FBI might be interested in, then burst out, "Oh, this oughta be good. Last time, you guys wiretapped my phone just because I danced with some agent's ex-wife at the Beach Bar. Brilliant use of our taxpayer money. What do you want with me this time?" He gestured vaguely, then narrowed his eyes. "Let me guess—Elana's charming ex-husband put you up to this?"

He wasn't angry. He seemed more amused than anything. Most Americans might've been pissed after learning the FBI tapped their phone just for dancing with the ex-wife of one of their own. But Ray? He thought it was humorous. Maybe even make a good story someday.

Jake held his ground. "Ray, I'm sorry—I truly don't know what you're talking about. But if you'll let me, I'd like to tell you about the project. It's confidential, and I'll need you to sign this NDA before we begin."

He reached into his satchel and pulled out a plain blue folder—no labels, no markings—along with a pen, and slid them across the table to Ray.

"So I'm going to sign this *Non-Disclosure Agreement*, in front of everybody at this bar, and then you are going to proceed to tell me about this top secret project, as I sign the NDA in front of 15 locals? I think you are missing the concept of an NDA. You guys are just brilliant, aren't you."

"After you sign the NDA, I was hoping we could go out to *Purrfection* and chat about it, privately."

Ray felt a wave of relief. The FBI showed no interest in Miami,

Dominica, or the real estate debacle in St. Thomas—just three recent activities best kept off any official transcript.

"We can, yes, but I've got to rotate my laundry into the dryer, and Alli just poured me another drink. Let's order some lunch, and I'll run over to the laundromat." Ray didn't give him time to answer. Although it sounded like a suggestion, it was the only logical course of action. Ray had a knack for making commands sound like suggestions.

After lunch—and three tequilas—Ray and Jake made their way back to *Purrfection*. Ray carried his blue mesh laundry bag, now filled with clean but crumpled clothes. As Jake descended the stairs into the cockpit, he noticed a small red spot, which he immediately identified: "Hey, Ray, you've got a little blood spot here on the deck."

Ray looked at it, somewhat puzzled, and shrugged it off. "This boat has blood all over the place."

"That doesn't sound like a good thing?"

"Just boat life. Could be from a fish? Could be one of our charter guests who didn't make it off the boat unscathed. But it's probably mine. I have a saying that a *boat project is never complete until a blood sacrifice is made.*"

"No need to get nervous, we know where all the bodies are buried," Jake stated.

Ray knew that was a lie. No way Jake would be on board if he knew the true details of all the misadventures. Ray deadpanned, "Oh, silly Jake. Why bury bodies when I've got a whole ocean? It's called Frenchie fishin'"

In the cockpit, Jake lounged facing aft while Ray began pulling out button-down shirts one by one, draping them over hangers and the lifelines.

"No iron on board," Ray muttered, almost to himself. "If I don't hang these right away…"

Jake didn't respond. He seemed focused now, the casual air of the bar fading as he shifted into work mode.

The FBI was after a thief - a female, they presume, who gains access to wealthy yacht owners and their bank accounts, then manages to steal their money through elaborate electronic transfer schemes. Sometimes in trickle amounts that are hardly noticed over years, other times in large chunks before the guy knew what hit him. Never the same method twice. A team out of Chicago caught the first case from a yacht on Lake Michigan, but then tracked her all over Florida and the Caribbean. The agents have nicknamed her 'The Siren', a mythical creature known for an enchanting voice and ability to lure sailors, or wealthy yacht owners, to their destruction.

He began without preamble. "We're targeting a young woman. Smart. Cunning. She's stolen a considerable sum from someone important."

Ray didn't even look up. "Don't tell me—Jeffrey Epstein?"

Jake sighed. "No, Ray. Epstein's dead."

"Is he, though?" Ray flashed a grin. "C'mon, man. On St. Thomas, we all know he didn't kill himself. The only real debate is whether he's sipping daiquiris on a private island somewhere."

Jake didn't bite. He pressed on, ignoring the jab.

The woman they were after, he explained, had a pattern: rich yacht owners, trust-funded playboys, retirees with more money than sense. She'd gain their trust, access their accounts, and drain them before they even noticed.

As Jake droned on in detail, Ray shook his head. "Okay, Jake, I'm not sure where you think I fit into that scenario. I'm clearly not rich—I own a f*cking boat. Some people think I'm rich, but I'm really just irresponsible. It's a hole in the water I keep shoveling money into. Yeah, technically, *Purrfection* is a 'yacht,' but she's a 1995 sailing catamaran, with no air conditioning, a broken water-maker, and a dated interior where the woodwork is water-stained. It's more like camping than luxury. I only came down here to run day charters because my boat isn't nice enough for the more profitable overnight ones."

Jake didn't flinch. "We know how you got here."

Ray froze. "How the hell did I get on your short list? Miami? My brief stint as a luxury yacht captain for that trust fund guy? Yeah, I bet the FBI was watching his shady ass."

He clipped another shirt to a hanger, chuckling without humor. "Two months of captaining his oversized floating ego. I had no business driving a 66-foot luxury motor yacht, but my motto is *just say yes*... and I needed the money."

He paused, realizing he'd rambled. "Sometimes you gotta say yes to something you're pretty sure is gonna be awful, just to prove to yourself you're better off without it."

Jake thought on Ray's philosophy, "That just doesn't seem smart though, does it?"

"In engineering, we call it prototyping. Sometimes you gotta prove the stupid ideas are stupid, just to get them out of your head and focus on the solution. But it's my life, the only engineering project that matters, and you think prototyping sounds stupid? Huh? Guess that's why I'm in the Caribbean, and you are going back to a cubicle in Chicago."

Jake didn't have time to debate philosophy with Ray; he was curious about Miami. The Siren Team had failed miserably there. He wanted more dirt on his fellow agents, but didn't even know what questions to ask.

The Chicago-based team had tracked the Siren to Ft Lauderdale, yachting capital of the States, as the hub of her operations, but wouldn't give up the case to any other team, with frequent trips escaping Chicago winters. But in Miami, they fumbled hard, not knowing the yachting industry.

They'd tracked her movements, her communications. It all lined up—until it didn't. They were about to arrest the personal chef on the yacht Ray was skippering. The real thief had been someone else entirely, right there in front of them. A misstep they didn't talk about publicly.

Jake pivoted back. "Look—our profilers think you're a perfect match for our target. Jessica. We'll engineer a match through a dating app. You've got a solid profile. We'll make sure it happens."

Ray raised an eyebrow. "You think I need help getting a date?"

Jake smiled. "We're just accelerating the timeline. She targets guys with boats. You qualify. Barely."

Ray let that sit a beat. "So what's this big plan, exactly?"

"You get her onboard," Jake said. "Let her think she's got access to your money. It's a controlled sting. We'll fund a bank account in your name—just over a million. You can spend up to $25k on boat stuff while she's with you. Make it look natural. Spend some. Let her see you log in. Buy her a couple of things, if it fits. But don't overdo it. She's not a sugar baby—try to buy her and she'll vanish."

The way Jake spoke—like he knew more than he was letting on—made Ray uneasy.

Ray gave a low whistle. "Oh, it's VERY natural to spend money on a boat, won't have to fake that part."

Jake pulled out his phone and tapped a few notes. "We'll need to clean up your dating profile. Lose the beard photos. Jessica prefers clean-shaven."

Ray frowned. "You serious? This scruffy, homeless pirate look is part of the charm. Silver hair, sun-bleached, a little wild—it's working for me."

"Is it, Ray? Really?" Jake gave a dry smile. "... Just passing on profiler notes. Might even help with your usual dating game."

Ray narrowed his eyes. He'd never said anything, but Jake seemed to know far too much about his private life.

It had taken Ray three years in the Caribbean to give in and grow the damn beard. It was as far from his corporate past as he could get. Clean-shaven reminded him of boardrooms and tee times. But he also knew the truth: he mostly kept the beard out of laziness. The heat made shaving a chore, and people seemed to like, almost expect it, for an island captain.

"You look too old with the beard," Jake added. "Jessica likes mature, distinguished. Not drunk Santa. She's younger than you; can't make that age gap seem too wide."

Ray hated the idea of working with the Feds. Hated being part of their machine. But his bank account was lean, hurricane season was coming, and even morally murky money still paid for haul-outs and rum. He exhaled sharply and gave a reluctant grin. "My motto, 'Just Say Yes'. Let's do this."

Jake nodded. "Still need a few more approvals from the higher-ups. But you're our guy. Until then, keep doing your thing. Just don't bring on any crew."

Ray stood, stretched, and grabbed the last hanger. "So sail around, fail at flirting with women, drink too much, occasionally catch a fish, maybe run a charter... I think I can handle that."

He glanced at his watch. "It's almost 3 o'clock."

Jake looked up. "What happens at 3?"

Ray stared at him like he'd asked why the ocean was wet. "Happy Hour."

"We just had drinks at lunch."

"Your point?" Ray asked, incredulous. "It's the Caribbean. It's Wednesday. What's not to like?"

"It's Tuesday," Jake corrected.

Ray's face lit up. "Is it? Even better. That means Alli's behind the bar today."

With a grin, Ray jogged below deck to stash his clothes. He returned with one shirt thrown over his shoulders, unbuttoned, and steadied the dinghy as Jake climbed in. The boat dipped under Jake's weight; Ray fired up the outboard and throttled forward until they got on plane.

Spray misted off the bow as they sped across Vessup Bay. Ray dipped a hand into the clear water, splashing his face and running wet fingers through his silver curls.

Jake looked back at him—shirt flapping open, chest hair out, aviators gleaming, wind-tangled hair like a movie extra who never left the set.

"You just look like the typical Caribbean captain out of some cheesy movie," Jake said almost in admiration.

Ray smirked. "I'm anything but typical, Jake. Anything but."

❖

Jake walked the short stretch from the dinghy dock to the ferry terminal, glancing over his shoulder to make sure Ray was nowhere in sight. Satisfied, he crossed the terminal drive and approached a rusty white panel van that looked more like a plumbing company reject than a federal surveillance unit. He knocked twice—quick, then slow.

The side door slid open.

Inside, two FBI agents sat in fold-up soccer chairs, hunched over mismatched monitors and tangled cords.

"Hell of a van you scored us, Jake," said a deep voice from a large man wedged awkwardly into one of the chairs.

"Agent Maxwell, this was all I could get from the local guys," Jake said, stepping in. "Pretty sure they gave it to us as a joke."

Kevin barely looked up from his laptop. "You're not wrong. This surveillance gear might be pre-Cold War. I had to—"

"Yeah, yeah, we get it," Maxwell cut in. "You waved your geek wand. Now tell me—what's your read on this jackass?"

Jake shrugged out of his damp shirt and dropped into the third folding chair. "Honestly, sir? I'm surprised he's our mark. The boat's old. Doesn't even look like the other cats in the marina. He's not flashing wealth—hell, he looks half-homeless. I don't see how The Siren's going to think he's a good target."

"I didn't ask whether we *should* use him, Agent Lawrence. I said, *how* do we use him. Director Beck hand-picked this guy. That's good enough for me."

Jake took a breath. "Okay. If this is the guy—"

Maxwell didn't blink. "He's the guy."

"Then it can work. He's Jessica's type, or he could be, once we clean him up. Adventurous, a little reckless, wild card energy. He's older, yeah, but she likes older men—especially the silver fox types. He's got that glint in the eye, like a kid who never grew up. She won't go for boring, we know that all too well. We prop up the bank account, frame him as frugal, not broke. We apply pressure on Jessica—stress her out a bit. I think we can sell it."

"Good." Maxwell leaned back in his absurdly red chair, which squeaked under the strain. "This is my last op before retirement. I want it to count."

Jake hesitated, then added, "Ray mentioned something about the FBI tapping his phone. Said he danced with someone's ex-wife."

Maxwell shrugged. "We tap a lot of phones, Jake. Don't need a warrant. Just say 'national threat.' He's got a boat. He's a threat."

Kevin looked up. "So we did monitor his texts?"

"Doubt it," Maxwell said. "Beck and Elana split five years ago. No reason he'd care who she's dancing with at a beach bar."

Jake and Kevin exchanged a look. They hadn't mentioned Elana or a beach bar.

Maxwell pulled out his phone. "Speaking of Beck, let me update him."

He thumbed out a quick message:

Did you really tap this guy's phone because he danced with Elana?! That's f*cking hilarious.

Sliding the phone back into his pocket, he stood. "Alright, let's get out of this tin can. Jake, you sure you've figured out the whole driving-on-the-left thing? Because that trip over here was sketchy as f*ck."

"I got it," Jake said, sounding much less confident than he meant to.

"Wait," Kevin said, scrambling to secure a tangle of devices resting on a TV tray. "None of this crap is anchored. I don't think this is even a real FBI van. It might belong to one of the local agents. Doesn't it kinda smell like...fish?"

Maxwell looked around, unimpressed. "Nice job procuring a mobile unit, Jake. What the hell are these chairs?"

"The van didn't have any. Just that rusted-out desk welded to the wall. One of the local guys told me K-Mart had plenty. So... here we are."

"K-Mart?" Maxwell snorted. "Did you pick up some underwear too?"

"What? No. Just the chairs. Did you need underwear?"

Maxwell rolled his eyes. "You gotta buy your boxer shorts at K-Mart. Cincinnati. 400 Oak Street..."

Jake blinked.

"Never mind. You two are too damn young. Good movie, though. You missed out." He rubbed his knees. "I am getting too old for this shit."

Kevin frowned. "Wait, hasn't K-Mart been out of business for like ten years?"

"I don't know. That's what is here on the island, and an insane number of soccer chairs. Wall-to-wall, like they are hoarding them."

Jake added, "You'd think with all the money this division got after Hurricane Irma, we'd have better gear."

Maxwell snorted. "Clearly didn't go to equipment. Wonder where it went. But hey, these are the same folks who sat on Epstein's file for years and took the payoffs."

He gestured toward the front. "Driver's seat, Jake. Go on."

Jake awkwardly clambered over the center console while Maxwell smirked at the struggle. The van wobbled as Jake finally dropped into place.

"Idiot," Maxwell muttered, then exited the sliding door, slammed it shut, and climbed into the passenger seat.

As Jake pulled onto the main road, both agents barked in unison: "Keep left!"

Alone in his hotel room, Maxwell stared at the burner phone, thumb hovering. He finally tapped out a message:

Talk now?

The reply came in the form of a call, just a few minutes later. Maxwell answered. "Good evening, sir—"

"Don't ever text me that shit again," Beck snapped. "You of all people know better. I hate texting to begin with, but if you have to, use Telegram. It's the only app the agencies don't have keys to—yet. Come on, Jimmy. You screw this up, and it's your ass. Literally."

"Yeah, I know," Maxwell sighed. "It was a dumb move. I get it. I know how critical this op is. It's $5k out of my pocket every week, and it's adding up."

Beck's voice dropped into something almost casual, but flat as ever. "The upside is solid if it plays out. High positives. High negatives."

"High negatives *for me*," Maxwell muttered. No reply. He filled the silence. "This Captain Ray guy is a character. Bit of a mess, but charming in a way. I get why you think he might work. Elana's not easy to impress, but if he was able to get close to her—"

"He didn't get *that* close," Beck cut in, fast. "I made damn sure. She's had her share of loser boyfriends, but this one? He had options. A boat. An exit plan."

Maxwell let out a short, knowing laugh. "Yeah. Her other losers couldn't just sail away with her."

That one landed. Silence on the other end.

Maxwell cleared his throat. "Well, sir. Good night."

A pause. Then, slightly off-beat—

"Good night."

The line went dead before Maxwell could say anything more.

CHAPTER THREE

April 2022 - Hilton Head
HHI Blues

The sun rose over the horizon, casting golden rays across the beach waters of Hilton Head, South Carolina. At the poolside bar of the luxurious Grand Ocean Oak Resort, Jessica felt the familiar buzz of anticipation. Her thick, dark hair was pulled into a loose braid, and her teal uniform was freshly pressed. Today, the bar felt like a stage, and she was ready to shine.

By 8:00 AM, Jessica was behind the counter, arranging garnishes—lime wedges, pineapple slices, and fresh mint. The air was crisp with a gentle breeze, the scent of blooming jasmine mingling with faint saltwater, occasionally overpowered by fresh chlorine. She turned on the sound system, opting for soft reggae to set a relaxed mood. Personally, she preferred Rufus Du Sol or Duke Dumont—anything electronic and dancey—but maybe she could sneak that in later, depending on the crowd.

Early risers trickled into the pool area, and Jessica greeted them with a warm smile.

Her first customer was Mr. Brun, a retired schoolteacher from Ohio who returned to the resort every spring. He approached the bar with his usual cheerful demeanor.

"Good morning, Jessica," he said. "How's the ocean today?"

"Calm as ever, Mr. Brun," she replied, sliding a cup of fresh coffee his way. "Perfect for paddleboarding."

"Thanks, Jessica. You're a gem," he said, settling into his favorite barstool. "I think I've told you before, I'm not a fan of all these tattoos these days, but yours—those sea creatures—look good on you. Kinda fits your personality. Like a mermaid."

Jessica smiled and turned away. Of course, she wanted to say something about his judgmental attitude, but it was early, and he was older. It was sort of a compliment?

By mid-morning, the pool area filled with laughter and splashing water. Families lounged on deck chairs while couples sipped mimosas. Jessica's hands moved deftly as she poured, shook, and garnished drinks. She loved the rhythm of her work and the chance to chat with guests, each one with a story to share.

A couple sat down at the bar, pale-skinned and buzzing with excitement.

"Good morning! We'd love two mimosas!" the woman said brightly.

Jessica nodded, already juggling a few orders.

"We're from Chicago," she added. "It's the first sun we've seen in months!"

"Now, hun, we were in St. Martin after New Year's," the husband corrected.

Normally, Jessica would jump at the chance to mention she was from Chicago too, but her circumstances wouldn't allow that anymore.

The woman went on, "If you're ever in St. Martin, whatever you do, don't go to a bar called the Dinghy Dock. Stupid name, and the owner, Seth, is an asshole."

"I've always wanted to go to St. Martin. Been to Puerto Rico and a few other Caribbean stops, but not there. I'll steer clear of the Dinghy Dock, you said?"

"Yes. We should know—he's our son."

Jessica paused for just a second and looked up to see the cheeky grins spreading across their faces.

"Well, okay then. You really are from Chicago. I'll have to stop in and get a proper dose of hometown abuse when I make it down there."

"You'll love it. The French food, the Dutch party vibes—it's a great island," the woman said, rising from the bar. "I know this is a pain, but we're going to sit closer to the pool and catch some sun."

"Yes, ma'am," Jessica said. At least she acknowledged it was a pain in the ass to transfer the ticket.

"Marissa, just in time. Can you transfer that lady's tab to the pool?" Jessica asked her coworker starting her shift.

"It's three buttons. Can't you do it?" Marissa quipped, but seeing Jessica still mid-rush, relented. "Okay, I got it. But seriously, you've been here two months—it's beyond time you learned how to use the pad."

Around 11:00 AM, a bachelorette party arrived, their energy infectious and ready for day drinking. The bride-to-be, radiant in a sparkling sash, approached the bar.

"We're looking for something fun and festive," she said.

"I've got just the thing." Jessica winked and whipped up a round of Mermaid Bliss cocktails—blue curaçao, passion fruit, and a splash of champagne. The group cheered as she handed them their glittering drinks.

By lunchtime, the bar was packed. Piña coladas, daiquiris, margaritas—Jessica kept pace effortlessly. Even Marissa was in a decent mood, manning the blender station.

But as the afternoon wore on, the tide shifted. The ice machine started acting up, forcing Jessica to make frequent trips to storage. The friendly crowd grew more demanding. A sunburned man in a Hawaiian shirt slammed his glass on the counter.

"Where's my daiquiri?" he barked. "I've been waiting forever!"

"I'll get that right away," Jessica replied, knowing it had only been a few minutes—and that his server was poolside. She hurried to the blender, which was now sputtering.

By 2:00 PM, dark clouds had gathered. The wind picked up, sending napkins and menus flying. Guests began complaining about the weather, as if it were Jessica's fault.

"Can't you do something about this wind?" a woman snapped, shielding her hair with a towel.

Jessica forced a smile. "Mother Nature's got the wheel, but I can whip up something to warm you up."

The drizzle became a downpour. Guests crammed under the cabana's high white ceilings and open rafters. Spacious on normal days —not today. Voices overlapped in a chorus of complaints.

"Is there nowhere else to sit?"

"This is ridiculous for a resort of this caliber!"

Jessica's manager stepped in, climbing onto a chair.

"Can I have your attention!" he shouted. "This is Hilton Head— an afternoon shower is practically tradition. It'll pass, and the sun will return. Meanwhile, you've got the best damn bartender in Chicago making your drinks. Isn't she kicking ass?"

The crowd erupted in cheers, the mood lifting. But it wasn't the kind of recognition Jessica wanted. She was trying not to be noticed in Hilton Head.

She pulled her young manager aside. "Dude. Why'd you have to announce I'm from Chicago?"

"It makes people feel connected to you, that's all. Makes them trust you, and know their drinks are in good hands. Why? You in witness protection?" he joked—then saw her face. She was dead serious.

Back behind the bar, Jessica never let her composure crack. Even after Marissa clocked out, leaving her to handle the chaos solo.

"Of course that bitch isn't staying to help," Jessica muttered, then glanced up to make sure no one heard.

The clouds parted. The sun returned. The tourists filtered back to their chairs. Jessica was relieved the bar area was empty again, but knew billing chaos would follow. She could punch in her own orders lightning-fast—but the rest of the system overwhelmed her. Technology was not her specialty.

The day picked up again. The bachelorette party was on round four, keeping the pool entertained. Jessica considered changing the music. Not so fast.

A group of rowdy college guys stumbled up, their slurred voices growing more inappropriate by the drink.

"What's the strongest thing you've got?" one asked, leaning on the bar.

"Tequila shots," Jessica said flatly, pouring without flair. Her usual charm had vanished. Jessica hated tequila shots. She was a Jameson girl—for shots. Tequila, in her view, was meant to be sipped neat. But these guys wouldn't appreciate a decent reposado anyway. At least tequila shots cost more. In theory: higher tip.

"Do you need training wheels?" she barked at the ringleader.

"What?"

"Lemons and salt?"

"Oh, yeah. Of course…"

Jessica slid over a plate of lemon wedges and two salt shakers she knew she'd never see again.

Jessica resisted taking a shot with them, but one of the guys gave a rambling toast that somehow included someone's mom who'd died of cancer. Some things were bigger than principle. She tilted her head and raised a glass.

By 5:00 PM, the crowd thinned. Guests retreated to shower for dinner. Jessica stood behind the counter, her feet aching, blouse still damp from the rain. The humidity refused to let anything dry.

"Rough day?" asked a man at the bar, his tone sympathetic.

Jessica let out a bitter laugh. "You could say that. Typical, really."

He nodded. "You handled it well. Not many could keep their cool like you did."

"Thanks," she said softly, though the compliment felt hollow. "Corona, Dillon?"

"You should know by now, Jess. I come here every day to see you. When are you going to let me take you to dinner?"

"I don't know, Dillon. My schedule's insane. I get called in all the time. If Marissa's dog sneezes, she calls out—and I need the money."

"You should come be the mate on my boat, bartend on a yacht. Get you out of this mess. Good pay, plus a cabin and meals—cut your costs."

Jessica gave a tired smile as she wiped the bar. The thought of being a kept woman had never crossed her mind, even if it was a paying position.

By 8:00 PM, she finally closed the bar. Rain had returned as a slow drizzle, the air cool but heavy. She walked the path to her apartment, sandals squelching in puddles.

❖

"Another Corona, Dillon?" Jessica asked the tall, slender man at the bar—yet another local charter captain who showed up almost pretending it was for the beer and not a thin excuse to flirt.

A large tourist in a straw hat and flamingo shirt waved her down to settle his tab. Jessica handed him the bill. He gave her his credit card, signed with a paltry tip, and waddled off. She glanced at the receipt—barely worth the eye roll. Small tips were the norm these days.

The tourist made his way across the Hilton parking lot to a white panel van with no windows. He flung open the side door, and late-afternoon sun flooded the interior.

"Dammit, Maxwell, now I can't see anything for the next fifteen minutes," muttered one of the younger agents, shielding his eyes.

Maxwell stared back, deadpan, waiting.

"...I mean, I've got screens to read, sir. You won't be happy if I screw up surveillance 'cause I'm blind," the agent added weakly.

"Shut up, Kevin. Yeah, I should've knocked. Well, f*ck you anyway," Maxwell grumbled. He turned to the other man. "Jake, she's not falling for Dillon at all. I thought you said he was her type. I thought this was gonna be easy. Six damn weeks of this shit. I don't have time for it. We need a new plan."

Agent Jake Lawrence gave a sympathetic shrug. "You gotta look at everything she's going through. Kicked out of Chicago. Her mother threatened. Romance might be the last thing on her mind. Dillon is trying to get her to bartend on a yacht, the same scenario that got her into this mess."

Maxwell scoffed. "You'd think she'd notice his money. That big boat is costing us a fortune. He's the provider type. That's what she needs. Why isn't it working? Dillon's a good-looking guy. He's had Emotional Manipulation training. He's pushing buttons—I can see it—but every time she flirts, she pulls back. He's even tipping big."

Jake stayed quiet.

"Maybe we need Campanelli to text her. Give her a little nudge," Maxwell said, voice rising.

"We all agreed—if Campanelli contacts her, she'll see it as a threat and disappear," Jake reminded him. "We need a place she'll run to that we control."

Maxwell grunted. "Well, shit. I'd love to get her out of Hilton Head. You got a suggestion?"

Jake shrugged again. "Not really."

Kevin piped up from the monitors. "Honestly, we don't even need to be here. I could monitor all this from Chicago. It's 2022. We've got the tech."

Maxwell spun to glare at him. "Yeah, and we've got a travel budget to burn. Plus, this $120,000 surveillance van. We're the FBI—it's what we do." He reached for the door handle. "I'm going out for a smoke."

Kevin scrambled for his sunglasses. "Didn't know he smoked."

"He doesn't," Jake said. "He's probably calling the Director."

Maxwell crossed the lot, distancing himself from the van and the resort. He pulled out his phone and texted:

Maxwell to Beck: **Got time to talk?**

Beck: **Give me 10. Wrapping up a Zoom.**

He ducked into a nearby shopping center to soak up some air

conditioning. Ten minutes later, the phone rang. He stepped back outside and answered.

"Hello, sir."

Beck's voice came in flat. "You've been down there a while. What's going on? Interest adds up every week."

"She's not taking the bait with Agent Dillon," Maxwell admitted. "Maybe it's time to change targets?"

"No. You start targeting someone new, and it's obvious something's off. That girl is perfect. Surveillance places her everywhere we need. When this wraps up, there will be an investigation. You have to think long term."

Maxwell hesitated. "It's just... difficult, given my situation. I'm trying to stay alive, week to week. Jake thinks we should get her out of Hilton Head. Somewhere more exotic, like Miami or the Bahamas."

"The Bahamas?" Beck snapped. "We don't have jurisdiction there. Are you stupid?"

Maxwell winced. "Just brainstorming, sir."

Beck exhaled. "Actually... maybe not a bad instinct. What about the U.S. Virgin Islands? We do have jurisdiction. Maybe it's time we use Captain Ray De Soleil after all. Let's amp up the pressure to get her to leave Hilton Head. She needs to loosen up, feel safe, for this to work, and the Caribbean is the place."

"Not Captain Dillon?" Maxwell asked, surprised. "That Ray guy is a wild card. He's not even an agent."

"We are only using Dillon because Campanelli scared her out of Chicago so fast, she had to drive somewhere. We were forced to use him. De Soleil was always my first choice. He's got the right appeal, and somehow people feel safe with that idiot."

Maxwell narrowed his eyes. "This is my neck on the line. Literally. You sure about this guy?"

Beck's voice cooled. "I'm sure. He even crossed paths with the real 'Siren' in Miami, months ago. Could come in handy if this op ever gets reviewed. And it will. You don't steal a million dollars of Bureau money and expect no one to look."

Maxwell stiffened. "He knows the real Siren? Doesn't that make him a liability?"

"No. He was too stupid to figure it out. He was just the captain of a yacht she targeted. We never got close to her. Do we ever? We tried to pin something on him, but nothing stuck. I'll check with Legal, make sure the De Soleil contract's still valid."

Jessica unlocked the door and stepped inside, the familiar jingle of her keys signaling her arrival. Instantly, she heard the excited scrabble of paws on hardwood as Rufus, her chubby Shih Tzu, bounded toward her. His fluffy tail wagged furiously, his entire body wriggling with joy. Jessica dropped her bag and knelt to greet him, laughing as Rufus nestled into her face, grunting.

"Miss me, buddy?" she asked, scratching behind his ears. The stress of the day melted away as she scooped him up, his warm weight a comforting reminder that no matter how tough things got, coming home to Rufus made everything better.

She immediately grabbed his leash and a water bottle from the fridge, heading out to the dog path behind her building.

As she walked, her phone vibrated. She didn't have to look—only one person ever made her phone ring (her mother), and only one person made it vibrate: her best friend Courtney in Chicago.

She swiped to answer with a smirk already forming. "What up, bitch!"

"Love you long time too! How the hell are you? I'm surprised you answered."

"You caught me walking Rufus," Jessica said, giving the leash a gentle tug as he sniffed the base of a palm tree. "I'm guessing you knew that."

"Yeah, I tried to time it for after work but before you pass out from tequila later on."

Jessica rolled her eyes, stepping over a crack in the sidewalk. "Come on, you act like I just sit in my apartment and drink alone."

"Well... don't you?" Courtney quipped.

"Yeah, but I'm doing arts and crafts while I do it, making lamps outta tequila bottles. I'm not just sitting there."

A beat of silence, then Courtney's deadpan:

"That's a difference? To you? Really?"

"Of course, I'm being crafty. Besides, the hotel has no idea what these bottles are worth," Jessica said, her voice picking up with excitement. "Some idiot businessman bought the last few shots the other day. It was a Clase Azul Ultra Añejo!"

"Shut the f*ck up! The black bottle?" Courtney gasped.

"Yes! It has, like, precious metal in the bottle itself. Like gold and shit. I bet I can sell it for $2k."

"But that's, like, a $3,000 bottle—how come only $2,000?" Courtney asked.

Jessica let out a dramatic sigh. "Well... let me think... because it doesn't have any tequila in it, and I've turned it into a lamp?"

"Smartass!"

"Better than a dumbass."

They both laughed. A warm breeze rustled the palm fronds overhead.

"So what else is up? How's tall, dark, and mysterious—Captain Dillon?" Courtney asked in her best seductive voice.

Jessica paused, slowing her steps. Rufus trotted a little ahead. "Dillon? I dunno. He's tall, dark, and... mysterious."

"So... you've friend-zoned him already?"

"No... no... I haven't. Yet," Jessica replied, hesitantly.

"He still coming by for happy hour every day after work?" Courtney asked, lowering her voice to a hushed, suggestive tone like she was narrating a scandal.

Jessica answered proudly, "Yes, he does."

Then her tone shifted, the confidence wobbling. "But... I dunno.

He's always so clean. You'd think someone captaining a boat wouldn't be cleaned up by 5 p.m. every day. It bugs me. He doesn't have many stories. He's kinda boring. Aren't captains supposed to be characters? It's in all the songs. I think it's even on the application. He's just kinda…"

"So he's too boring for you?" Courtney teased. "Maybe he pays people to get dirty for him. You've seen his boat—it's big and nice and expensive. I doubt he's down there changing the oil himself. So, what, are you looking for Captain Jack Sparrow?"

Jessica huffed a laugh. "Yeah, I've seen it. Looks nice—from the dock, I guess."

Courtney paused. "You've never been on it?! Girl… you don't warm up very easily, now do you?"

Jessica stopped at the corner, letting Rufus sniff a fire hydrant like it held government secrets. "Well, you remember what happened the last time I got on a yacht!"

"That was by NO means or measure a normal situation," Courtney fired back instantly. "You were bartending for a mafia boss. You got wrapped up in shit no normal human would ever believe, let alone witness. Captain Dillon just wants you on his boat for your sexy body and those massive heavenly ta-tas."

Jessica covered her mouth, trying not to cackle into traffic. "Does your mind always go to the gutter? Every time?"

"Does yours, *ever*?"

"Touché, bitch." Jessica laughed again, tugging Rufus back onto the path. "I need to get you down here for some shots before I get kicked out of my apartment."

"Kicked out? What'd you do now?"

Jessica sighed, shifting the phone to her other ear as Rufus tangled himself around a palm trunk. "I didn't do shit. But I'm getting kicked out July 1st."

"You've only been there a few months. They can't do that."

"Apparently, they can. It's in my lease—if the owners sell, they can ask me to vacate. The new owners don't want a renter, so…"

Courtney let out a sympathetic groan. "Why don't you come back to Chicago, just for the long weekend? Your favorite DJ has a show."

Jessica froze mid-step. The breeze stilled for a second, too. "You know I can't come back to Chicago... and thanks for that minor PTSD incident you just gave me by bringing it up again."

"Campanelli wouldn't even know you're in town. How could he?"

"Uh, I'm sure he's got ways," Jessica muttered, lowering her voice as if Campanelli himself might be hiding in the bougainvillea. "My phone shows me ads for things I just *talk* about. All kinds of ways these days. He's probably got drones and shit. Why would I risk that?"

Courtney started to argue, then stopped short—remembering there was absolutely no point in debating technology with someone who thinks her mom hacked her Fire Stick, but really just gave up her password to Amazon Prime. "I'm not sure that's how drones work—it's usually the government—never mind." She exhaled loudly. "Yeah, yeah, I guess I need to come down there. You make it sound so damn exciting..."

"It's not. It's really not."

"See... you sold me. I'll be on the next flight... to Vegas. Why don't you just go sell your lamp."

"Yep, I need to. I gotta pick up after Rufus here."

"Ok, love you, girl. Stay strong."

"Love you too. Take care in the cold."

CHAPTER
FOUR

Flashback - August 2021
I Give You the F.B.I.

A bright, hot, stagnant August morning. Ray rolled out of his bunk, stood up without swaying, and thought, *Okay, not as bad as I thought it would be... I survived another crazy night in Red Hook*. Just a slight pounding in his head. Manageable.

As he climbed the four steps from the port hull to the main salon, he spotted his wallet sitting safely in its usual spot on the windowsill.

Good... at least my wallet made it back. Hmmm... now where is my phone? It wasn't on the charger.

He scanned the room for his phone. He looked around the salon. No luck. Ray always left his phone in the salon—his rule to avoid any chance of late-night drunk texting—or worse, drunk dialing.

Oh shit, he thought, pivoting back down the four steps to the port hull, then forward through the galley to his bunk. He felt around the bed until he found the phone wedged between the mattress and the wall.

This is not good.

He unlocked the screen nervously. *Huh… no new messages. Cool. Crisis averted.*

Moving on to his standard morning ritual, he pulled up the National Hurricane Center's website. The Seven-Day Graphical Tropical Weather Outlook loaded slowly, but eventually showed the reassuring message: "*Tropical cyclone activity is not expected during the next 7 days.*"

Still, Ray knew better than to relax. In August, storms started brewing off the coast of Africa and swept across the Atlantic. *Just because it says 'not expected' today doesn't mean tomorrow won't be a different story.*

He was about to check the local forecast when a new text notification popped up:

Elana: Good morning…. Who is Me? I love Me's.

Ray frowned. He didn't know an Elana. He scrolled up to see the rest of the conversation from the night before:

Ray at 11:42 pm: Elana it's me.

That's fairly early in the evening to be forgetting people.

Elana at 11:48 pm: Me?

Clearly, whoever I met was not impressed by "me."

Ray at 12:05 am: lol. Hi. How are you?

That's just brilliant drunk texting, Ray. Genius-level stuff right there. No wonder she's falling all over you.

Ray at 12:07 am: St Thomas?

Oh great. I was so drunk I don't even remember meeting her last night? What the hell?

Then the text from this morning.

Elana at 7:39 am: Good morning…. Who is Me? I love Me's.

Ray stared at the screen, baffled. But not alarmed. The exchange was odd, but not out of the ordinary enough to trigger any real concern. He shrugged.

He had no clue who Elana was—and didn't much care. If the encounter hadn't even registered in his usually obsessive mind, it probably wasn't worth the energy to chase the mystery.

He went about his day, turning his focus to boat chores and oil changes.

Flashback - August 2021

Ray checked the dipstick again—clean and golden—and gave the old starboard engine a final pat. Oil change complete. Sweat poured off him in sheets as he climbed out of the engine room and stepped into the full slap of the Caribbean sun. The engine hatch clicked shut behind him.

Three horn blasts echoed from the ferry terminal.

Three o'clock. Happy Hour.

He didn't even bother peeling off his shirt—just walked straight to the sugar scoop and dove in. The water had lost its early-summer chill and now hovered in that disappointing, body-temp zone. Not exactly refreshing, but enough to rinse away the worst of the sweat and grime.

By the time Ray strolled into Tap & Still, still damp and wearing his Sail Purrfection buff as a makeshift COVID mask, Bud Light Bob was already in his usual seat.

"Who was that hot blonde you were dancing with at Duffy's last night?" Bob said by way of hello.

Ray slid into the seat across from him, tugged down the buff, and grinned. "You know me, Bob. A f*cking Ray of sunshine."

It was August 2021. The USVI still clung to its COVID rules, including the bar scene's two most sacred commandments:

Rule #1: Ass up, mask up. Walk around - better have a mask on, until you sit down. Rule #2: No sitting at the bar—but sitting at a table pushed up to the bar? Totally fine.

Of course, bartenders couldn't hand drinks over the bar; they had to walk the long way around to deliver them. The logic made no sense, but the Health Department didn't deal in logic—only shutdowns and dollars.

Ray pulled out his phone, a little slower than usual. He scrolled through his contacts until he found the name that might explain Bob's blonde: Elana. He tapped out a message to Elana.

Good afternoon... late night at Duffy's I guess.

Her reply came almost instantly.

Omg!! Did I meet you there?

Ray: **I gotta be honest, I don't know how I got your name and number in my contacts... I'm Ray. I own a catamaran called *Purrfection*.**

Elana: **Well I'm glad you have my number. I'm from Illinois. My name is Elana. It's nice to meet you. I moved to St. John today. Staying at a boutique hotel. I think we met last night. My boyfriend and I were out. I don't remember much. How long are you here?**

Boyfriend? Ray thought. *No wonder I don't remember much of this.*

Ray: **I live here, on *Purrfection*. I thought I was doing okay today... I feel fine, but apparently I don't remember much either.**

Elana: **From what I hear, I was taking my top off last night... I don't recall, but I was told we all had fun! Are you full-time in St. John?**

Ray: **I'm full-time on my boat, yeah. But the boat moves. I was just in St. Maarten for three months. I'd surely remember topless. But now it's coming back to me a bit. Your boyfriend looked kinda pissed, so I said, 'don't worry mate, she's just having fun and still going home with you.' But he didn't seem too sure about that.**

Before Ray could overthink his last message, Tara appeared at the table, holding a Heineken like it was a bottle of vintage wine.

"For you, good sir, we have the finest bottle of Heineken available in the Caribbean," she declared, eyes smiling above her Sail Purrfection buff.

"Hmm, Tara, that's not quite true. But I love you anyway," Ray replied, accepting the bottle with a bow of his head.

"What do you mean? I grabbed it from the bottom of the cooler. Coldest one I could find. Feel my hand—it's still freezing."

"I was just in St. Maarten. Their Heineken is a pilsner—sharper, crisper, and made for hot days. This one's a lager, a little heavier. But yes, it IS cold, and after sweating through an oil change, much needed hydration."

"You finally changed starboard oil?" she said. "You've been talking about that since you got back."

Ray ignored her tone. She knew full well *Purrfection* had been booked near-solid all summer, running charters for a parade of COVID stimulus check tourists.

"Another Bud Light, Bob?" she asked over her shoulder.

Bob nodded. "You shoulda been there, Tara. Ray was on fire, dancing with this hot blonde at Duffy's. She kept trying to unbutton her blouse—and Ray's shirt too. Her boyfriend was getting pissed."

"That must've been something," Tara said. "Dancing with masks on but no shirts."

"We weren't topless," Ray said automatically. Then paused. "... right, Bob? We weren't, were we?"

"You were as close as you could get. Her blouse was unbuttoned all the way, white lace bra, nice rack. She kept rubbing your chest hair."

Ray squinted. Bob might've been full of shit—but he did remember saying something to a jealous boyfriend. Maybe it wasn't total fiction.

"No wonder the guy was pissed," Ray said, playing along, but not knowing the extent of Bob's exaggeration, he added, "I'd better lay off the texts. I don't need another physical altercation with a jealous boyfriend."

February 2022

A few months after Elana left for the mainland, she called Ray out of the blue—ostensibly for advice on getting her Captain's License, though the conversation wandered far beyond that. They talked for hours, catching up on everything from sailing to life plans. Somewhere in the middle of it, she casually slipped in that she'd dumped her dead-weight boyfriend and was looking for a fresh start, maybe even on St. John.

For months, Ray humored her texts and late-night calls as she wavered—half-committed to selling her business, half-tempted just to visit for a season. He'd learned more about her than he expected, including the fact that she'd been married for nearly two decades to a senior FBI official. That detail never sat comfortably with him; Ray's natural distrust of the Feds left a quiet unease in the back of his mind.

Elana finally showed up in St. John, hoping to find a property that spoke to her, though she spent most nights with Ray at the Beach Bar in Cruz Bay. They danced to every band that came through, his favorite being his buddy and fellow sailor, Moss Henry. By the end of the week, Ray sailed *Purrfection* back to her mooring in Red Hook and hopped a flight back to Ohio for a week.

Upon his return to the island, Ray hopped out of the overloaded, steamy taxi van full of tourists and headed straight for the cool air of the Salty Siren. He fell easily back into his usual spot with the FOGs (F**cking Old Guys) — Happy Hour wine.

As soon as Ray opened the door, from his corner barstool Bud Light Bob greeted him in classic fashion. "Well, is she gone?"

"Bob, *I've* been gone a week. Elana flew out the same day I did, about 10 days ago. Remember, I flew back to Ohio the same day she left."

Bob shrugged. "I can't keep track of you. I gave up a long time ago. Any good stories?"

"Oh, I've got a crazy one, yes!" Ray leaned against the bar. "I had the f*cking FBI monitoring my text messages because of Elana!"

Bob squinted. "C'mon... why would the FBI give a damn about you?"

"Elana was married to the FBI for almost 20 years. She told me she has agents watching her 24/7. She knew exactly what I was texting my buddy back in Ohio."

"That sounds like a load of crap. Sell that to some tourist." Bob scoffed.

Ray pulled out his phone and thumbed through messages. "Here. See for yourself."

Elana: **Wow!! You are scaring them.... Don't do that...**

Elana: **They can read your texts!!**

Ray scrolled to a photo of a well-built man in a tight blue t-shirt, partially hidden behind a pillar at Beach Bar. The guy had that unmistakable stance—arms crossed, gaze locked, as if he were scoping something out.

Elana: **My bodyguard**.

Ray: **lol**

Elana: **I'll meet you at the airport... It's not a lol... he's real. He was watching you like a hawk the other night. I had an EarPod in my ear all night. You need to slow down, cowboy... behave... Just saying.**

Elana: **Be lucky. I like you...**

Elana: **Don't text anyone else... you're making them nervous for no reason.**

Ray tucked his phone back into his pocket. "See? I'm not bullshitting. That's creepy proof."

Bob eyed the photo, "That guy could be anybody. That bar's full of tourists who look like that."

"Grumpy tourists? Not usually. She knew exactly what I was texting Braxton. Well, almost *exactly*! Makes me nervous. All the shady crap I get dragged into down here, I don't need the FBI poking around. I doubt she ever moves down here anyway."

"I don't think you have much to worry about, Ray." Bob surmised, "That's hardly proof. Not very specific. Light on details. I think she's the one bullshitting you, trying to be the girl you actually remember this time."

CHAPTER
FIVE

April 2022
Culebra

Three rumbling horn blasts from the car ferry marked the hour—three o'clock. Happy Hour.

Ray grabbed a white linen button-down shirt, sniffed it to make sure it was still fresh enough, then threw it on unbuttoned. Hopping into the dinghy, he untied it and yanked the engine cord. A quick twist of the throttle sped him up, bringing the boat on plane, his shirt flapping in the wind. He dipped a hand into the salt water, running it through his hair and across his face—a quick refresh before reaching shore.

Once tied up at the dinghy dock, Ray made his way toward Tap & Still, unsure who he'd run into but also knowing exactly who would be there.

He pulled up a chair at the bar next to Bud Light Bob, nursing a Happy Hour Bud Light.

"Any new crew?" Bob greeted him without preamble.

"No new crew, but I think Tara has a lady friend coming to the island, and she wants to take her on a sailing trip. I'll probably take them somewhere. Haven't been out in a while, and I haven't caught a fish in even longer. Feels like time to move. A boat isn't meant to sit still, and neither are sailors. Maybe St. Croix, maybe Culebra."

Bob took a sip of his beer, then asked, "So... anything ever come from your top-secret meeting?"

Ray exhaled sharply. "I haven't heard shit in two months from that FBI prick."

Bob's eyes widened. "FBI?! They're back bugging your phone again? Who'd you dance with this time? Is Elana back on the island?"

Ray shook his head. "No, Bob, I don't think they are. Elana isn't back on the rock. It was some unrelated charter thing." He paused, then reconsidered. "Well... I think it's unrelated. Who knows with those idiots? Point is, I haven't heard anything, so it's time to move on to the next adventure."

Bob wasn't satisfied. "What was it about?"

Ray hesitated. He shouldn't say anything- signed a Non-Disclosure Agreement. But, as usual, his tendency to over-share won out.

"They wanted to run some kind of sting operation off my boat. Crazy, right? This hot bartender from Chicago has been going around stealing bank account info from wealthy yacht owners, and they wanted to use me as bait to catch her."

Bob burst out laughing. "But you're not wealthy! What were they thinking?"

Ray smirked. "Beats me, Bob. Maybe they figure I'm decent enough that she'll trust me. Maybe they know she's thinking of moving to the Virgin Islands. Maybe they know she's into older guys." He took another sip of tequila. "Who knows, Bob. It's the FBI—look at how much time and resources they wasted on Elana's behalf."

Bob leaned in. "Was she at least hot? Got a photo?"

Ray pulled up the picture the FBI had given him. The woman in the photo had long dark hair, striking eyes, a full sleeve nautical-themed tattoo that complemented her look, and—most notably, from Bob's favorite feature—an ample chest prominently displayed.

"Wow!" Bob whistled. "No chance, Ray. No chance. She's so hot."

Ray scoffed. "Come on, man. I got this. Beautiful ladies are always out on my boat."

"You land in the friend zone every time," Bob cracked, grinning. "So... are you gonna look her up?"

Ray hesitated, then nodded. "I never really thought about it, but I guess I could. I know she's in Hilton Head. Shouldn't be too hard to find her."

Bob leaned back, satisfied. "Well, that should be entertaining."

Then he added, "Wanna head over to Salty for a glass of wine? Alli's working. You know you can't resist Alli. And I like my Happy Hour wine price."

Ray chuckled. "Don't give me that shit. You get your Happy Hour price all night long anyway. You just wanna see Alli."

Bob grinned. "So?"

Ray sighed. "It's a little early for wine, and Alli will just feed me tequila if the sun is still up. But sure, let's go see her before her shift ends."

Bob and Ray crossed the street and climbed the small, steep hill into Duffy's Love Shack parking lot, heading towards the small shopping center where the Salty Siren Bistro was located. The door read 'Pull,' but Bob jokingly pushed it, mocking the tourists who did the same. Sometimes, locals played a game where if the next person pushed instead of pulling, someone had to buy shots.

For Happy Hour, the bar was nearly full, but Bob and Ray managed to claim their usual corner seats—Ray facing across the bar and Bob facing down it, both with a prime view of Alli. Ray's tequila appeared in front of him as if by magic.

Before Alli could open a Bud Light for Bob, he stopped her.

"Wine, please, Alli."

"Early night, boys?" Alli asked, raising an eyebrow as she returned the Bud Light to the cooler.

"We just came to see you," Bob said smoothly.

Alli turned her head over her bare right shoulder, giving Bob a devious look as she poured his wine.

"Probably not early. You know us," Ray added. "We're just as likely to close this place down."

Through the big glass window, Ray caught sight of a familiar figure crossing the parking lot. Tara made a beeline for the two seats closest to the door, sliding in beside Bob and Ray.

"Bob! Ray! Just the man I wanted to see!"

Of course, Bob assumed she was talking about him, but Ray knew that tone. That was the unmistakable tone of *Let's go sailing!*

"Tara!" Bob exclaimed, his New England accent in full swing. "Our favorite bartender!" He said it just loud enough for Alli to hear.

Alli snapped her head over her right shoulder again, nailing Bob with a pointed *F*ck you, Bob* glare—a sharp contrast to the peace sign inked on her shoulder.

"I haven't been your bartender for months, Bob," Tara countered. She had transitioned from bartending to working on several boats in St. Thomas, joining delivery crews from the Virgin Islands to North Carolina, and even earning her US Coast Guard Captain's License.

"Ray!" she continued. "So I've got this friend coming into St. Thomas, and I thought it would be great to take her sailing! Maybe even St. Croix?"

"A lady friend this time, Tara?" Ray teased. "Okay, okay, let's see what I can do. I haven't been sailing for a few weeks, and it's about time *Purrfection* gets out on the water before she gets grumpy with me."

"You're the best, Ray!" Tara grinned. "Hey Alli, I'll have an Espresso Martini, and put Ray's next tequila on my tab, please!"

Ray checked the app on his phone for the upcoming wind conditions.

"You know, we've never flown the spinnaker with you on board, have we?" Ray asked.

"No, we haven't! Let's do it," Tara said eagerly.

"It just so happens we have some light wind days coming up. Not strong enough to sail south to St. Croix. *Purrfection* is a big girl—she needs at least 15 knots to move and 20 knots to have fun. But we could fly the kite downwind to Culebra, then easily motor back in the light winds. Normally, it's tough to motor back against the stronger Easterly Trade Winds, but the forecast says we could return without beating into the waves."

"Well, that didn't take any convincing at all, did it?" Bob quipped in his snarky New England tone. "Only one tequila in."

"You know my motto, Bob...*Just Say Yes*."

With that, Ray took a sip of his tequila, finishing the glass just as Alli placed another in front of him.

After two months of silence from the FBI and no response from Jake, Ray assumed the plan was off. He'd only been ghosted once before—by a feisty blonde—and this felt eerily similar. In hindsight, it did seem overly dramatic to use the FBI to catch a 35-year-old yacht-hopping con artist. She was only swindling rich, gullible old men. Hardly seemed like an FBI priority. But apparently, she'd pissed off the right rich, gullible old man—one with enough influence to get the FBI involved.

With no charters on the horizon, Ray and Tara finalized their sail plan to Culebra. Tara's friend was visiting the island and wanted to go sailing. Ray knew it would be a fun downwind sail to Culebra, with a chance to fly the spinnaker. It didn't take much arm-twisting—one tequila, to be exact—for him to commit. Besides, he was craving Zaco's Tacos.

The morning of the trip, Tara and her friend Lindsey hopped aboard with their luggage. Tara carried a small dry bag with essentials;

Lindsey, on the other hand, had a carry-on stuffed with outfits she'd never wear in a week. Tara always prioritized food and alcohol over clothes—one of the many reasons she was always invited back.

The day started cloudy, typical for the lee of St. John. Ray fired up the engines while Tara took the helm. Lindsey earned her keep by untying the mooring lines. Tara guided *Purrfection* through the mooring field under Ray's close supervision, then motored past Cabrita Point into Pillsbury Sound. They passed Great St. James, and, as tradition dictated, Ray and Tara flipped double middle fingers at Little St. James Island. Lindsey looked confused. In unison, Ray and Tara clarified, "Epstein's Island."

Once south of St. Thomas, the skies turned clear and blue. A steady 12-knot breeze out of the east made for perfect spinnaker conditions. Tara set the autopilot slightly southwest and went forward to help Ray deploy the sail.

Purrfection's spinnaker, a bold red, white, and blue star-patterned triangle, unfurled beautifully against the sky. They held steady at seven knots—almost too fast to fish. But Ray always had lines in the water. Tara and Lindsey lounged on the bow's tanning nets, sinking into a beanbag while the deep blue sea slipped silently beneath them. Ray hesitated to disturb them, but then—

Zzzzzzzzzzzzzzzzzzz.

"Fish on!" Ray shouted, but Tara was already at the stern.

Ray started reeling, muttering, "They always hit the rod, never the hand lines. Gotta make it difficult."

Tara had this routine down. While Ray fought the fish, she grabbed a towel and an ice pick. "Want me to get the cutting board and fillet knife?"

"You know better than that, Tara. If we're too prepared, we'll jinx it and lose the fish. Respect the process."

Lindsey, watching the struggle, gasped. "Wow! That must be huge!"

Tara shook her head. "If it were big, we'd have lost it already. This is a sailboat, not a fishing boat. We can't slow down like a fishing boat would. We're still moving at seven knots. Ray has to get its head above water and surf it in."

Sure enough, Ray landed a ten-pound tuna—not massive, but perfect for a fresh meal for the three of them. Tara filleted the fish and stowed it in the fridge while the crew returned to the bow to relax. Three hours down, three to go on their 35-nautical-mile journey.

Ray chose to anchor in Bahia Linda, a small bay that could only fit three or four boats. If it were full, he'd have to backtrack and circle the island to anchor in Ensenada Honda. But he preferred this little bay—better protected, shallow, with turtles bobbing in the water. The charts for the main bay ominously warned: "POSSIBLE EXISTENCE OF UNEXPLODED ORDNANCE." Both Culebra and Vieques had been US Navy bombing practice sites.

Once anchored, Ray grilled the tuna while Tara poured wine. They feasted on their fresh catch.

The next day, the crew explored the sleepy little island, renting a golf cart to drive around. Later that evening, they had a nice meal and a few drinks, but Tara was a bit anxious to get back to *Purrfection*. Nothing much was happening in Culebra on a Saturday night, and they weren't staying out late enough for the only bar in town to get busy, called The Spot.

After returning to the boat, Tara and Lindsey made their way to the bow, eager for some quiet cuddle time under the stars. Ray lingered in the cockpit, giving them space.

Alone, Ray reached for his phone and went through the usual social media checks before flipping over to the dating apps. With no promising local matches, Ray remembered Bob's challenge, that Jessica —the FBI target—was out of his league. He switched his location to Hilton Head and narrowed the filter: women aged 34 to 39.

Within minutes, Jessica's profile popped up.

She was stunning. Long, straight brunette hair, deep brown eyes, a bright, wide smile, and a nautically themed arm sleeve tattoo that made Ray's pulse tick up a notch. She had the striking contrast of dark Puerto Rican features mixed with the freckled, sparkly-eyed charm of an Irish girl. Just his type. Her profile photos were well-chosen—mostly snapshots of her traveling the world.

One detail caught Ray's eye: her profile mentioned wanting to move to Puerto Rico. That was his opening.

Ray: **How about the US Virgin Islands instead?**

Minutes later, she responded.

Jessica: **That's another possibility. I have friends there.**

Ray: **Well then, I might just be your guy! I'm on Instagram as @SailPurrfection. Based in St. Thomas, Red Hook area.**

Jessica: **That's exactly where my friend is. He's opening a new restaurant there.**

Ray hesitated, then took a guess.

Ray: **Trevor?**

Jessica: **Yes! Trevor! He's an old friend from Chicago. I was a bartender there for years.**

Ray: **Small world. The more you explore this big ol' world, the more you realize. Stalk my Instagram a bit and see what you think.**

Ray kept it brief. No need for endless back-and-forths on the dating app—he wanted her to check out his Instagram. His feed was a highlight reel of island life: turquoise waters, white sandy beaches, and, of course, sailing adventures and turtles. The ladies love turtles. He used it for business—advertising his day charters—but also to showcase his personal Caribbean lifestyle. Instagram was also a helpful filtering tool. No sense wasting time chatting with a woman who preferred open fields, horses, and the smell of dirt.

His most recent posts? A shot of *Purrfection* gliding effortlessly under a billowing red, white, and blue spinnaker on the downwind sail to Culebra. A fresh tuna catch. A candid moment of his crew exploring the island.

Satisfied, Ray shut down the app. Whatever happened next was up to Jessica. He figured he might hear something in a day or two—if she was even interested. But within minutes, his phone buzzed: a notification from Instagram.

Jessica had viewed his profile. Then, a message—this time, through Instagram.

Jessica: **Very jealous of all this!! I need that in my life! Hi! It's Jessica, btw!**

Ray: **Yes, ma'am! We can make that happen!**

He smiled as he typed his next message, keeping the momentum going.

Ray: **Culebra is actually a sleepy little island. Pretty chill. We're all in our bunks already. I'd rather take you to Vieques for the bioluminescent bays.**

Jessica: **I've done the one in Fajardo. Wasn't the best... I've seen it way better in Holbox, Mexico. But I would like to see Vieques. I've only been to Flamenco Beach a few times in Culebra, but never really explored the island.**

Ray: **We were just at that beach today. Rented a golf cart, hopped around a bit. But honestly? Not much to see or do. The beaches just aren't as nice as St. John. I'm spoiled.**

Jessica: **My friend works at the Dinghy Dock.**

Ray sat up a little straighter.

Ray: **Oh yeah? We just ate there tonight. I bet she was our server. She was from Chicago, moved to Culebra seven years ago with her boyfriend?**

Jessica: **Kayla!**

Ray: **Yes, Kayla! That was her name. See? Small world... She was sweet to us. But this place is just sleepy. The bars didn't even open until 2:30 pm on a Saturday, even though the signs said 1 pm. Everything's closed tomorrow, so Sunday Funday will just be on the boat.**

Jessica: **You need a bartender for your boat. Then you don't need a bar!**

Ray's fingers hovered over the keyboard, a grin forming. Was this her first hint at wanting to meet up?

Ray: **You applying?**

Jessica: **I am! Been in the service industry 20 years!**

Ray: **Purrfect.**

That was the note to end on. A smooth sign-off, playing off his boat's name, leaving just the right amount of intrigue. It was Saturday night, after all. No need to linger in conversation and risk seeming like he had nothing else going on—even if, admittedly, he had just confessed to an early bedtime.

Satisfied, Ray set his phone down, wondering where this might lead

Sunday morning, Ray was up with the sun, as usual. The girls slept in a bit, and when they finally woke around 9 AM, the conversation quickly turned to whether they should just motor back to St. Thomas that day. The beach on Culebra wasn't anything special—St. John had better ones—and with everything closed on Sundays, there wasn't much to do anyway.

So they began the upwind journey back to St. Thomas. The crew sprang into action.

Tara moved to the bow to handle the anchor, with Lindsey watching in case she needed backup. Ray shifted the boat into forward gear, putting slack on the anchor chain. Tara pressed the UP button on the windlass control, slowly bringing in the chain. As she worked, she pointed with her right arm, signaling the direction of the chain so Ray could steer accordingly.

Moments later, she gave a firm fist sign—stop. Then, she twirled her right finger in the air—the signal that the anchor was up and Ray was free to maneuver.

Clearing the narrow entrance of the bay, they rounded the point of Culebra. Ray engaged the autopilot, setting a course for St. Thomas.

The wind was stronger than predicted, and the waves bigger, but *Purrfection* could handle it.

With autopilot holding the course and the fishing lines in the water, Ray fired up Instagram and posted a story about motoring back to St. Thomas, beating into the waves under somewhat windy conditions. Within minutes, Jessica commented on the post.

No Sunday Funday? she asked.

Ray smirked at his phone and typed back: **It's always Sunday Funday on a boat. We just happen to be motoring back.**

After a brief pause, he added another message: **Actually, that's not technically true. I don't drink when I'm in charge of the vessel and responsible for people. So, shit, I guess it's not Sunday Funday for me... until we get back.**

His fingers hovered over the screen before he sent another text: **So when are you coming down to see me?**

Jessica replied: **Sooner than you think! I'm getting kicked out of my apartment July 1st, and I don't want to stay in Hilton Head. I'll be moving somewhere—probably Puerto Rico.**

Ray raised an eyebrow: **Oh wow. Seems like you'll have to come down for a tour so I can talk you into the right decision.**

Jessica: **I have to decide soon! I won't have time to visit. That's what's stressful! I have a friend in St. Thomas who keeps telling me the same thing—that I just need to come check it out. He also warned me it might be harder to find a rental with a dog, but he's a service animal, so hopefully that helps. Flights are insane right now, though. I just paid the same as a round-trip to Tahiti.**

Ray considered that for a moment before replying: **You're welcome to stay with me. The guest cabin should be back open soon. Who knows, might even like me a little.**

Jessica responded quickly: **Thank you, I appreciate that! Is a small Shih Tzu named Rufus welcome also?**

Ray grimaced. The last thing he wanted on board was a dog—especially a little one. When he first bought the boat, his own dog had lived aboard for two years, but that was mostly at a marina with easy shore access. A dog on board now meant dinghy trips to land multiple times a day, rain or shine. Then again, the Caribbean was mostly sunshine. After a moment of hesitation, he sighed and tapped out a reply.

Of course, a dog is welcome... I love dogs.

He's been with me almost ten years now, so yeah, we're a package deal. Jessica's response was exactly what Ray had expected.

Ray admitted: **I had my dog on board when I first set off to the Bahamas. Taking a dog to the beach a couple of times a day isn't so bad. But you'll have to take him to shore every so often by yourself.**

Jessica: **Wait... take him to shore? What does that involve?**

Ray leaned back and ran a hand through his hair. **Well, the boat isn't at a dock. It's usually on a mooring ball or at anchor. I don't like marinas—too crowded, everyone up in your business. So you'd hop in the dinghy, fire it up, drive to shore, tie up at the dock, take the dog to some grass—if you can find it—and then come back. Not too difficult.**

She shot back: **I don't know shit about driving a dinghy! I'm from Chicago!**

Ray: **It's not difficult. I'll teach you. I'm thinking of sailing to Grenada for September—avoid the worst month of hurricane season. Then, explore the islands in October on the way back north. St. Vincent, St. Lucia, Dominica, St. Barth's, St. Maarten. Didn't get to do that in 2020 because COVID shut everything down.**

Jessica: **That sounds amazing!**

Ray didn't miss the opportunity: **Could use a crewmate. Someone to sail with me.**

She hesitated before asking: **You got Wi-Fi on that thing? Luckily, I have two remote jobs, but I mostly rely on bartending since my rent and car payment are so high.**

Ray: **Yes, I have Wi-Fi. I run a software company. I always need to be connected. You wouldn't have those bills on the boat.**

Jessica's next message came after a moment: **We might just have to meet up and plan something.**

Ray grinned at the screen, sensing skepticism in her words. She thought he was just flirting.

Ray: **I'm coming to the States next week to visit my family in Ohio. Might have to swing by Hilton Head to meet you.**

He left the conversation there, waiting to see if she would respond. She didn't. Neither did he.

By 4 PM, *Purrfection* pulled into Vessup Bay after an uneventful, fish-less slog against the easterly trade winds. Ray navigated through the mooring field and turned upwind, making it easier for Tara to grab the mooring ball. Tara stood at the bow, boat hook in hand, pointing at the mooring like she was about to spear it. The gesture wasn't just for show—it helped Ray keep track of the ball, which disappeared from view about fifteen feet away.

After securing to the mooring ball, Tara called out, "Time for a *Safe Arrival* cocktail!"

Lindsey raised an eyebrow. "Safe Arrival? Has it ever not been safe?"

Ray grinned. "Any time we make it back and nobody dies, that's a *Safe Arrival*. So yes—technically always safe."

Lindsey nudged him. "Technically? Sounds like there's a story there, Captain."

Ray shook his head. "No stories... that I can share. Let's just say nobody's ever climbed aboard alive and left dead... well—guests, anyway."

Tara handed Ray his first drink of the day—tequila and water—while the sun slipped lower, painting the bay gold before they eventually ferried back to shore.

CHAPTER
SIX

May 2022
Ohio Sting

Ray left *Purrfection* for the week and made his way to the St. Thomas airport. Thanks to his ex-wife, a flight attendant, he was still listed as her preferred travel companion, allowing him to fly standby for free. Standby travel, however, was never guaranteed. If there was an open seat, he was on; if not, he waited. His ex pushed for frequent visits, eager for him to spend time with his grandchildren.

As he navigated through the underground walkway between Concourses A and B at the Atlanta airport, known for its artificial 'rain forest' ambiance, Ray posted an Instagram story. Almost immediately, Jessica commented.

Jessica: **Where you headed now?**

Ray: **Ohio for a week. Play some golf with my dad and brother. Want me to stop in Savannah on my way back next week?**

Jessica: **You just hop on a flight last minute? That's expensive.**

Ray let her assumption stand. No need to explain the perks of being a flight attendant's ex. Let her think he had the means to drop cash on a spontaneous flight.

Ray: **It would be nice to meet up, see if we vibe in person as well as we do over text. Hell, you might not even like me. Doubtful, but possible.**

By the time he boarded his flight to Dayton, he'd left Jessica's message hanging and turned his attention to his other friends, seeing who was free for golf or drinks. He never made plans before he was seated on the flight. The standby game was unpredictable; one canceled flight could shift an entire passenger list. His friends understood. If it worked out, great. If not, next time. The hardest thing to manage with this lifestyle? Dentist appointments.

Spending time with his grandkids was the real reason for these trips, but when they weren't available, golf provided the perfect distraction from not being in the Caribbean. He teed off at Walnut Grove Country Club, an old-school track where he had once been a member.

The course was a blue-collar country club, mostly filled with self-made millionaires—contractors, business owners, guys who started with one truck and built an empire. The kind of place where the only two doctors in the club didn't even want to be called Doctor. On Friday nights, the club had a couples tournament, usually involving more drinking than golf.

At the club, Ray reconnected with many of his old golfing buddies, each one eager to hear about his Caribbean adventures. He had spent years talking about buying a boat and making the move, yet most were still shocked when he followed through.

That evening, after golf, beers, and catching up with old friends, he finally posted an Instagram story about his day. He had learned to delay these posts while in Ohio; otherwise, his phone would explode with messages from people wanting to meet up. Sure enough, within minutes:

Jessica: **I don't know much about golf, but aren't you supposed to wear shoes?**

Ray: **I'm a Caribbean boy. I rarely wear clothes, let alone shoes.**

Immediately, he regretted that text; he backpedaled quickly.

Ray: **I mean, I'm in board shorts most of the time. Rash guard when the sun gets too intense. Never wear shoes on the boat.**

Jessica: **Well, at least you're having fun in Ohio. What else are you up to?**

Ray: **Golf, golf, and more golf. Dinner and drinks with friends. Trying to see my granddaughters as much as I can, but they're all so busy.**

As soon as he hit *send*, he winced. *Shit. Did I just reveal my grandpa status?* He wasn't sure if he had mentioned it before. Too late now.

Ray: **So you're still trying to move to the Caribbean?**

Jessica: **I have to decide soon! So stressed! Flights are costly, can't afford an exploratory trip. Flights to Puerto Rico are much cheaper, though.**

Ray: **I'll have to come pick you up in Puerto Rico then, sail you back to St. Thomas, after stopping in Culebra, of course.**

Jessica ignored that and continued.

Jessica: **That's one thing I didn't think about when moving to Hilton Head! I used to fly cheap from Chicago.**

Ray: **Yeah, but the weather?**

Jessica: **That's why I traveled so much! But I'm trying to finally make paradise my home! Hilton Head is great, but the water sucks! I'm a mermaid—I need to dive and snorkel whenever I want.**

Music to Ray's ears. The Virgin Islands were full of mermaids.

Jessica: **Practicing my frog kick in my pool with my snorkel gear isn't cutting it!**

Ray: **You should at least try the USVI. It's not for everyone, but it sure sounds like it's for you.**

Jessica: **I honestly just want to live in a hut by the beach! I'll build one if I have to!**

Ray: **A catamaran anchored just offshore isn't a bad option either.**

Jessica: **That's always been my dream—either learn to sail and live on a boat or open my own beachfront bed and breakfast.**

Ray: **Seems like we have a lot to talk about. I'll keep you updated on my travel plans. Let's see if I can swing by and meet you on my way back.**

Ray left it at that. No need to push. Timing was everything.

Ray left pre-dawn for the Dayton airport, knowing the flight to Atlanta was completely booked. At least he was the only passenger on standby—the only one bold enough to try it. All he needed was one person to *not* show up.

As boarding time neared its end, he heard the gate agent call out a name. That was the missing passenger he needed. If nobody sprinted up to the counter in the next few minutes, the seat was his.

Ray waited, heart steady, eyes on the clock. Then, the gate agent waved him aboard - the excitement and thrill of standby, space available travel.

Once the wheels hit the ground in Atlanta, he pulled out his phone.

Ray to Jessica: **Hey there. I made it out of Ohio and to Atlanta.**

Jessica: **Nice! Are you coming out this way? You never finalized anything.**

Ray: **I'd be coming to see you, and I never really properly asked you out.** He added a panicked emoji.

Jessica: **Well, when? Lol.**

Ray: **I'd get in tonight, but you're working, so tomorrow night?**

Jessica: **Okay, I could probably do that. I just have a bunch of stuff to do during the day, but nighttime should be fine.**

Ray: **Great. I won't get on this flight to St. Thomas. I'll just come see you instead.**

As he hit send, he realized her answer to *Will you go out with me?* was just *probably*.

Jessica: **You're crazy! I love it.**

Ray rolled into Hilton Head and booked the cheapest room he could find—a Days Inn with a lingering musty funk, wedged across the road from the ocean. The air outside felt like a wet towel to the face. Classic coastal South Carolina.

Ray: Good morning, Jessica!

Jessica: Morning, Ray. Where'd you end up staying? I probably could've gotten you a Marriott discount or something, but it was so last minute!

Ray: No worries. Ended up at a Days Inn. Kept it cheap.

Immediately after sending, Ray winced. He thought Jessica was into guys with money, and here he was proudly declaring his allegiance to budget motels. *Smooth, Ray.*

He scrambled to recover.

Ray: **But I've got a sweet hybrid minivan with your name on it. Candy apple red, black rims, leather seats. Absolute chick magnet. Vroom vroom.**

Jessica: **Oh boy. Can't wait. Even Days Inn is probably pricey around here. Everything is stupid expensive.**

Ray: **Just let me know what time works tonight. I still need to shave—probably rocking too much scruff for your taste.**

Jessica: **I have no idea. I'm awful at making decisions, FYI. But 7:30-ish should work. Also, can you just text me? Might be easier than Insta.**

Ray: **You got it. Sending a text now to lock it in.**

He flipped to his text app and typed: **Hi, this is Ray on *Purrfection*.**

Moments later:

Jessica: **Yep, got it.**

As soon as Ray switched to texting, he immediately received a text:

Jake: **Ray, what are you doing?**

Ray: **Hey, good to hear from you too, brother. Promise me money and adventure, then ghost me like a Tinder date. What a tease.**

Jake: **This isn't a joke. We were about to call you. We're finally ready to kick this operation off.**

Ray: **Call me? Jake, it's been two months. Not a word. Meanwhile, I've been floating around crewless like Tom Hanks. I've been talking way too much to Wilson. Oh, wait, that's right, you are the government.**

Jake: **Why are you messaging Jessica? How did you find her? Where'd you meet?**

Ray: **Honestly? Didn't even flinch when you texted. Figured you guys still had my phone monitored. Any normal American would be pissed right now, but I've come to expect the surveillance state.**

Jake: **We're not tapping your phone, Ray. It's not always about you. So, how did you meet her? What's going on?**

Ray typed proudly: **Well, Jake, I have our first dinner date scheduled for tonight at 7:30ish. I met her on a dating app a few weeks ago, and we've been messaging on Instagram. I guess you guys don't have Instagram tapped?**

Jake: **Tonight? We won't have any chance to get a team in place.**

Ray: **A team? Jake, are you sure you've got the right girl? I haven't met her yet, but she doesn't seem to have a lot of money. If she's a thief, she's terrible at it. Or she's really good at working three jobs to cover up the fact that she's got millions in the bank.**

Ray knew that Jessica could have been lying to him this entire time. Just because she told him about multiple jobs doesn't mean she's working at them.

Jake: **We've been tracking her for months. Tried placing one of our own as a captain, but she wasn't buying it. Wouldn't go for him.**

Ray: **Jake, Jake. Is he a real sailor? You can't fake the kind of shit we've experienced. Nobody ever knows if all our crazy stories are true or not. You can't make this shit up, Jake, and you definitely can't fake it.**

Jake took a few minutes before replying, totally ignoring the fact that he just revealed the failure of their operation to date: **We just won't have time to get a team in place, but maybe I can find a wire for you to wear.**

Wait a minute, Jake, you still want me to go through with this operation of yours? You really think this bartender from Chicago is some kind of experienced electronic bank thief? Ray stared at the message on his phone, thumb hovering over the send button.

His mind was spinning. Jessica didn't seem like a criminal—she seemed lost, maybe running from something, but not the kind of person who knew how to reroute international wire transfers or hack banking passwords. He liked her. More than he should, probably. Something in the way she talked about the ocean had stuck with him. Not just the usual tourist daydreams about sandy beaches and piña coladas, but something deeper. She'd told him she wanted to sail, to disappear into the blue, to leave the noise behind. She'd said it like someone who meant it.

That didn't sound like a criminal to him. But what did he know anymore?

He sighed and deleted the message.

The truth was, it didn't matter what he thought. The FBI was already in play. The Bureau had its hooks in this thing, and if Ray had any chance of protecting Jessica—or even finding out what she was really involved in he needed to stay close. He needed to play along. That was the only way he might be able to steer this in a direction that didn't end with her in handcuffs. Or worse.

Then he remembered the number Jake had thrown out. That kind of money could buy a whole lot of repairs for *Purrfection*. Boats were beautiful, but they were also giant floating holes into which you poured your soul and your savings. *Purrfection* had eaten through most of his savings already, and the off-season, hurricane season, was always a tightrope walk over an empty wallet. He loved his life down in the Caribbean, but it was hanging by a fraying dock line most days.

He took a breath, thought to himself, *"just say yes"*, and retyped his message.

Ray: **But if you need me to do it, Jake, I guess I'm in. I've served my country before; I can do it again. Do I need to sign any more paperwork to get paid like we discussed, or no?**

Jake texted Ray some more details on where to meet him to get set up and sign whatever paperwork needed to be signed. They coordinated details of where and when to meet Jessica; luckily, the FBI had some pull, because no reservations were available at any decent restaurant in Hilton Head during season.

Ray texted Jessica: **You were right. Reservations are a bit hard to come by.**

Haha, Yes, I know, I live here. Jessica texted like a smart-ass, scoring another point with Ray.

Ray: **Looks like I've got Crane's at 8:30 at the bar.**

Ray figured Jessica was a 'sit at the bar' girl at heart. Ray typed, Is that ok?, but did not hit send. He remembered Jessica was bad at decisions, so he decided to take away any question.

Jessica: **I'm cool with Cranes at 8:30.. I've been on the phone with a friend I booked Hawaii for and had to help them figure out some stuff... literally in a towel, need to get ready.**

Ray *really* wanted to fire back something about the towel; she tossed it up for an easy flirt, but stopped himself. The FBI was probably reading every message; he was on a mission now, not a real date. This was the first time Ray realized he might be in trouble, not following his natural instinct to flirt back.

Ray: **Ok, Crane's at 8:30. See you then.**

CHAPTER
SEVEN

May 2022
First Date

Jessica adjusted her gold hoop earrings as she stepped into the dimly lit restaurant, the warm sea breeze trailing in behind her. The scent of grilled seafood and tropical spices mingled with the gentle hum of chatter and clinking glasses. She paused just inside the entrance, scanning the room until her eyes locked on Ray.

He was seated at the bar, leaning casually against the polished wood, his short-sleeve shirt revealing tanned forearms. When he saw her, his face lit up in a smile that crinkled the corners of his eyes. Jessica felt a warm flutter in her chest as she made her way toward him.

"Jessica," he said, standing to greet her. "You look stunning."

"Thank you," she replied, her voice smooth but tinged with a hint of playful confidence. "You clean up pretty well yourself."

Ray laughed, a low, easy sound, and motioned toward the barstool next to his. "I hope you don't mind the bar. Reservations were impossible, but they said it was the best seat in the house."

Jessica slid onto the stool and leaned toward him slightly, her eyes sparkling. "The bar is my favorite spot. Better view of the action."

To Ray's delightful surprise, Jessica didn't turn to face the bar; she sat sideways, facing him. When Ray took his seat, their legs were almost intertwined, though just a little too much space at the bar kept them from actual physical contact.

"What can I get you to drink?" Ray asked.

Jessica looked at the bartender and said, "I'll do a Casamigos Reposado, please."

"A tequila girl? I love it." Ray turned toward the bartender. "Same for me, please."

"I usually drink silver tequila with water, ice, and a lime. But I love a good reposado."

"That sounds... hydrating?" Jessica teased, questioning Ray's boring drink of choice.

"It is! A friend on the island got me drinking it. It does prevent hangovers—or helps, anyway. Those island rum drinks hit hard, sneak up on you. That sugar drunk? That's a bad hangover."

The bartender placed two glasses of golden tequila in front of them. Jessica picked up both, handed Ray his glass, and said, "Cheers." She made an awkward movement toward Ray's face, almost as if coming in for a kiss, her eyes strangely wide open. "You gotta make eye contact when you clink the glass, or else it's seven years bad sex. My glass is up here, mister."

Ray was slightly embarrassed, not exactly sure where his gaze had been. "I did make eye contact. My eyes were on yours—until you freaked me out with that wide-open eye thing."

"I know they were. I saw you looking up... mostly." Jessica seemed to congratulate Ray, as if he had just passed some kind of test—or as if she had been disappointed too many times by men caught *not* looking in her eyes.

The drinks and the conversation flowed effortlessly.

"Have you read or heard of the book *The Swell*?" Jessica asked.

"I've heard of that book in the sailing community, but I don't know anything about it."

"The lady who wrote it lives on the island I go to in French Polynesia. She's from California but lives there now. It's a good read if you have some free time—it's about her sailing journey."

"I'll have to find time to read it. Unfortunately, I don't read much —too busy fixing things. A few classics, like Hemingway..."

"How about the documentary *Chasing Bubbles*? On YouTube. So good!" Jessica said excitedly.

"I have seen that. Such an epic journey," Ray answered. "That boat is in our mooring field."

"Wait—the boat, *Bubbles*?"

"Yes, you'll pass it every day. Multiple times a day, handling your dog's business."

"I'm not sure where my obsession with the ocean came from. My mom is deathly afraid of the water, and my hillbilly father—I'm not even sure he knows where the ocean is," Jessica said, contemplating.

Not wanting to dive into family just yet, Ray kept the "have you seen..." competition going. "Have you seen the YouTube channel *Sailing Doodles*?"

"*Sailing Doodles*? No, I'll have to look that one up."

"In the beginning, it was about a guy sailing around with his two Golden Doodles. But now it's basically T&A, still good, just a different direction. I know the creator, Bobby. We met in the US Virgin Islands during COVID and had some good times. I was actually on an episode —we had a pizza party on the beach, just the four of us: Bobby and Taylor, Punky and me. The episode is called *Goodbye to Punky*, and it's one of the most awkward goodbyes, a little bit of drama. I didn't realize when I was picking her up that he'd be filming it—but hey, it's what he does."

"Oh, so it's like *Girls Gone Wild* on a boat? Wait... you were in the video showing your T&A too?" Jessica teased. "I guess I could see the ass part... not bad."

Ray could tell the tequila was hitting her—especially with no food yet.

Jessica shifted topics quickly, pivoting hard from her comment about his backside. "So, when's your birthday?"

"January 19th. Why?"

"What year?"

"1967. If you ask me the time, I'm running out of here."

"The time? Why would I need the time? Why would you run out if I asked?"

"Oh, it's a funny joke. The son texts his mom and asks, 'Mom, what time was I born?' She texts back, 'Son, I don't care how pretty or sexy she is—RUN!'"

"I don't get it," Jessica replied with a blank stare.

"The mom knows—the girl is into astrology, and she's about to look up his *chart*. You know, she thinks the position of planet Earth in a massive universe at the exact time of his birth determines his personality—and their compatibility..."

"Oh, that's funny." But Jessica continued as if it wasn't connected, "Nah, I'm just going to look up your spirit animal. I don't need the time of birth for that."

Ray thought to himself, this could be disastrous, or it could be fun to play along. He remembered the old saying: *At some point in his life, every man has to choose between arguing about astrology or getting the girl.* He waited to hear what spirit animal he'd been assigned.

Jessica typed in his birth date. "Looks like you're a Salmon. Wow. I'm a Stingray, and I've never really met another water spirit animal. No wonder we get along so well so quickly."

Relieved that he could now play along—and maybe even use this to his advantage—Ray replied, "Well, of course we are. We're talking about the ocean and sailing and beaches, and living our lives around that. Makes sense we're water animals—the charts wouldn't lie!"

"Hard-working, resilient, and independent, those born under the sign of the Salmon are always on the move," Jessica read. "Well, that sounds like you." She continued: "Like their animal namesake, those born under this sign are willing to fight an uphill—or upstream—battle regardless of what the end goal is. Once they set their mind to something, there's almost no stopping them. Inside, they may have doubts and fears, but those rarely, if ever, come to the surface."

As she finished reading, Ray's logical brain was about to start arguing—but damn, that sounded like him. Too much.

"OK, OK, so what does it say about this Stingray—besides the obvious?" Ray asked.

"What's the obvious?" Jessica questioned.

"It's my name? Ray?" he said.

Jessica seemed to realize that for the first time, then returned to her app and read: "A seeming contradiction in terms, those born under the sign of the Stingray are adventurous, humanitarian, generous, sincere, rebellious, and emotionally fragile all at the same time. To some, this energy may come across as chaotic and wild—which it certainly can be—but Stingrays are also deep thinkers, dreamers, and idealists. Though they can be sullen and elusive at times, members of this sign always stand up for what they believe in."

Ray thought to himself, *Well, that sounds like me, too. But I'm not going to argue this.*

"Does that ring true to you?" Ray asked Jessica.

"I think it does, yes."

"Perfect. Some of my favorite red flags. We shall get along famously."

Their conversation flowed effortlessly—a mix of teasing banter and thoughtful exchanges that hinted at the depth of their connection. At one point, Jessica leaned forward, the glow from the overhead pendant lights catching in her hair. "Tell me something you wouldn't normally share on a first date," she said, her tone curious yet daring.

Ray's smile faltered just a bit, replaced by something more thoughtful. "I've never dreamed of living on a sailboat," he admitted. "It was never something I thought about, and now, I can't shake it. A line in a Jesse Rice song goes, *'I've sailed the waves, and given up my soul'*, and I feel that so deeply sometimes. Just me, sails up, the open water, and... maybe someone who doesn't get seasick."

Jessica's eyes widened. "That's bold. Romantic, though."

"What about you?" he countered. "What's your secret dream?"

She hesitated, swirling her glass again. "I'm simple. I just want to travel the world—unencumbered by my past."

"Sailing's a good way to accomplish both."

Ray had to remind himself, through the fog of the tequila, that the FBI was listening—and this was still an FBI operation.

"It's getting a bit late, and my flight is early tomorrow."

"I was thinking of taking you to another local bar—kind of a dive bar. Seemed like it would be perfect for you," Jessica said with enthusiasm, then added more subdued, "But it *is* late, and I have a long day of torturous work tomorrow."

"Next time, then," Ray said boldly.

"Next time, huh?" Jessica couldn't help but challenge his confidence.

"Oh, definitely," Ray said, standing and offering her his arm as they prepared to leave. "This was just the beginning of our story."

Jessica looped her arm through his, feeling the heat of his skin against hers. "Good," she said, her voice low and teasing. "Because I'm not done with you yet."

As they stepped out into the balmy Hilton Head night, the electric energy between them was undeniable, promising more to come, but not tonight.

Maxwell sat in the front passenger seat, casually sipping his coffee while Kevin fiddled with the monitoring gear, trying to clean up the signal from the restaurant bug. The faint clink of silverware and muffled laughter played through the speakers—Ray and Jessica, mid-date.

Maxwell twisted in his seat, projecting his voice toward the back of the van. "This couldn't be going any better. She's really into this guy, huh, Jake?"

Jake gave a dry, forced laugh, eyes fixed on the monitor. It wasn't funny.

"I mean, she's falling hard—first date—and this clown set it up all on his own. Didn't need our help. Guy's got natural game, doesn't he, Jake?"

Jake stayed quiet.

Maxwell smirked, clearly enjoying himself. "And we've barely even helped him."

Jake cut in, defensive. "What do you mean by *barely*? We made sure her lease didn't get renewed. Got the auto dealership to overpay by seven grand for her Jeep. The FBI paid full price for that expensive lamp she made. That's not nothing. We're pushing her out of Hilton Head—right toward this guy."

"I gotta admit," Maxwell said, leaning back, "when you pitched the idea to *not* hit her with the Campanelli threat, I thought it was weak. Thought you were going soft. But letting her move to the Caribbean on her own terms..." He nodded, almost impressed. "It's solid. We couldn't afford for her to get scared and disappear. Smart."

He let the moment hang, then turned, his grin sharp. "She's our Siren, right? The one who'll sing us straight to the treasure."

Jake shifted in his seat, jaw tight. He shot a glance at Kevin—still wearing his headphones, luckily oblivious to the turn in the conversation.

Maxwell leaned in slightly, voice dropping to a taunt. "Still... gotta sting a little, doesn't it? Watching her fall for the guy *you* recruited. Especially when you were probably hoping he'd blow it."

Jake didn't answer.

But the silence said plenty.

❖

Back in his hotel room, Ray lay on the bed, replaying the evening with Jessica—every laugh, every look. He'd never been the type to wait when it came to texting. So he started typing:

Ray: **I could miss my flight tomorrow and stay another day… Good Night.**

He was thinking she'd be asleep and he'd get no response, but then.

Jessica: **If I didn't have to work all day tomorrow, I would say miss it. But doesn't make sense since I have to slave away all day tomorrow. night night! Safe travels to the airport.**

Ray smiled at the ceiling, surprised by the buzz of another incoming message.

This time, it wasn't her.

Jake: **That went well. The team is impressed.**

Ray smiled as he texted back: **I kinda forgot all about you guys. I had a blast. Yeah, I think it went well. Kinda hesitated on the good night kiss, but keeping it professional for now.**

Ray suddenly remembered that the FBI was reading all his text messages as well.

Jake: **Probably best. We will make sure that when she checks your references that she hears more about your wealth.**

Ray: **That's a tall order, Jake. It would help if you guys made a nice deposit in my account already.**

Jake: **I can't see how that would help. She won't see your account until you log in from your computer, back on your boat. We just need to make sure she has the right perception of you.**

Ray: **You mean the right deception of me.**

Jake: **Just keep her interested. She needs to want you to be the mark. She only hustles people she likes. Doesn't matter how much they're worth.**

Ray: **Good to know.**

He stared at the ceiling, thumb hovering over the screen. Part of him wanted to press Jake about Jessica—a talented electronic thief with money in the bank, and she is working so many legit jobs? Bartending. Travel Agent. With a side-hustle making lamps out of tequila bottles.

But he knew better than to ask. He wouldn't get a straight answer. He didn't want to screw up his payday.

CHAPTER
EIGHT

May 2022
Call of the Sea

Ray stared down at his phone, thumb hovering over the screen. *Too soon?* he wondered. He sent the text anyway.

Ray: **Good morning. Hopefully not waking you up...**

The reply came faster than he expected.

Jessica: **Morning! I'm up! Half asleep but up. I was up way past my bedtime!! I'm an old lady! Haha.**

He grinned. Her energy came through, even in text. The kind of woman who could tease him before her first cup of coffee.

Ray: **My bad. Totally my fault. Hopefully it was worth it. What time does your shift start?**

Jessica: **10. Totally worth it. Are you in St. Thomas, or at least Atlanta?**

Ray: **Made it to Atlanta. Wouldn't be the worst thing if I missed this next flight to St. Thomas and had to come back and see you.**

He hit send and immediately wondered if he sounded too eager. *Chill, man. Let it breathe.*

Jessica: **You're crazy. You'd be welcome, but get back to Paradise! You were supposed to kidnap me and Rufus and bring us with! What kind of pirate are you?**

The smile on Ray's face deepened. He could practically hear her saying it.

Ray: **I've got a plan. Just gotta be careful with the whole pirate-kidnapping thing these days... Epstein kind of ruined the vibe. But... I hope that means you're still interested.**

He caught himself holding his breath, just a little.

Jessica: **I should probably get my own flight. Keep you out of trouble. When's your flight?**

Ray: **Got a few hours... unless I miss it and have no choice but to return to you.**

This time, he *knew* she was rolling her eyes. But then her reply surprised him.

Jessica: **I had to spend nine hours in that airport once! Never again. I blew so much money bar crawling solo just to stay sane.**

Ray laughed aloud in the terminal. Yeah, she was his kind of chaos.

Then her next text hit a different note.

Jessica: **And yes, I'm still interested. Extremely interested.**

He blinked. Read it again. A warmth lit up somewhere in his chest, uninvited but welcome.

Ray: **Good. Seemed like you were having fun enjoying my company. You know how I can tell when a bartender' is ACTUALLY flirting with me?**

Jessica was an experienced bar tender, and she knew full well all the bartender tricks for getting bigger tips.

Jessica: **How?**

Ray: **Yeah... she's NOT! She's really not.**

Jessica was impressed that Ray had this realization about bartenders. Most guys tend to believe they have a chance, and that's exactly what the good bartenders want them to think.

Jessica: **I wasn't your bartender last night, now was I? I was on the same side of the bar as you. That's a big difference. No bar to protect me—just open to you.**

Ray let that one sit for a beat, confirming that she was actually flirting with him last night.

Ray: **I'm learning. Sounds like we need to get you down here as soon as possible.**

Jessica: **That would be fabulous. Otherwise, I'll figure something out. I need to figure my life out anyway. Hilton Head's not it.**

Ray's fingers tapped faster now, momentum building.

Ray: **I thought we had a plan for hurricane season:**
— **Come to St. Thomas as soon as you can.** — **Check out the boat (and the captain).** — **If you like it, put your stuff in storage and come with me to Grenada.** — **July 1st: move aboard.** — **August 10th: start heading south.** — **October 1st: sail back north through Dominica, St. Lucia, St. Barth's, and St. Martin.** — **Back to St. Thomas by Nov 1st. I cover all food and drinks onboard.**

Jessica: **That sounds awful.** 😏

She's still playing. Good, he thought.

A couple hours later, just before boarding, one last confirmation he should get on this flight.

Ray: **I'm getting on the flight back to St. Thomas, boarding now.**

Jessica: **Safe travels! I'm about to walk out of my job. I'm so over it here. Not good, but I honestly don't even care. They're pushing me like they want me to quit.**

That made Ray pause. The playful rhythm between them flickered, replaced by something heavier. *Her life's unraveling faster than I expected,* he thought. *FBI influenced? Nah... that's crazy.*

Still, he didn't like the pit forming in his gut. So he pivoted.

Ray: **Well damn. I would've stayed if I'd known.**

Jessica: **Just decided this now. I can't keep showing up and being this miserable. It's not healthy.**

Ray: **Sounds like you've got new motivation. A new direction. It's what a stingray would do.**

He waited. The reply didn't come. Somewhere over the Bahamas, he leaned back in his seat and stared out at the clouds. His mind wandered: *Was this something real forming, or just fantasy stirred by sun and tequila?*

Just before touchdown, his phone buzzed again.

Jessica: **I just left work. Told my managers I'm giving two weeks, but I can't work those two weeks.**

Ray: **Congrats?!**

Jessica: **You'll think I'm crazy, but I've been so unhappy. I had nothing left. One coworker—total conniving bitch—shows up late every day with some excuse, and today I was like, "I don't want to hear it."**

She goes, "If you're so unhappy here, then don't be here."

So I left. I bust my ass and get treated like crap. I'm done.

Ray read the message twice. This wasn't a flirt. This was a line in the sand. A woman walking away from what wasn't serving her.

Ray: **Not crazy at all. I love it. Too many people stay stuck. Plugged into the Matrix. You're breaking free. Now let's get you to blue water.**

But as the plane began its descent into St. Thomas, Ray's thoughts wandered. Was Jessica really coming because she liked him—or, as the FBI suggested, to steal from him? In just a few weeks, she'd gone from a bartender pouring drinks to a full-blown fantasy—talking about sailing the world with him. Was it real? Or just part of a long con?

None of it made sense.

If she'd stolen millions, where was the money? Why juggle multiple jobs? Why all the side hustles? That's what gnawed at him. *Unless... maybe it wasn't about the payout. Maybe it was the thrill of the game.*

Either she's an Oscar-level actress, or the FBI is cluelessly chasing the wrong girl.

Ray leaned against the varnished wood rail of the dockside bar, a tall glass of silver tequila over water with a squeeze of lime in hand. The sun dipped low behind the masts, painting the harbor gold. He swirled the drink, watching the light catch on the clear liquid—a clean, sharp taste he'd come to favor.

Waiting for Bud Light Bob to arrive from St John, he snapped a photo—Tap & Still's open-air deck buzzing with chatter—and posted it to his story.

Jessica replied to his post within minutes.

Jessica: **It looks right up my alley.**

His heart gave a stupid little jump. It had been like that ever since they met—too much gravity between them, too fast. He wanted to play it cool. He never played it cool.

Ray: **Soon. Soon my lady. Soon.**

The three "soons", really Ray? Too eager. Too transparent.

Jessica: **I definitely feel like I should come out to visit first before making decisions! But I have done crazier things in my life.**

The tease in her words lingered once again, the maybe-maybe-not in her tone. Ray was caught between desire and caution. He wanted her to come. He *wanted* her, period. But he couldn't afford to scare her off. Not with pressure. Not with expectations.

He typed, erased, typed again.

Ray: **That's totally up to you. I understand. No pressure. I'm overly excited, I know. I thought we had a really good connection and I need to chill my ass out.**

He stared at the screen, grimacing. Too much again. He backpedaled.

Ray: **You can always bail out. Meaning you could just plan on coming to the boat, check it out, see how you like it. See how it goes with me. See how you like St. Thomas. Then choose: sail to Grenada with me for hurricane season, stay on land in St.**

Thomas, maybe you like St. Croix or St. John or Culebra better. Or ship your stuff to Puerto Rico.

It felt like a sales pitch disguised as reassurance. He told himself he was offering her options, but really, he was trying to build her a runway—to make it easy for her to say yes.

Then he waited. Finally:

Jessica: **I had a great time yesterday! I honestly would love to sail with you for months! I would love to learn about boats and all of that! I mean, it's really crazy how this is all kind of happening when I got put into a shitty situation! But I need to be smart and figure out all angles!**

There was a yes buried in there. A yes wrapped in caution, wrapped in circumstance. He could hear the conflict in her tone—logic warring with impulse.

Ray tried to ease her worry.

Ray: **You should check with Miranda too. She was my mate on my trip to Grenada in 2020. Ask her whatever questions you want—about me, about the boat, about sailing.**

If she needed to vet him, let her. He had nothing to hide.

Her next message stopped his breath cold.

Jessica: **Can we just keep going and go to the Galápagos? With a stop in Panama at Bocas del Toro and Isla Colón??**

Then, as if afraid of what she'd just said:

Jessica: **Just a thought.**

Ray stared at the screen, stunned. That wasn't just a whim—it was *his* dream. A dream he had long folded up and shelved away with the other impossible things. A crossing to the Pacific. A partner. A reason.

His thumbs trembled slightly as he typed, remembering she still might be a thief. She still might be saying all this to play him:

Ray: **Oh don't tease me. Finding somebody to do that journey with has been a dream of mine.**

His mind flashed ahead—Jessica at the helm, barefoot, hair wild in the salt air. Nights under foreign stars. The two of them sharing silence, storms, stories.

He reeled it back in.

Ray: I know I'm very poorly trying to flirt but you will have your own cabin, your own space, on the other side of the boat.

He didn't want her to think he was luring her down here for anything she wasn't ready for. But even as he said it, his thoughts drifted—what if she *did* want more? Would he even know how to handle it?

Jessica: Good to know! Because I'm very independent and used to being by myself. So these were things running through my mind—how I would deal with another person everyday!? Haha not like deal? I guess that's bad verbiage. I'm just so used to being by myself.

Ray smiled to himself. It was the first time they'd even discussed the cabin layout, and now that it was out in the open, he found himself wondering—had she assumed they'd be sharing a cabin? Had he?

That fantasy crept in again—waking up with her beside him, tangled legs, coffee in the cockpit, no walls between them. He shook it off. Too soon. Too much.

Then the message that undid him:

Jessica: Sign me up! We're doing this!!! How did I become the lucky winner?

He read it twice. Three times. His grin could've lit up the marina.

Was she serious? Was this it? He didn't want to jinx it by celebrating too early. Yet, it could still be a set-up for her to get to his FBI-funded bank account.

Jessica: I already have a life jacket for Rufus! Umm this might be a random question? But how do I get my guns there?

Of course. Of *course*, her next concern would be about her dog and her weapons.

Ray laughed aloud, startling the couple next to him.

Then, with his heart in his throat and more truth in his fingers than he meant to send:

Ray: Omg I love you.

Teasing, or maybe it was too much. Maybe it was the silver tequila working overtime in his chest. Or maybe it was just the truth slipping past his guard. He didn't mean it in the forever kind of way. But he didn't *not* mean it, either.

The typing bubble appeared. Disappeared. Came back.

Ray was nervously hoping she didn't take that last text too seriously. Then two photos dropped into the thread.

The first—Jessica lying in a hot pink hammock, hair twisted in a messy bun, sun-kissed and radiant. She wore a snug gray tank top, the curve of her smile a little crooked, a little dangerous. Her eyes were alive —bright and daring—and the swirl of ink down her shoulder gave her that defiant edge he was so drawn to. She looked wild and grounded at once. Like someone who could shake the whole world loose and still land barefoot on deck without flinching.

The second photo made him laugh out loud.

Rufus, nestled right between her tan legs, was flopped upside down in a tropical-patterned doggie life jacket, looking equal parts confused and proud. His tiny teeth peeked through his underbite as if to say *I didn't NOT sign up for this.*

Then her message came:

Jessica: **You're trouble, Captain. But I think I'm in.**

Jessica stood in her condo, adjusting the angle of her phone to snap pictures of her latest creations—lamps made from empty tequila bottles. Her signature piece was the tall, elegant Clase Azul bottle, its white ceramic body adorned with hand-painted blue florals. With precision, she drilled a hole in the base for the power cord and topped it with a perfectly chosen lampshade. Just as she framed the next photo, her phone lit up with a text from Courtney, her friend back in Chicago.

Courtney: **Hey, how's it going in Hilton Head? I need to come visit.**

Jessica: **Too late bitch! I'm moving on.**
Courtney: **Wait, what? Moving to where, Puerto Rico?**
Jessica: **Nope, I'm moving to the US Virgin Islands.**
Courtney: **What?? That's fabulous. Did Trevor hook you up with a place to stay?**
Jessica: **No. He did not. I haven't told Trevor I'm coming yet.**
Courtney: **You are confusing me. What's going on?**
Jessica: **I met this guy, and he's a really good guy, and he lives on his catamaran in St Thomas, and he needs help for hurricane season, so yeah. I'm going to be his crew.**

Jessica saw the dots coming from Courtney's text. Then no dots. Then more dots.

Courtney: **WTF?! So many questions... Maybe just call me?**

Jessica hit dial. "Hey, how are you?"

Courtney didn't even pretend to ease in. "I'm great. What the *hell* are you doing? Who *is* this guy? How did you meet him?"

Jessica hesitated. "He's this well-known captain down in the islands. Runs day charters out of St. Thomas. Red Hook, I think it's called. Same area Trevor is in."

"That's not what I asked. Did Trevor introduce you? I thought he didn't even know you were coming?"

"No, not through Trevor."

"So, how do you go from bartending in Hilton Head to knowing a charter captain in the Virgin Islands? Was he on vacation?"

"No." Jessica exhaled, already bracing for impact. "I met him on a dating app, okay? He found my profile in Hilton Head. We matched. We texted. We vibed. He's got good energy."

Courtney pounced. *"Texted*? Have you met this dude in person, or are you moving to a postcard with good lighting?"

"I'm not an idiot. He flew to Hilton Head to take me out to dinner."

"He *flew in* just for you?" Courtney paused. "...Okay, that's a little impressive."

Jessica had thought about saying he was on his way from Ohio back to the islands. But *"flew in just for me"* played better. So she let it sit.

"We had a great dinner. Talked all night. He's got that... grounded energy. I'm excited."

Courtney grinned through the phone. "Great. So, how was he in bed?"

"Gesh bitch, what kind of girl do you think I am? It was one date, our first date."

"Ok, ok, you are a little frigid at first, aren't you. How was the goodnight kiss?"

"Can we *not* make this about sex? I'm spiraling. I'm losing my place, I quit my job, and it's a complete shit show down here."

"You're dodging. Which means it was either awful... or—oh no. Did you *scare him off*? He didn't even try, did he?"

"I didn't scare anyone. It was a sweet night. I think he didn't want to mess it up. I mean, we're talking about moving in together. Not like... dating. More like roommates. Crewmates? Boat mates? Are we just supposed to make out in the parking lot?"

"That is *a lot*, Jess. You hate Hilton Head that much? Why not just come back to Chicago? It's been a few months, I'm sure Campanelli has forgotten all about it."

"You *know* I can't go back. Antonio Campanelli hasn't forgotten anything. Even if he forgave me, his crusty-ass uncle never will. I gotta go somewhere. The condo I'm in is getting sold. I quit my job last week. I don't even have rent for June—but hey, that's what security deposits are for, right?"

"Damn. What happened to that other guy—Captain Dillon?"

"Oh, please. That was nothing. He loitered at the bar, flirted a little, but never asked me out. I only brought him up because he was the first halfway decent-looking human I'd met here. But his vibe was off. Like, used car salesman energy. I'm not even sure what he was captain *of*."

"So now you're just peacing out to the Caribbean?"

"You know I've always wanted to do this. Gypsy soul and all that. This guy, Ray—he's smart, funny, easy to be around. Good energy."

"Okay, okay," Courtney said, sighing. "Send me a photo and every scrap of information you have on him. I'll at least cross-check with Trevor. Maybe run a background check. Trevor has ways."

CHAPTER NINE

June 2022
Second Date?

Ray was up early, just as the sun peeked through the hatch above his head. He rolled out of his bunk and hopped to the floor, walking the two short steps into the galley, naked as usual.

He flipped the propane safety switch next to the stove, grabbed the grill-style lighter from the utensil basket, and turned the knob until gas whispered out. A flick of the lighter, and the flame caught. He filled the kettle with just enough water for one full cup, then set it on the burner. He prepared the French press, adding coffee grounds and placing it over his favorite mug—one he'd picked up years ago on his first sailing trip to Green Turtle Cay, Bahamas.

Sipping his morning coffee, looking out over the water for his turtle friends, Ray fired off a text to Jessica: **Any news on flights? It'd be great to get you here by May 30th for the Rock De Boat raft-up concert on the water.**

Jessica's response was less optimistic. Flights were a mess. She was too busy just trying to tie up loose ends. Her next hurdle was figuring out how to get her stuff to the islands. Shipping was expensive.

Ray reminded her that space on a boat was limited: **We won't be making lamps out of tequila bottles or anything.**

But he had a solution: one last trip back to Ohio before hurricane season. A golf tournament with his buddy Fireball Bill, a visit with family—and maybe a swing through Hilton Head to pick up a couple of suitcases for her. The perfect excuse for one more dinner date.

Jessica replied with: **Why doesn't that surprise me? You're getting predictable. How boring...**

Ray could feel the flirtation in her words. It tugged at him. He knew he should keep things professional, but Jessica's teasing hit all the right notes. Still, he reminded himself: when she comes to the Caribbean, it might not be for him—it might be for the money.

Meanwhile, Jessica bit her lip as she texted him. She wanted to invite him to stay with her, remembering his gentle touch on her arm at dinner that had left an impression. But she couldn't bring herself to say it.

Instead, she wrote: **I'm not working at the Marriott anymore. Can't get you that discount.**

Ray read it and felt the absence—no offer to stay at her place. But maybe that was for the best. One awkward night could jeopardize everything. They both knew it. He resisted the urge to send a cheeky reply about staying on her couch and simply said:

That's okay. I'll stay at the Holiday Inn Express near your place. Easier to get your luggage that way.

Hilton Head Island shimmered under the weight of a soft, amber evening. The faint scent of salt and jasmine lingered in the air as Jessica adjusted her dress and stepped out of her Jeep. The waterfront restaurant loomed in front of her, a sprawling expanse of glass and wood that glowed warmly against the deepening twilight. Ray was already there, leaning against the railing near the entrance, his broad shoulders silhouetted by the fiery remains of the sunset.

"You're early," she said as she approached him.

"Or you're late," he countered, though the grin tugging at his lips softened the words. He was dressed simply—white linen shirt, sleeves rolled up, khaki pants—but the confidence with which he wore it made her wonder how he always seemed so comfortable, no matter the setting.

They stepped inside together, the soft murmur of conversation and the clinking of crystal filling the space. The hostess guided them to their table, a secluded spot near the edge of the terrace overlooking the marina. The view was breathtaking—sailboats rocked gently in the harbor as a crescent moon began to rise—but Jessica's attention was pulled to the table itself.

Wide. Far too wide.

Ray pulled out her chair for her, and she murmured a thanks before sitting down. He slid into his own seat across from her, leaning back casually as he scanned the surroundings. But the width of the table created an odd distance, as though the space itself was reminding them to stay in their respective lanes.

A waiter arrived almost immediately, offering them water and a wine list, but Ray held up a hand. "We'll start with Casamigos Reposado, neat," he said.

Jessica raised an eyebrow. "Ordering my drink for me? Bold move."

Ray grinned. "We both know you aren't a white wine spritzer kind of woman."

"Fair enough," she said, smiling despite herself. "It's what I would have ordered anyway."

"I know." He stated. She found herself wanting to smack that smirk right off his face, but could not hold back her smile.

The waiter nodded and disappeared, leaving them with their menus. Jessica pretended to study hers, but her thoughts drifted. It wasn't a date. It couldn't be. Or was it? Yet, here they were, staring across an expanse of white linen and candlelight, the pull between them tangible even in the moments of silence.

"So," he said after a moment, "how is the packing? You have a suitcase for me to take back?"

Jessica sighed, setting down her menu. "Exhausting. I didn't realize how much junk I'd accumulated until I had to fit my life into two suitcases. I have something for you to take back, yes."

"Welcome to boat life," he said, his grin returning. "Minimalism isn't a choice; it's a necessity."

She smirked but didn't respond, her mind flitting back to the small, utilitarian quarters of Ray's boat. She'd seen pictures, and while it was tidy and well-maintained, the thought of squeezing her life into such a confined space with a man she barely knew still felt surreal. Necessary, yes, but surreal.

The waiter returned, balancing two small glasses of golden tequila on a tray. He placed one in front of each of them, then added a small plate of lime wedges and a pinch of salt on the side.

Ray raised his glass, tilting it slightly toward her. "To hurricane season," he said with a wry smile.

Jessica hesitated, her fingers curling around her glass. "To surviving hurricane season," she corrected, lifting hers.

But when Ray leaned forward to clink his glass against hers, Jessica froze. "Wait. Hold on."

"What?" He lowered his glass slightly, puzzled.

"You didn't make eye contact," she claimed, her cheeks flushing. "When you toast, you have to look the other person in the eyes. It's seven years of bad sex if you don't. I thought I taught you this already?"

"Yes, ma'am, you did. We can't afford seven years of bad sex," he blurted out, his lips twitching with amusement, Jessica ignoring the comment. "I'll make it awkwardly obvious this time."

His eyebrows rose, but he complied, locking eyes with her as their glasses met with a soft clink. The moment lingered, her eyes holding his a beat longer than necessary, and suddenly the tequila felt like an afterthought.

The tequila was smooth, smoky with a hint of vanilla, and it warmed her from the inside out. She set her glass down, feeling the tension in her shoulders ease slightly. For all her reservations, there was something undeniably easy about being around Ray, even when they were actively avoiding the undercurrent pulling them closer.

"If you had reached for that lime, this date would be over!" Jessica couldn't believe she had just said the word 'date'.

"Of course not, no training wheels for this sailor, and never with a good Reposado."

The waiter returned just in time to break that bit of awkwardness to take their dinner orders—grilled mahi-mahi for her, steak for him—and then retreated again, leaving them in the soft glow of the candlelight.

"I eat a lot of fish, you know, in the Caribbean. I just had one of the best steaks back in Dayton at the Pine Club, but I won't get good steak for a while, so... I probably should have warned you, we'll eat a lot of fish." Ray stated as the silence returned expeditiously.

"This isn't how I imagined my life turning out," Jessica said abruptly, her fingers tracing the rim of her glass.

Ray's gaze sharpened. "Moving onto a stranger's boat during hurricane season wasn't part of the five-year plan?" In the back of his mind, he was wondering if being a thief was part of her plan.

She laughed despite herself, the sound light but edged with weariness. "Not exactly. But I guess life has a way of... rerouting you. I've always wanted to travel and spend time in the Caribbean... just wasn't expecting this, under these circumstances."

He nodded, his expression unreadable. "Tell me about it."

It was the kind of moment that invited honesty, but neither of them stepped into it. Instead, Jessica reached for her tequila, letting the warmth settle in as it slid down her throat.

"What made you decide to stay in the Caribbean year-round?" she asked. "Most people would pack up and head north for hurricane season, or south, right?"

Ray leaned forward slightly, resting his forearms on the table. "It's home," he said simply. "I can make some extra money running charters while all the other boats leave. Besides, that's why I've got you, to run south if anything major comes at us."

"You couldn't just... hire someone to help? A first mate or whatever you sailors call it?"

He shook his head. "First mates are paid by charter, and I don't know if we will have any. I hope we do, but I couldn't guarantee. Besides, I need someone I can trust, somebody who is ready to go. I can't afford somebody backing out at the last minute."

"Ah," she said, raising an eyebrow. "And I'm supposed to trust you with my life in return?"

"You're here, aren't you?"

The words hung between them, neither of them willing to admit how much weight they carried. Jessica wanted to argue, to point out how desperate circumstances had forced her hand, but she knew it wouldn't change the truth. She was here. Part of her—the part she didn't want to examine too closely—did trust him. Or at least wanted to.

Their food arrived, a welcome distraction. For a while, they ate in companionable silence, the clinking of silverware and the hum of conversation from nearby tables filling the gaps between them. But as the plates emptied, the tension returned, coiled and unspoken.

Jessica set down her fork, her appetite fading. "We need to set some ground rules," she said abruptly.

Ray looked up from his nearly demolished steak. "Ground rules?"

"For the boat. For... us. If this is going to work, we need boundaries."

He leaned back in his chair, crossing his arms over his chest. "That's usually the Captain's job, but all right. Let's hear it, Admiral."

She hesitated, the words tangling in her throat. "For starters, no... entanglements."

His brow furrowed. "Entanglements?"

"You know what I mean," she said, her cheeks flushing. "This is a practical arrangement. I need a place to stay; you need help for hurricane season. Let's not complicate things."

A slow smile spread across his face, and she resisted the urge to throw her napkin at him.

"Relax," he said. "I'm not in the habit of complicating things. No expectations."

"Good," she said firmly. "Because I'm not looking for anything. Not right now. Not yet."

"Message received," he said, though the teasing glint in his eye made her wonder if he was taking her seriously.

She exhaled, relief and frustration warring within her. "What about you?" she asked. "Any ground rules you want to set?"

He considered her for a moment, his expression softening. "Just one," he said finally. "Be honest. If something's not working, if you need out—whatever it is—just say so. Don't let it fester."

Jessica blinked, caught off guard by the sincerity in his voice. "Okay," she said softly. "I can do that."

They fell silent again, but this time the quiet felt less strained, as though they'd both taken a step closer to the fragile middle ground they were trying to build.

The waiter returned to clear their plates, offering dessert menus, but Jessica shook her head. "I think I've had enough for tonight."

Ray nodded in agreement, signaling for the check. When it arrived, he reached for it, but she beat him to it with quicker hands and a smirk.

"Split it," she said, holding up a hand to stop him.

"Jessica—"

"This isn't a date," she reminded him, her tone firm but light. "Remember?"

"If it is a crew meal, the Captain pays. It's tax deductible." Ray couldn't believe the words that came out. If there was one way to kill any romance, THAT was it - *tax deduction*.

As they stepped back into the cool night air, the marina stretched out before them, its boats swaying gently under the moonlight. They walked in silence for a while, the only sounds the faint lapping of waves.

"You sure about this?" Ray asked suddenly, his voice cutting through the stillness.

Jessica stopped, turning to face him. "About moving onto your boat? Or about trusting you not to complicate things?"

"Both."

She studied him for a long moment, searching for cracks in the easy confidence he wore like armor. But all she saw was a man who, for better or worse, was offering her a lifeline.

"I'm sure," she said finally, though the words felt as much like a challenge as a reassurance.

He nodded, a small smirk tugging at his lips. "Good. Let's hope we don't regret it."

They stood there for a moment longer, the space between them humming with unspoken possibilities. Then Jessica turned, heading toward the parking lot, and Ray watched her go, his hands in his pockets and his thoughts as restless as the sea.

Inside the cramped FBI surveillance van parked discreetly behind a cluster of palm trees, the air was thick with tension and the hum of machinery, and humidity, the AC unable to keep up. The faint aroma of coffee and the sharper tang of overused electronics underscored the hushed conversation among the three agents.

Agent Maxwell, the grizzled veteran, leaned back in his swivel chair, the dim glow of the monitor lighting up his face. He scratched at his graying beard, a smirk tugging at his lips. "Well, that was cozy," he said, nodding toward the audio feed coming through their headphones.

"C'mon, man," Jake muttered, shifting uncomfortably on the bench seat, the faint redness creeping up his neck betrayed his embarrassment.

"Oh, Jake. Admit it," Maxwell pressed, his voice laced with amusement. "Jessica sure seems to have a soft spot for our boy Ray. She practically melted when he ordered that fancy tequila. You taking notes on how to sweep a lady off her feet?"

Jake shot Maxwell a glare. "This is work. Professionalism, remember?"

Maxwell chuckled. "Sure, kid. Professionalism."

At the other end of the van, Kevin, the tech guy, didn't even look up from his console. His fingers flew across the keyboard, and the screen displayed a barrage of data: financial transactions, boat registrations, and the Siren's digital breadcrumbs. A half-eaten donut sat precariously close to his keyboard.

"You two done?" Kevin asked without turning around. "Some of us are trying to figure out how our suspect manages to drain a yacht owner's bank account without leaving a trail. You know, actual FBI work."

"Relax, Kev," Maxwell said, waving a hand dismissively. "A little banter never hurt anyone. Besides, it's not every day you see a con artist like Jessica flirt her way onto a boat. The lady has skills."

Jake shifted in his seat again, his jaw tightening. He stared at the small monitor in front of him, where a grainy live feed showed Ray and Jessica at the marina restaurant. The pair appeared relaxed, laughing over some shared joke, their body language effortlessly intimate.

"Ray's just playing the part," Jake said, his voice a little too firm.

"Oh, absolutely, he's got the charming Caribbean captain thing nailed." Maxwell agreed, his tone dripping with sarcasm. "But you've gotta admit, they've got chemistry. He's good. Almost too good, huh?"

"Ray is working for us on this operation; he just needs the damn charter fee," Jake snapped, finally turning to glare at Maxwell. "Unlike some people who can't seem to stay focused."

Maxwell's smirk widened. "Easy there, tiger. Just calling it like I see it. You're not worried Jessica might like him, are you?"

Jake clenched his fists, but Kevin cut in before the conversation could escalate.

"Will you two knock it off?" Kevin said, his voice sharp. "I've got something here."

Both agents leaned forward, the playful tension evaporating instantly. Kevin tapped a few keys, and a series of bank statements appeared on the screen. He pointed to a line of suspicious transactions.

"This is from one of her previous marks," Kevin explained. "She siphoned money in small increments over a few months, routing it through offshore accounts before it disappeared entirely. Looks clean at first glance, but see these timestamps? They correspond to the GPS locations of her burner phone. On this other yacht in Miami, she transferred it all at once, one big score, bouncing off accounts in 3 different countries before I lost track of it. It's different every time."

Maxwell whistled low. "Impressive work, Kev. But when she takes Ray's funds, I bet she does it in one swoop. Ray is too tied to his account, he'd noticed."

Kevin glanced over his shoulder, his brow raised. "You sure about that? If Jessica likes this guy, she might not even…"

Maxwell cut Kevin off, "It will be one big grab, as long as Ray holds together and she doesn't bolt."

"Ray can handle himself," Maxwell insisted. "He's been navigating tricky waters long before he got involved with us. He knows how to charm and disarm better than all of us combined."

"True," Kevin agreed. "But even the best can be outplayed. Jessica is not just any con artist. She's smart, manipulative, and… let's face it, she's damn charming herself."

Jake's jaw tightened again, but he said nothing. The silence in the van grew heavy, broken only by the faint crackle of static from the surveillance equipment.

"Speaking of charming," Maxwell continued, clearly unable to resist, "Jake, what was it she called you when you met her at that Chicago yacht party? Handsome? Or was it something else?"

Kevin snorted, trying and failing to hide a grin.

"Enough," Jake said through gritted teeth. "Can we focus on the case?"

"Sure, sure," Maxwell said, holding up his hands in mock surrender. But the twinkle in his eye said he wasn't done teasing his junior agent just yet.

Kevin cleared his throat, drawing their attention back to the screen. "Look, I've got Ray's account set up, sitting there with a million in it. He's authorized to use $25k. Before Jessica makes her move, we will need to unlock it. I'm setting up alerts on her known account. Her account is limited to $100k transfers, so once in her account, she won't be able to easily move it, giving us plenty of time to lock it before we arrest her. We learned that trick from the Chicago disaster."

Maxwell nodded. "Good. Jake, keep an eye on their texts, especially Ray's. If anything seems off, I need to know immediately. This operation is too important, and I can't afford any slip-ups."

Jake gave a curt nod, his eyes fixed on the monitor. On the screen, Jessica leaned closer to Ray, her laughter ringing through the audio feed. Ray responded with a charming smile, his hand brushing hers across the table. The intimacy of the moment made Jake's stomach churn, though he'd never admit it.

"You okay, Jake?" Maxwell asked, his tone uncharacteristically soft.

"I'm fine," Jake replied, his voice flat.

"Good," Maxwell said. "Because we're just getting started. We need this buddy. We need it. Let's make sure we're the ones writing the ending to this story."

Kevin cracked his knuckles and got back to work, his eyes glued to the screen. Maxwell leaned back, crossing his legs and watching the feed with the patience of someone who'd seen it all before.

Jake, however, couldn't shake the gnawing feeling in his gut. He told himself it was just concern for the mission. He needed it to be a success. But deep down, he knew it was more than that. Jessica wasn't just another suspect. That terrified him more than he cared to admit.

Maxwell placed his nightly call to Director Beck.

Beck answered on the first ring. "Report."

"She's definitely moving to the boat," Maxwell said. "So we've activated Ray's fake account. Once she's settled—and we're sure she can't just bolt—we'll have Campanelli text her the instructions."

"Bolt? Why would she run?"

Maxwell gave a half-laugh. "It's the Caribbean, sir. People vanish all the time. People go there TO vanish. That's why the real Siren operates there—easy island-hopping, fragmented customs, some ports still use carbon copy forms. No real need for a fake passport; nobody has a passport scanner anyway. If someone wanted to disappear? This is still the place to do it."

Beck grunted. "Right. We *want* her to vanish once the money's transferred. Don't forget that."

"I know the plan. It was your plan." Maxwell paused, then added, "Yeah, I think Ray can keep her around long enough. He's smooth. I can see why you didn't want Elana anywhere near him."

He said it lightly, teasing like they were two rookies back in a surveillance van—but then remembered he wasn't that guy anymore. Beck sure as hell wasn't.

Maxwell pivoted. "On a more serious note, Kevin has found something on the real Siren—how she siphons funds slowly over time. We didn't know that already? Wouldn't that make our version look... off?"

Beck didn't miss a beat. "The Siren task force isn't trying too hard to catch her. They like their junkets to Miami and Barbados. She's careful, but Kevin must be good. Still, if they found something obvious, they'd have acted. I wouldn't stress about the details."

He added, almost as an afterthought, "No one's going to miss a million dollars. Not in our budget."

They exchanged a few fading pleasantries from their days in the field, then ended the call.

CHAPTER TEN

June 2022 - St. Thomas
Welcome Aboard

Ray shifted nervously in the Jeep he borrowed, his fingers tapping a rhythm against the steering wheel as he idled in the arrivals lane at St. Thomas airport. He'd only met Jessica a few weeks ago, but their conversations had quickly escalated from polite pleasantries to something that felt deeper, even real. Now she was here, and he couldn't help but feel the flutter of anticipation—and maybe a hint of anxiety—in his chest. Somehow, this did not feel like it was an FBI operation - all set up and staged.

The sliding doors of the terminal whooshed open, and there she was. Jessica stood out against the crowd, even the St. Thomas crowd, her dark hair catching the light, a vibrant floral sun dress brushing her thighs. Her face lit up when she spotted him, and she waved with the kind of enthusiasm that made Ray's stomach flip. Beside her, waddling in a slow, determined gait, was Rufus, her Shitzu. The dog looked as out of place as a snowman on the beach, but his flat face held an air of unbothered dignity.

Ray jumped out of the Jeep, waving back. "Hey! Welcome to paradise."

Jessica beamed. "Thanks for picking us up. Rufus has already had enough of traveling for one day, haven't you, buddy?"

Rufus grunted in response, his tongue lolling sideways. Ray bent down to scratch behind his ears, earning a grunt of approval. "He's a champ. Let's get you two out of this heat. There's no way a taxi would take you with a dog, so I had to borrow a car to come get you."

Jessica handed him Rufus's leash while she wrestled her suitcase into the back of the Jeep. Ray opened the passenger door for her, she stooped down to pick up Rufus, and hopped in. Once they were all settled, Ray pulled onto the main road, the shimmering ocean coming into view almost immediately.

"So, what do you think so far?" he asked, stealing a glance at her.

"Well, you're driving on the wrong side of the road. It's making me a bit nervous, and I'm from Chicago."

"I kinda meant the island."

"It's gorgeous," she said, her voice tinged with awe as she took in the turquoise water and swaying palm trees. "Even more beautiful than the pictures."

"This is just the airport beach. Wait until you see St. John beaches, and the turtles, and the sunset," Ray said. "But first things first. You must be thirsty after that flight. There's a great spot just down the road where we can grab a drink. It's actually called the Dog House. Most places on the island are not going to be dog-friendly, but I'd think Dog House should be? I'm not sure."

"Rufus is a Service Dog, so..."

Ray cut her off with a laugh.... "That isn't going to matter down here. It's the US, but it's a territory, not the real US. You won't find disability access, handicap parking spaces, service animals - none of that matters down here."

He turned into a parking lot with a steep entrance, typical for the island, and found a good spot to park in the main paved lot, not always an easy task. Jessica exited the Jeep with Rufus tucked under her arm, a familiar resting place for him. Ray looked over at her, carrying the dog, not knowing what to say, so he didn't.

Like most bars in the Caribbean, the Dog House was open-air, with no walls or doors to walk through. It was across the street from the cruise ship terminal and had absolutely no view whatsoever. But it had good food and drinks, and was a dog-friendly locals spot - unless cruise ships were in port.

They were able to get two seats at the bar. Rufus settled under her barstool with a huff, his expression suggesting he approved of the venue, or he was pissed at being left on the floor. Ray didn't know the bartender and was trying to get her attention when Jessica stopped him.

"Shift change." She said. From her professional experience, she could tell the bartender behind the bar was trying to close out, and a new bartender should be around here somewhere.

Ray heard a giggle coming from behind the swinging door, not far from where they were sitting.

"Oh shit," he told Jessica. "Forgive me now, because we might be in trouble."

"What are you talking about?"

As Jessica asked, the swinging door flung open, and Izzy sprang forth. She saw Ray and immediately came running around the bar. Ray stood to hug her, and in typical Izzy exuberance, she hopped into Ray's arms and wrapped her legs around his waist, giving him sloppy kisses on his cheek.

Isabella was in her mid-twenties, with smooth, sun-kissed skin that glowed against the backdrop of the Caribbean sun. Her straight, chestnut-brown hair fell effortlessly to her shoulders, with deep brown eyes that exude both mischief and warmth, framed by naturally arched brows. A small, delicate nose ring added to her vibrant personality, while an intricate floral tattoo danced across her shoulder. And that giggle…. That infectious Izzy giggle.

Before Ray could say anything, "Is this Jessica?! The boys have been talking about you all month! Welcome to the island!"

"I did NOT realize you'd be working at Dog House today. I borrowed a car and need to be able to drive us back to Red Hook!" Ray pleaded. "Jessica, this is Izzy, Isabella, my favorite local bartender. She's usually over in Red Hook."

"You think I'm usually in Red Hook because that's where you see me. I probably work as many shifts here as I do over there." Izzy stated, then turned to Jessica, "Kinda gotta work two jobs around here to pay the rent.... So..... Shots!" as Izzy danced her way back behind the bar.

"Was that a question," Jessica asked.

"I don't think so," Ray replied, then realized Jessica's response wasn't a question either. "Oh shit," he mumbled to himself.

"Ting bombs?" Izzy asked.

"With Jameson, sure!" was Jessica's answer.

"That's different, but I like it!" as Izzy giggled and proceeded to add Jameson and Ting, a Jamaican grapefruit soda, and just a little ice to a shaker, sealed it up and shook it by the side of her head, releasing the cap and pouring it into 3 shot glasses.

The three picked up their respective shots and simultaneously exclaimed "Cheers!", at which time Jessica made sure she made awkwardly obvious eye contact with first Izzy and then Ray. Ray did likewise. Izzy's eye contact was a little suspect, so Jessica just had to tell her.

"You gotta make eye contact when you say Cheers, Izzy. Otherwise, it's seven years bad sex."

"Well, shit, has that been my problem? I've been blaming Ty." Isabella giggled as she turned to serve some other customers, leaving them in the pleasant hum of the bar. Ray leaned back, his gaze lingering on Jessica. She looked radiant, her cheeks flushed from the heat, her eyes sparkling with curiosity as she took everything in. He realized he was staring and quickly looked away, focusing on the beautiful view of the parking lot instead.

Ray had to keep reminding himself of the FBI sting operation. But was she really *'this'* good, to get him all out of sorts and thinking this could be real? He had to snap himself out of it.

"So, what else do we want to drink? I must warn you that shots may appear at any point in time, without us asking." Ray asked, just as Izzy reappeared in front of them for their order.

"Casamigos Reposado, neat". Jessica said.

"Make that two, please, Iz."

"Aw, upgrading your tequila, ay Ray? Not going with the usual. I gotcha".

The tequila arrived, golden liquid in a short glass.

"Did we order a double?" Jessica asked, her eyes becoming wide, looking at the island pour.

"To new adventures," Ray said.

"To good company," Jessica added, her voice warm. The eye contact from the unspoken cheers now not nearly as awkward.

They sipped their drinks, the conversation flowing as easily as the breeze through the open walls. Jessica told him about her life in the city, her demanding job, and her dream of one day leaving it all behind for a simpler life. Ray shared stories of his move to the island, the challenges of adapting to a slower pace, and the unexpected joy of discovering new places.

Rufus, ever the opportunist, perked up when a basket of tater tots arrived. Jessica laughed as she slipped him a small piece, earning a satisfied grunt from the dog. "He's a food critic in another life," she said, shaking her head.

Ray leaned back, watching her with a growing sense of ease. The energy around Jessica—her laugh, her openness, the way she seemed to fit into this island setting as if she'd always belonged—that made him feel like he'd known her much longer than a few weeks. It all seemed so real, like she really was coming to the island to get to know him, not for some opportunity to steal his money.

"We gotta get moving. I need to get this car back to Red Hook before my friend gets off sunset charter, and we need to get out to the boat yet. Luckily, Izzy knows I'm driving; otherwise, we'd be stumbling out of here. She takes great pleasure in watching me stumble out of the bar in Red Hook."

The drive back to Red Hook was quiet, the kind of comfortable silence that spoke volumes. Jessica leaned her head against the window, her eyes heavy-lidded but content. Rufus snored softly in the backseat, his day of travel and adventure finally catching up with him. Ray stole a glance at Jessica, her profile softened by the glow of the dashboard lights, and felt a quiet thrill. This felt like the beginning of something good.

As Jessica approached *Purrfection* for the first time, she immediately fumbled for her phone to take photos of her new home. A traveler at heart, she wanted all her friends to know about the adventure she was starting. Ray thought this a little suspicious for an electronic bank thief to be so forward with her whereabouts and doings, but he figured a key to being a good thief was to act normal.

Jessica's smile was beaming, a true joy that could not be faked or manufactured.

As they approached, Ray began the first of many lessons to come.

"As we approach the stern, I'm going to come in at an angle toward the port sugar scoop, aiming right at that cleat there. Then you'll grab the painter and cleat us off right there."

"Port? That's the left side, right? Like on a cruise ship?" Jessica asked.

"Well, yes, if you are facing forward, it's the left. If you are facing aft, it's the right side," Ray explained.

"Wait, what? It's the right side?"

"It all depends on which way you are facing. That's why we say port and starboard, and stern and bow, and aft and forward. These are all in relation to the ship itself, not which direction you are facing."

"Ah, gotcha. Now, what am I painting? I do love to paint," Jessica claimed.

"The painter... It's the line coming off the bow of the dinghy."

"You mean this rope here?" Jessica asked.

"Ok, ok... whew. I forgot how steep this learning curve is. One thing you will hear quite often is 'There's no such thing as a rope on a boat.' They are called 'lines,' which is basically a rope with a job."

"What? I'm looking, and there are ropes all over this boat."

"Yeah, I know. Sailors are very particular about terminology and generally pretentious. Me, not so much, but I also don't want it to look like I've taught you nothing. First things first, let's get you and Rufus on board. So, see that shiny metal thing that kinda looks like bull horns? That's called a cleat. You're going to lasso the rope from the dinghy bow and loop it around a few times. I'll show you the 'right' way to cleat later on."

Jessica stood up in the dinghy, her legs a little shaky, so she could wrap the painter around the cleat a few times. Once secure, Ray stepped toward the bow of the dinghy so he could hold it steady against *Purrfection*. Jessica placed her hand on Ray's shoulder to climb aboard for the first time, with Rufus tucked under her arm. She let the dog down on the sugar scoop and helped Ray get her luggage out of the dinghy and over the sugar scoop wall.

"Welcome to *Purrfection*! Head on up the stairs, then down again to the cockpit area," Ray said.

Jessica climbed up the stairs, then back down into the cockpit. She looked around at her new home and was overcome with elation. She stopped suddenly and turned abruptly, with Ray following so closely behind; they were face to face with no space between. Thinking quickly, she hugged Ray and said into his ear, "Thank you for bringing me here. This adventure is going to be amazing." Ray couldn't help but hear a bit of flirtiness in her tone. As she pulled away from the embrace, she paused for what seemed an eternity, face to face with Ray. The perfect moment for a first kiss, perhaps. Ray fought off the urge quickly, snapping back into teaching mode.

"This area is called the cockpit. These two teak tables need refinishing, and the teak door into the salon needs it, too. But, the boat is roomy and a sturdy sailing vessel. Through these doors—inside here—is called the salon. That's my stand-up work desk. These cushions kinda suck; they were never attached properly. On the trip from St. Augustine to St. Thomas, the crew decided to start the cushion Velcro project once we anchored in the Bahamas. I didn't realize they were both high as kites, so it's a pretty shite job; they aren't properly secure, so watch them sliding on you."

"Down the port stairs to the port hull, this is the galley. Please don't call it a kitchen. I know it's a kitchen, and you know it's a kitchen, but on a boat it's called a galley, so that's the term we use. Port forward is my cabin."

"Your cabin is on the starboard side, so if you wanna go down those stairs... To the aft is a spare guest cabin, then forward is your cabin."

Jessica descended the four steps into the starboard hull. She looked aft at the guest cabin, then started forward toward her cabin.

"Aw... look at what you did for me! A welcome package! I love it. You are so sweet."

Jessica entered her cabin to find several welcome gifts neatly arranged on her bed. From left to right: a Sail Purrfection rash guard, two books Ray had chosen just for her, another rash guard, and—taking center stage—the crown jewel, two bottles of Jameson.

"This book is Chapman's Piloting and Seamanship. It's frequently called 'the bible.' You'll have a test on that at the end of the week," Ray teased.

Jessica lifted a book from the bed. "And this one—World Cruising Routes? I thought we were only going to Grenada for hurricane season. Or are you trying to tempt me?" Her voice carried a teasing lilt, just enough flirt to make Ray's chest tighten. For half a heartbeat, the moment hovered on the edge of something more... But Ray couldn't afford to gamble.

If he misread her, if he pushed too far, he risked not just scaring her off but losing the only crew he could count on for hurricane season. That wasn't a chance he could take.

He forced himself to turn away. "I'll grab your gear so you can start figuring out where to stow things." With that, he ducked into the starboard hull, moving fast before his notoriously unreliable manly instincts convinced him to blow everything.

Ray returned down the starboard stairs. "Here's the luggage you brought with you. I just need to go get the one I brought back last trip."

Jessica giggled. "Oh... I won't need that one down here."

"Okay..." Ray said cautiously, not knowing what could be in the other suitcase. "Did I smuggle your guns? I never did look. I should've looked, now that I think about it."

"No, nothing like that. Although I do think there's an extra bottle of Adderall in that suitcase."

"Oh great. You know that could probably affect my captain's license. I can't be a drug smuggler—not through the airport, anyway. Even if they are prescription, it's not my prescription."

Jessica wanted to get off the subject, and she knew the contents of the suitcase would do the trick. She opened the case in the salon, revealing a bright pink plastic float of some kind.

"It's Francine!"

"Francine? Oh shit, that flamingo float thing you told me about? I thought you were teasing me about bringing that."

"Nope. You brought her—for us."

"Us?"

"Well, she does fit two in just the right configuration," Jessica hinted.

Ray felt that butterfly thing again and had to snap himself back into FBI operations mode. He thought to himself, *Wow, she is good...* as he headed back out to the cockpit to get some air.

As the two relaxed in the cockpit, barely touching their first sips of Jameson, the night settled warm and still around them.

"That was a pretty good first day, don't you think?" Ray asked.

"Best I've had in a while—but a long one. I might turn in soon," Jessica said, stretching.

"That's good to know," Ray replied. "Stuff like that's worth saying out loud. If I don't know where you are and can't find you, that's an emergency. Like I said—your cabin, your space. I won't go in unless something's really wrong."

"Totally fair," Jessica nodded. "My cabin, my space... except for the hidden camera in the shower for your OnlyFans page."

"OnlyFans?" Ray blinked. "What?"

Jessica smirked. "My mom was convinced you'd rig up a camera in there and start streaming me."

Ray laughed. "Your mom thinks I have an OnlyFans? Huh... does she know how much money we could make off that? I mean, you've gotta earn your keep somehow."

"Good night, Ray."

"Good night, Jessica. First sleep on a boat should be super relaxing."

CHAPTER
ELEVEN

June 2022 - St. Thomas
Fun in the Sun

Jessica's first week on *Purrfection* slipped into a rhythm she hadn't expected—mornings with coffee on deck, dinghy runs to shore to walk Rufus, and laughter that came easier than it had in years. Ray taught her the quirks of island life and boat handling, from zipping the dinghy across Vessup Bay to the local bar scene, and of course, the Happy Hour routine.

They made the swim over to a sunken monohull near their mooring, a coral-crusted ghost resting in twenty-five feet of water. Ray dove through the broken hatch with the ease of experience, while Jessica hovered above with the GoPro, catching the wreck's eerie beauty on screen. She couldn't match his dives, but from the surface she filmed the shimmer of the hull, schools of fish circling, and Ray checking the dark hull for lobster.

Mid-week, after crossing the choppy chaos of Pillsbury Sound, Jessica picked up a mooring at Honeymoon Beach with surprising ease for her first time. They dropped the dinghy and headed for Scott

Beach, Rufus leaping ashore only to retreat in defeat when a wild donkey flicked its ears at him. Jessica's laughter echoed as the little dog hid behind her legs, the donkey resuming its seaweed hunt unfazed.

In the shallows, masks on and camera in hand, Jessica slipped beneath the surface first. Ray found her a turtle grazing on seagrass, its calm rhythm mesmerizing as she filmed. Deeper still, she discovered a stingray half-buried in the sand, its stillness and quiet strength resonating with her. When she surfaced, whispering that it was her spirit animal, Ray teased her gently, but the weight of the moment lingered. Between Rufus's antics on shore and the silent grace of the sea, Jessica felt herself being pulled deeper—not just into the water, but into this new life.

Friday evening, they prepared for the chaos of an off-season night in Red Hook - not as many tourists, but perhaps friends drinking heavily because they didn't have to work on Saturday. Virgin Islanders are eco-conscious citizens of the world. Locals knew to bring their own tumblers to the bar to save on plasticware, which also resulted in an even bigger island pour. Jessica pulled out the plastic coconut cups she'd brought, complete with metal straws to save the turtles.

"Those are purrfect", Ray stated, stretching out the 'r'.

As they returned to the *Purrfection* after a tipsy night ashore, one straw slipped overboard into the dark water. Jessica groaned at the loss, only for Ray to shrug and promise he'd find it. True to his word, he dove in first thing the next morning, despite the hangover, and surfaced with it in hand.

"If I can't spot a shiny metal straw in twenty feet of the clearest water in the world," he said with a grin, "go ahead and revoke my Island Boy card."

Maxwell paced the hotel room, fingers steepled. "Alright — we've watched those two lovebirds all week. She's comfortable now. Hell, maybe too comfortable. Time to have Campinelli text her."

Jake glanced at the door, making sure Kevin wasn't about to wander in. "Not yet. We need her to see Ray's bank account first. Give her a day to sit on it, let the doubt settle in. Then, when Campinelli applies pressure, it all snaps into place in her little bartender head — that was the plan."

"Fine. Text that idiot captain and make sure he lets her see it," Maxwell snapped. "We've been watching them swim and drink, drink and swim all week. Let's move this operation."

Jake nodded and reached for his phone, eyes still on the corridor.

As he handed the metal straw to Jessica, water still dripping from his eyelashes, he received a text from Jake.

Jake: **How's it going?**

Ray smiled and typed back: **Touch of a hangover, but going great, we've had a helluva week. I think I agreed to a birthday party on the boat tomorrow.**

Jake replied almost instantly: **Just make sure to log into your bank account. Let her see it.**

*F*ck*, Ray thought. It was a quick reminder of why Jessica was really here—this whole trip wasn't just about sea breezes and sea turtles. He was still on an active FBI mission, and Jessica was part of that equation, whether he liked it or not.

"Hey," Ray said casually to Jessica, "I think I agreed to host Ty's birthday party on *Purrfection* tomorrow. Tara is going out on charters today, so we are gonna borrow her car for a quick provisioning run. Just gotta check my funds."

He opened his laptop at the salon table and pulled up his bank account. Then he got up to rinse his coffee mug, leaving the screen clearly visible.

Jessica passed by, glancing toward the screen out of habit more than curiosity. Her eyes caught on the number: over a million dollars.

She blinked, kept walking, but in her head the thought echoed loud and clear: *What the hell kind of provisions do we need? It's not like he's going to run the account dry anytime soon.*

Still, she couldn't help but admire him. Ray had money in the bank—more than she would have guessed—but he wasn't flashy about it. He lived like a barefoot pirate, sun-kissed and salty, a little rough around the edges. Just a kind man with laugh lines and calloused feet who knew how to free dive for a lost straw and didn't seem to care what anyone thought. That sense of steadiness drew her in more than any flashy display ever could.

CHAPTER
TWELVE

July 2022 - St. Thomas
The Secret Travel Agent

Ray and Jessica relaxed in the cockpit after a full day of crazy adventure, hosting Ty's birthday party on *Purrfection*. Izzy had a terrible reaction from an unknown crab allergy, but Ray saved the day by stuffing antihistamine down her throat before it swelled up. Hours later, they were all doing shots at Bernie's in celebration, Ty and Izzy tighter than ever after the ordeal.

"That was one hell of a day to cap off my first week. I'm spent. Good night."

"Good night Jess," Ray stated as he stretched and yawned.

Jessica stood, gathering her phone and drink, and headed down the starboard steps toward her cabin. Rufus, her little shadow, followed with tiny, determined clicks of his nails on the fiberglass. The door eased shut behind them with a quiet click.

She grabbed the folded blanket at the foot of her bunk, then sank down with a tired groan. Rufus curled up immediately beside her, snuggling into the curve of her hip.

She snapped a photo of her bare legs stretched out on the blanket, with a bottle of Jameson and a grumpy Shih Tzu in frame, and sent it to Courtney with a caption:

Nightcap. Full week, crazy day. Still buzzing.

Courtney replied in seconds. **Bitch I'm stressed AF. You're glowing like a f*cking mermaid.**

Jessica smiled, thumbs dancing. **This week has been amazing. Snorkeled a sunken boat and found sea turtles. Stared at stars on the bow. It was annoyingly magical.**

Then, after a beat, she added:

I think Ray saved our friend's life today. But nobody takes it seriously, so it's hard to tell, like this shit happens all the time here. And get this... this guy with the homeless pirate look has over a million dollars in his bank account.

Courtney's typing bubble popped up instantly.

WAIT WHAT.

JESSICA MARIE

YOU FOUND A SUGAR DADDY AND DIDN'T EVEN KNOW IT

Jessica rolled her eyes, glancing down at Rufus, who raised his head and blinked at her like *Don't drag me into this.*

He's not a sugar daddy. He's just... Ray. Weird, kind, stargazing, free-diving, tequila-lovin Ray.

Courtney fired back:

Girl. KIND is rich. WEIRD is rich. RAY is now code for 'secretly loaded yacht man' and I love this journey for you.

Jessica grinned and rolled onto her side, phone still glowing in her hand.

Don't be a brat. But yeah... might be something here, even without the bank account.

Kevin kept his eyes on the scrolling text messages while Maxwell dozed in the chair, head tilted back, not quite asleep but not on duty either. Jake had already checked out for the night.

Leaning closer, Kevin spoke softly. "Sir, sorry to wake you—but you said you wanted to know. It's confirmed. Jessica knows about the bank account."

Maxwell stirred, rubbing his face as though he'd never really been asleep. "Okay, okay. Good. Good. That means we can move on with the rest of the plan."

Kevin blinked. Plan? As far as he knew, their only mission was tracking down the Siren, waiting for her to steal the funds, and catching her when she did. Whatever Maxwell was mumbling about, Kevin hadn't been briefed.

The sun was high overhead, casting a golden glow across the turquoise waters as *Purrfection* bobbed with the waves coming from Pillsbury Sound. The wake from the ferry rocked the boat side to side. Jessica sat in the cockpit, her laptop open on the table, fingers tapping aggressively at the keyboard. Her brow furrowed, lips pursed in irritation as she scrolled through a long list of emails, and she let a frustrated grunt.

Ray popped out of the salon, watched her struggle with a small smirk. "You okay over there?" he asked, sipping his coffee, thinking the ferry wake might have been the frustration.

Jessica exhaled sharply, clearly exasperated. "No, I'm not okay. I sent two emails and forgot to add my name and phone number. Makes me look like an idiot. I'm trying to run a Travel Agency business here. Every time I send an email, I have to cut and paste my name and phone number, and sometimes I forget. It's driving me insane. There has to be a better way."

Ray chuckled. "You don't have an email signature?"

Jessica paused, looking at him blankly. "A what?"

Ray shook his head, setting his coffee down and moving toward her. "Let me see your laptop," he said, holding out a hand. Jessica handed it over, watching as he navigated through her email settings with ease. "Here, you just create a signature. That way, every email you send automatically includes your name and contact info. Do you have a logo and website you want to add?"

Jessica's eyes widened. "Wait—so I never have to paste it again?"

Ray grinned. "Never again."

She let out an exaggerated sigh of relief. "Why did no one tell me about this sooner? This is life-changing."

Ray laughed, handing the laptop back to her. "You're welcome." Ray struggled to understand how a 38-year-old didn't know about basic email, but he reminded himself that she's been behind the bar since she was 17. Was she really '*The Siren*', playing Ray as if she wasn't an electronic bank thief? It was so simple a task, it almost seemed like a set-up.

Jessica glanced at her screen, admiring her brand-new signature at the bottom of a test email. "This might be the greatest thing anyone has ever done for me."

Ray shook his head with a grin, stepping back to the helm. "I'll take that as a thank you."

Later, as he lounged in the cockpit alone, Ray pulled out his phone and shot a quick text to Jake.

Ray: **Just taught her how to set up an email signature. A signature, Jake. This can't be the tech-savvy 'Siren'. No way. How is she going to log in to my bank account when she can't send an email?**

Jake's reply came fast:

Jake: **It's a ruse. Classic misdirection. Don't fall for it, Ray.**

Ray stared at the message, the island breeze brushing against his skin. He wasn't sure whether to laugh or worry.

Jessica nestled into her bunk, letting out a contented sigh as she shifted beneath the soft weight of her sheet. At her feet, Rufus curled into a warm, compact ball, his tiny snores already starting to fill the quiet cabin. She reached up, her fingers finding the fan switch before flicking it on, the gentle whirr blending with the distant lapping of waves against the hull. She unlatched the hatch above her, pushing it open just enough to welcome the cool, salty night breeze. The air carried the faint scent of the ocean and a whisper of laughter from the other nearby boats, a soothing reminder that life on the water never truly slept. As the breeze ruffled her hair, Jessica let her eyes flutter shut, drifting into dreams with the comforting presence of her little companion beside her. Before she could drift off, her phone made a 'ding' notification sound. Her phone only makes a noise for one person, her mother.

Jessica unlocked her phone screen with a hint of a smile on her face, expecting to hear from her mom. Instead, her face dramatically changed to a doom. It slipped her mind on who else could break through her 'do not disturb' setting...

Campanelli to Jessica: **Johnny is going to text you. Unblock him.**

A tear rolled down Jessica's cheek as she replied what she knew she had to reply.

Jessica: **Yes sir.**

A life that she thought she left behind found her in the middle of the Caribbean Sea.

Jessica entered her contacts app and found Johnny. She hesitated, her thumb hovering above the screen, glowing in the darkness of her gently rocking, serene cabin. Finally, with a deep sigh, she slid her thumb across the screen to unblock him. She closed her phone, placing it on the bookshelf above her bunk, knowing that Johnny would make her wait in agony most of the night.

The next morning, Jessica woke, her sleepy hand reached for her phone like any other morning, then remembered the dread that might await her. She stared at the device, not sure if she wanted to unlock it, but knew she must check. She had received a text.

86775: **Security Code 567090o.**

Jessica knew the number and what the code was for. The only part that mattered was the last 4 digits, the time Jessica needed to be alone to text Johnny, 0900, 9 am. It was 7:35 am, still time to agonize.

At 9 am precisely, Jessica opened her phone. She stared at the screen, dreading the text she must send.

Jessica to Johnny: **Hola!**

Johnny: **Ciao Bella!**

Jessica: **What do you want now? Why is Campanelli texting me? WTF?**

Johnny: **Campanelli has a job for us. You didn't think you ended up on Ray's boat by chance, did you? You'll get instructions later. But this time, we are going to get a piece of the action.**

Jessica bit her lower lip, her face filled with anxiety. She knew the texting protocol - open with a greeting only the two would know, to verify WHO was texting, then two messages back and forth. That's it. She wasn't supposed to send a second text, but she could not resist.

Jessica: **What job? Campanelli knows Ray? What did you get me into this time? I don't want any action! I just want you people to leave me the f*ck alone!**

She knew Johnny would ignore the second message, but needed him to hear it. She deleted the messages and locked her phone.

CHAPTER
THIRTEEN

July 2022 - St. Thomas
Courtney Rizzo Problems

"Courtney gets in today! I'm so excited to see her," Jessica announced as she bounded into the galley.

"She already texted—she's on her first flight. Are you *sure* we shouldn't go pick her up? I bet we could borrow someone's car."

Ray shook his head without looking up from his computer. "It's just easier for her to pay the $25 for a taxi van to the ferry dock. She'll have company on the ride, and it saves us a bunch of time. I've got things to do, lady."

"But *you* picked *me* up!" Jessica protested, eyes wide in mock betrayal.

"That's because you're special to me, and you know it," Ray replied a little too quickly, the words slipping out before he could filter them. His tone softened, but he pivoted fast. "Besides, you had a dog. Taxis won't take dogs. Let's be real—every time I've had a friend pick me up from the airport, I end up buying lunch and shots at Dog House. It's honestly cheaper—and safer—for me to just grab a taxi.

But if a friend *is* available... well, it usually turns into one hell of an afternoon."

Courtney to Jessica: **I landed bitch! Come get me!**

Jessica: **Great! You are taking a taxi to Red Hook ferry dock, remember?**

Courtney: **A taxi? Just like in Chicago, eh? No airport pickups. Ever. Shut up and take the Blue Line. Got it.**

Jessica: **See you in a few.**

Courtney had unpacked and settled into the starboard aft guest cabin. Jessica invited her to the cockpit for drinks, proudly displaying the prized plastic coconut glasses.

"Sorry, Ray—only two of these, and the guest takes priority over the captain," Jessica said with a playful grin as Ray emerged from below deck, holding his own drink in a white thermal tumbler stamped with the Purrfection cat logo.

"At least you've got two straws again," Ray replied, eyeing their tropical setup. "I've got my drink, thank you very much."

"Oh yeah!" Jessica turned to Courtney with sudden enthusiasm. "Ray is so good at going down."

Courtney choked on her straw and immediately shot Ray a look, slowly raking her eyes over him. His brows raised slightly, caught somewhere between pride and embarrassment.

Jessica, oblivious, kept going. "The other night, I dropped one of the straws off the back of the boat. The next day, Ray went snorkeling and actually *found* it! The boat had moved overnight, like thirty feet, and he still managed to track it down. Then he just dove, held his breath, and grabbed it from like twenty feet down. No big deal."

Ray shrugged modestly. "It's not that complicated. I just paid attention to the wind and current when we lost it."

"I wanna hear more about these 'going down' skills," Courtney teased, nudging Jessica with a wicked grin.

Jessica blinked, suddenly processing what she'd said. "Oh shit—your mind is *always* in the gutter, bitch!"

Courtney laughed. "Hey, it's hard to find a man with solid skills. I thought maybe you'd found one..."

"I meant he's really good at free diving. You know, holding his breath and diving down." Jessica clarified, flustered now, quickly adding "Under water!"

Courtney gave a slow nod, eyes twinkling. "Is that what you call it down here in the Caribbean? Got it. So he's really good at holding his breath for long, deep stretches of time?"

Ray noticed the pink rising in Jessica's cheeks and debated stepping in—but honestly, he was kind of enjoying himself.

Courtney pivoted like the mischievous little sister she was, eyes glinting with curiosity. "So you're a good-looking guy, living solo on a catamaran, sailing around paradise... Come on, Ray. You *have* to have some stories."

Ray chuckled, sipping his drink. "Oh, I've got stories. Might even write a book someday. Most are about my ridiculous, drunken friends and our antics. The stuff that happens down here, the stuff that *CAN* happen down here. But most stories come because I've just learned to say 'yes' when most people would hesitate."

Courtney wasn't letting him off that easily. "C'mon, Ray. How many hearts have you stolen on this boat, you sun-kissed, blue-eyed, silver-haired pirate?"

Jessica nearly choked on her drink, laughing.

Ray sighed, realizing she wasn't going to quit until he revealed something. "Okay, okay... Just a few months ago, I was dancing with this beautiful blonde—amazing energy, great smile, whole vibe. I thought it might go somewhere, right? I'm texting my buddy about her, hyped up like a teenager."

Jessica raised an eyebrow. "Let me guess. She saw the texts?"

"Oh, worse," Ray said, grinning. "Later that night, she tells me to *stop texting about her*. Now I'm thinking—that's a little presumptuous. But then she quotes *exactly* what I texted. Word for word."

Courtney leaned in. "Nooo. How?"

"She says the FBI had tapped my phone. They were reading my texts in real time."

"What?!" Courtney gasped. "Why the hell would the FBI be spying on *you*?"

"Well," Ray continued, enjoying the dramatic twist, "her ex-husband was a high-up at the FBI. Some kind of director. They'd been divorced for five years, but married for nineteen. I guess he still kept an eye on her... and any man who got too close. Maybe he thought I was gonna whisk her off to sail the world."

Jessica whistled. "That's intense."

"She even had a bodyguard traveling with her," Ray added. "Guy was watching me like a hawk the whole night."

"Creepy as *f*ck*," Courtney said, wide-eyed.

Ray nodded. "I gotta admit... wasn't that creepy, because I didn't notice him that night. She sent a picture of him to me later, lurking behind a pillar. We talked more at the airport about it, in person, and yeah.... My phone was tapped, texts were monitored, easily, no warrant needed."

Satisfied that he'd sufficiently derailed the interrogation, Ray gave Courtney a grin. "So, what about *you*? Got any mafia stories from Chicago? Al Capone's nephew ever stroll into your bar? Pizza wars? Or maybe some impassioned rant about the 'correct' toppings for a hot dog? Cubs or Sox?"

Courtney snorted. "You *do not* want to get me started on Chicago hot dogs."

Jessica leaned back with a smile. "Too late now."

Courtney took a sip from her drink and shrugged. "I don't have any good stories. Jessica and I did bottle service for years in the clubs— crazy stuff probably happened all around us, but with the music blasting and everyone shouting, you couldn't hear anything anyway. We mostly just smiled, looked cute, and tuned it all out."

She shot Jessica a look. "*But* Jessica's got a recent story."

Jessica's smile faltered. "Courtney..."

SUN, RUM, AND STOLEN FUNDS

Undeterred, Courtney waved a hand. "I don't know why you won't tell it. It's been a while, and no one's after you."

Jessica's eyes narrowed. "Yeah. *No one's after me* because I kept my damn mouth shut. Like I was told."

Her tone was sharp, but underneath, there was a flicker of something else—relief, maybe. Like, part of her *wanted* the secret out.

"So..." Courtney dragged the word out, watching for one last red light from Jessica. Seeing none, she plunged in. "Jessica was bartending on this yacht in the harbor. Belonged to this mafia guy, Antonio Campanelli. Total classic—legit businesses on the surface, like a cute little winery and one of the smoothest liquor distribution setups in Chicago. But his family? Deep in all kinds of shady stuff."

"Oh wow," Ray said, intrigued. "The name doesn't sound mafia. But let me guess—it didn't end well?"

Jessica studied Ray's face as Courtney mentioned the name Campanelli, but she saw no flicker of recognition. She exhaled and finally spoke up. "It was boring. Great money for Saturday afternoons. Nothing much happened... until it did. Until Johnny."

"Johnny?" Ray echoed, his ears perking up—first he'd heard of any men in Jessica's past.

Courtney jumped back in. "Johnny was this stiff little accountant. Total beige energy. But he got Jessica mixed up in something sketchy. Turns out, he wasn't just any accountant—he worked for *the family*. Whatever mess he dragged her into, it got really ugly. She had to leave town."

Jessica rolled her eyes. "I didn't even *like* him that much. He was just a lost puppy after a nasty divorce."

Courtney leaned back and raised her glass. "You're probably the first guy in a while Jessica's been attracted to who *isn't* a lost puppy."

Jessica squirmed in her seat, clearly uncomfortable.

Ray tried to lighten the moment. "Oh, I'm not all that 'found' either. Just someone to fix - like the rest of us down here." He glanced at Jessica, his voice softer. "But they *let* you leave? That's not very mafia. Sounds more like cowboy stuff—'leave town by sundown.'"

"It was a weird situation," Jessica admitted. "Antonio's text was short but... chilling. He said, *'We know you didn't take the money. My uncle is old school. Snitches get stitches, that kind of thing. You should get out of town.'* That was all I needed to hear."

Courtney raised an eyebrow. "So you finally tell Captain Ray De Soleil the full story... something you wouldn't even tell me? I see how it is. Gotta trust your man."

Jessica shot her a glare, but said nothing.

Ray, still trying to make sense of it, asked, "That's a pretty intense message for someone who was *just* bartending. What money? Sounds like there's more to it."

Jessica hesitated, then exhaled, voice shaking a bit. "There *is*. I did something I shouldn't have. Johnny backed me into a corner. They... threatened my mom. I didn't know what else to do."

Ray and Courtney stayed quiet, letting her speak.

"Johnny forced me to install something on Campanelli's laptop. I didn't even know what it was. He said his boss needed it. I was scared. Johnny said they knew my mom's address. So I did it. I had to. I messed with the laptop. Later, I found out Campanelli had video of me doing it."

"Damn, Jessica..." Courtney whispered, eyes wide. "It's kind of amazing you're still alive. Antonio must really have a soft spot for you. I can't imagine anyone else walking away from that."

The weight of her words landed too hard. Jessica's expression tightened, and the playful glint vanished from her eyes.

Courtney winced, realizing she'd gone too far. She motioned for Ray to move closer. His protective instincts had already kicked in. He shifted beside Jessica, gently brushing her knee with his. "You don't have to talk about it anymore," he said quietly.

Jessica nodded, staring down at her drink. The tropical evening around them had gone still.

❖

SUN, RUM, AND STOLEN FUNDS

Early that morning, Jessica received a text — a time code for when she was supposed to message Johnny later that evening.

86775: **Security Code 6671855.**

Jessica saw the message and realized that time would not work for her. Per her protocol, she replied.

Jessica to 86775: **STOP**

A few minutes later, another code arrived; the new time was acceptable, so no reply was necessary.

The sun had barely cleared the morning haze when *Purrfection* skimmed across the turquoise sea, slicing through the waves on her way to Culebra. The breeze was light but steady—perfect for a relaxed sail—and Ray stood at the helm in his favorite oil-stained rash guard, sunglasses perched on his nose, grinning like a kid who'd just pulled off a magic trick.

Jessica lounged near the bow, legs stretched out, toenails glinting metallic teal. Courtney had taken over the Bluetooth speaker and was DJ'ing a playlist that bounced from early 2000s hip-hop to yacht rock without shame or apology.

They were headed to Ensenada Honda, the protected bay where Ray liked to anchor when visiting the island. But this trip wasn't just for scenery—they were swinging by to see Kayla, a Chicago transplant and longtime friend of Jessica and Courtney's. Ray had met her once before, on the trip where he first found Jessica on a dating app - but the girls talked about her like she was part myth, part legend.

They dropped anchor near the Dinghy Dock and headed ashore for a quick dinner. The place was lively as always, with music drifting through the air and chickens darting underfoot. Over grilled fish tacos and strong rum punches, they caught up with Kayla, swapping island gossip and laughing over old stories from their city days. It was a short visit, but full of warmth and energy, like no time had passed at all. Jessica and Courtney sensed the new island vibe Kayla was sporting, even through the exciting regaling of Chicago adventures passed.

Back on *Purrfection*, the island vibe set in.

Courtney popped up from below deck with a grin and two

absurdly large inflatable microphones. "Ladies and gentlemen ... and sailors," she announced, "prepare yourselves for the *SS Nasty* Talent Hour."

Jessica immediately struck a pose, one arm skyward, the other on her hip. "Just sing bitch!"

Ray leaned back with a fresh drink, already laughing.

Courtney cued up the music—classic girl power anthems, 90s hip-hop, and Millennial bangers. The two of them put on a full-blown show: karaoke from memory, belting off-key harmonies, dancing around the deck with the blow-up mics like they were headlining Madison Square Garden.

Ray applauded every ridiculous moment, his cheeks sore from smiling. The Dinghy Dock restaurant wasn't but 100 yards away, and the patrons had to be wondering about the absurdity.

The stars wheeled overhead, the water lapped gently at the hull, and *Purrfection* swayed to the rhythm of three people who, at least for tonight, had nothing to prove, nowhere to go, and nowhere to be.

Jessica disappeared mid-performance to use the head. She descended the stairs and closed her cabin door.

At precisely 9:45 pm, Jessica sent a text

Jessica to Johnny: **Hola!**

Johnny: **Ciao Bella! You are going to receive a package from your mother. It will contain a thumb drive. Keep it hidden for now. Instructions to follow.**

Jessica: **A thumb drive? For like a laptop?**

Johnny: **Yes. Just keep it hidden for now.**

Jessica knew the contact protocol - she wasn't supposed to send a second message, but often did to piss Johnny off.

Jessica: **You never said when this package is coming. We are sailing around a bit. We are in Culebra. We won't be back in St. Thomas for a few more days.**

But then Jessica paused, contemplating the thumb drive. What the hell was it for this time? Last time, she had to plug it into Campanelli's laptop—clear enough. But now? Plug it into Ray's laptop? Her head spun with possibilities. The only remedy, she decided, was the sea, a little Jameson, and—as she was starting to realize—a little Ray of sunshine didn't hurt either. She shook it off and popped back up to join the performance.

Late in the evening, Ray finally looked at his phone, with a text from Jake:

Jake: **What are you doing in Culebra? How are we going to catch Jessica if we don't know where she is?**

Ray, somewhat tipsy: **How did you know we went to Culebra? I don't broadcast AIS. Can't be a pirate and broadcast your position.**

The sail from Culebra to St. Croix was anything but smooth.

The trade winds howled steadily at twenty knots, and the seas stacked up in confused six-footers, slapping against *Purrfection*'s hull with the force of a grumpy god. Courtney, normally excited for adventure, had turned a distinct shade of green somewhere south of Vieques. She lay curled on the leeward settee in the cockpit, moaning softly with her eyes closed, a damp towel across her forehead.

Ray and Jessica, on the other hand, were in their element. Salt spray flew over the bow as *Purrfection* crashed through the swells, and they just laughed—two sun-drenched kids on a roller coaster made of wind and water.

"Hold on! One hand for you, one for the boat." Ray shouted over the wind as another wave lifted them, the boat surfing briefly before settling back into the chop.

Jessica whooped, arms in the air like she was on a ride at a carnival. "This is *awesome!*"

That's when Ray spotted them—a fluttering cloud of movement in the distance, just off the starboard bow. "Birds!" he pointed. "Gulls and frigates. Means bait fish. Something big is feeding down there."

He gave autopilot a 10-degree shift, adjusting their course just enough to skirt the edge of the frenzy. "Let's see if we can pick up dinner."

As *Purrfection* sliced closer, the water churned in oily flashes—something large pushing the bait balls up from below. The hand line stretched taut behind them gave a sudden, jerky twitch. Then the other. Both lines started dancing.

"We're on!" Ray shouted, springing into action. "Make sure you secure your harness before pulling it in."

Jessica grabbed one line and began hauling it in, her muscles straining against the pull of something powerful. Ray worked the other line, grabbing tight, turning his hand 90 degrees to gain friction, pulling, then reaching forward again, hand over hand. Not as sporting as a fishing rod, but much more practical to get dinner onto the boat.

After a quick fight and plenty of splashes, Jessica hauled in a gleaming wahoo, its silver-blue body striped like a torpedo, teeth still snapping at the air. Ray was impressed that she managed to slide the big fish onto the sugar scoop with no instructions, while he battled the other line. She nearly dropped it trying to lift it up the sugar scoop steps.

"Whoa there, killer," Ray chuckled. "That one is big, and it's got sharp teeth!"

He stepped in to take the wahoo from her, grinning like a proud fisherman. Jessica didn't mind. She was beaming, flushed with the thrill of it.

Ray's own line produced a decent mahi—green, gold, and gorgeous in the sunlight.

Courtney roused just long enough to raise her phone from her lap, blinking through the haze. "Smile," she croaked, her voice hollow but determined.

Ray posed with Jessica's wahoo because it was too big for her to hold, while Jessica, beside him, held the mahi; both of them were wet, giddy, and windblown.

Snap.

Courtney slumped back down and groaned, her work on this world done.

By the time *Purrfection* reached the lee of St. Croix, the seas had mellowed. The wind softened, the swell flattened, and the sun glinted off the now-gentle water like melted glass.

That's when the dolphins came.

First one, then two, then a whole pod—darting and leaping in the bow wave, playful and curious. Jessica ran to the bow and climbed out onto the pulpit, sitting with her legs stretched forward, just inches from the sea. She giggled with joy as the dolphins danced below her, twisting and flipping in the clear water.

"They're *so close!*" she cried.

Ray smiled from the port-side pulpit, watching her with the kind of quiet pride that sneaks up on you when life aligns just right.

Courtney groaned from her cocoon of towels. "I don't care if dolphins are juggling flaming torches. I'm not moving."

Jessica glanced back and shouted through her laughter, "You're missing *magic!*"

Courtney just waved a weak hand, surrendering to her queasiness as *Purrfection* sailed on toward the anchorage.

As the big catamaran dropped anchor close to the beach off the coast of St. Croix, Jessica turned to Ray with a mischievous grin. "We should have a dress-up party," she declared, her eyes sparkling with excitement.

Ray groaned, rubbing his temple. "Jessica, I just filleted those fish, I'm not really feeling—"

"Oh, come on! It'll be fun!" she insisted, nudging him playfully. "Courtney will love it, and she deserves it after that rough passage. I have a surprise for you."

Ray sighed but relented, not catching Jessica's mischievous tone. "Fine. But if this ends up as another one of your ridiculous schemes..."

"It absolutely will!" she chirped before disappearing below deck, giggling as she grabbed Courtney's hand.

As they descended the stairs, Ray yelled, "Courtney, you better be feeling better, no puking down there."

In Jessica's cabin, the girls prepared their costumes. Jessica's was elaborate, while Courtney opted for something much simpler: a t-shirt with a comical print.

"Okay, take Ray and Mr. Jameson and Rufus out on the bow. I want to pop out of my hatch and make an entrance."

"In that costume... I'll have to make sure Ray doesn't fall off the boat," Courtney stated, as she looked Jessica up and down.

Up top, Ray was adjusting the billowy sleeves of his black pirate shirt, still grumbling about his lack of a proper hat, or any other effects a pirate might need. "This pirate came for the Jameson, not the authenticity," he said out loud to himself, as he raised his glass. Rufus scrambled at his feet, squeezed into a little red crab costume, and was none too pleased about it.

Courtney appeared in the salon doorway, striking a playful pose with one hand on her hip and a teasing grin. Ray took a sip of his drink, then nearly choked as he caught sight of Courtney. His eyes widened in disbelief before he burst into laughter. She was wearing bikini bottoms, but over her top was a t-shirt that looked like a hairy man's chest, complete with hairy armpits and naval. Ray could not control his outburst.

"Come on, let's take the music out to the bow. Jessica might take a while." Courtney suggested, "Don't forget the whiskey."

As Ray and Courtney lounged on the starboard net, the hatch to Jessica's cabin creaked open. It swung wider, and Jessica emerged slowly, rising like a siren from the sea. Ray froze mid-sip, eyes widening at the sight of her—bright red wig, strapless bikini top studded with white seashells, and a shimmering mermaid skirt that promptly caught on the hatch. Her grand entrance stalled as she wrestled the fabric free, muttering under her breath.

Courtney stood to help, but Jessica toppled backward into the hatch, laughing at the sheer absurdity of Courtney's hairy-chested t-shirt looming toward her like some deranged lifeguard. Once their giggles subsided, Courtney managed to guide Jessica through a series of awkward twists and turns, finally helping her pivot her tail clear of the hatch.

Jessica struck a pose with mock elegance, arms lifted in a dramatic flourish. "Nailed it," she declared.

Ray raised his drink in salute. "Ten out of ten for commitment. Four out of ten for execution."

Jessica grinned. "I'll take it."

The Bluetooth speaker crackled to life, then dropped into a lively reggae beat. Courtney, never one to miss a good groove, grabbed Jessica's hand and spun her into a twirl. Jessica laughed, her sequined tail catching the moonlight as she wobbled straight into Ray—who caught her with exaggerated flair.

"Ah-ha! You've been captured by the dread pirate Ray De Soleil!" Courtney bellowed, striking a pose like an unhinged buccaneer.

Jessica groaned, mortified. Ray gave her a swift spin and released her—directly into a not-so-graceful flop onto the pile of bean bags.

"Graceful," she muttered, legs tangled in faux scales.

"Mermaid down," Ray said, raising his drink in mock alarm.

Meanwhile, Rufus barked excitedly, caught in the middle of the madness, his tiny crab legs flopping as he spun in circles.

The bottle of Jameson made its lazy rounds, and each swig was met with a new burst of laughter. The night sky unfurled above them like black velvet, stars blinking in quiet amusement at the nonsense below. They were absurd. Half-drunk. Slightly sunburned. And completely, unequivocally happy.

On *Purrfection,* anchored off the Frederiksted pier in St Croix, with nothing but each other and a good bottle of whiskey, life was magical.

CHAPTER
FOURTEEN

July 2022 - St. Thomas
Bernies For One

Courtney zipped up her duffel bag, then flopped back onto the narrow bed with a dramatic sigh. "You know, after this past week, I hope you realize how special this is—what you have here, with him."

Jessica looked up from folding a sundress. "What do you mean?"

Courtney propped herself on one elbow, eyes gleaming. "Girl, you *caught fish together*. Two of them—*at the same time*. You helped him clean 'em in that rough-ass ocean like some sea goddess. You watched dolphins together. You snorkeled that creepy-ass pier in pitch-black darkness like a crazy bitch. You dressed up like a mermaid in front of him. We sang—badly, I might add—all night with him just watching like he'd never seen anything better."

Jessica smirked. "It *was* a good week."

"I'm not even done!" Courtney wagged a finger. "I've never seen you this at ease. This... you. Hell, it feels like we're in some damn Nicholas Sparks romance. We just need Crazy Johnny to crash the party with a machete or a love letter, and we'd have the full plot."

Jessica laughed nervously but then sighed. "Court, it's not as simple as you make it sound. We're on this boat 24/7. If anything goes wrong..."

Courtney sat up. "Exactly. If he were an asshole, wouldn't you know by now? Seriously, could you even *stand* to be around him constantly if he weren't such a sweetheart? You generally like to be alone."

Jessica hesitated, her voice softer. "Can you understand, though? I'm scared to screw this up. If he gets mad or things get weird... I don't have anywhere else to go. Okay, fine, I'll say it—I *do* have feelings for him. He *is* wonderful. But I'm not just gonna throw myself at the guy. He's *the guy*. He should make the first move."

Courtney gave her a flat look. "Well, that ain't happening, sister."

"What?! You don't think he's into me?"

"No, *I'm* not saying that at all. I think it's obvious he's fighting it."

Jessica narrowed her eyes. "You are so full of shit right now."

Courtney held up both hands. "Hear me out. He's got the same fears you do. What if he makes a move and you don't feel the same? Then he's stuck on the boat with you, looking like a damn fool. Or worse, what if you're offended, pack your stuff, and leave? Then he's alone for hurricane season. The stakes are high, babe. You two are *this close* to something great... but also one misstep away from a shipwreck."

Jessica groaned. "Well, shit. That's super helpful. So... what the hell am I supposed to do?"

Courtney grinned and tossed her duffel bag over her shoulder. "So just dance, bitch. Dance."

Ray stood in the dinghy, already untying the painter and holding the dink against *Purrfection*, when Jessica and Courtney surfaced from the cabin. The sun hung high, painting the water in sharp glints of silver and blue. The ferry from St. John had just docked in the distance, and a string of passengers was already spilling onto the pier like ants off a log.

"Clock's ticking," Ray called over his shoulder. "If we're gonna get her into the taxi stampede, we gotta go *now*."

Courtney rolled her eyes but hustled down the stairs, tossing her bag ahead of her with a thud. "God forbid I miss my flight and have to stay in paradise another day."

Ray throttled forward, guiding the dinghy toward the dock, then the short walk to the ferry terminal. As they approached, the chaos of the arriving ferry crowd grew louder—wheeled suitcases rattling, kids yelling, taxi drivers shouting destinations over each other like auctioneers. A driver in a red polo waved at them from a twelve-passenger taxi van, already half full. "Last call for Cyril E. King Airport!"

"That's me, since I can't catch a ride to the airport," Courtney said, hefting her bag. She turned to Ray first. "Thanks for everything, Cap. Seriously, if you ever decide you're sick of this boat and want to write that romance novel, give me a call."

Ray chuckled. "Romance? I'm an engineer, can't write worth shit. But I got stories. Hopefully entertaining."

She turned to Jessica and gave her a quick, tight hug. "And *you*—don't overthink it. Just... dance, bitch."

Jessica laughed into her shoulder. "Shut up. I hate you."

"I know. I'm amazing." Courtney winked, then turned and jogged to the van, waving over her shoulder. A ferry passenger slid in behind her, the sliding door already closing before she even sat down.

Just like that, she was gone—swallowed up by the buzz of tourists and taxi horns and island heat.

Jessica stood on the ferry terminal curb beside Ray, watching the van merge into the exit traffic.

"You okay?" he asked quietly.

Jessica nodded, tucking a strand of hair behind her ear. "Yeah. Just thinking."

"About what?"

She glanced up at him with a half-smile. "How am I supposed to dance without music?"

Ray gave her a curious look but said nothing, just a small smile, and gestured back toward the dinghy dock, but of course, it was almost Happy Hour.

❖

Courtney had flown out the day before, leaving Jessica to return to her morning ritual—walking Rufus along the quiet parking lots of Red Hook. She texted Johnny per the usual schedule.

Jessica to Johnny: **Hola!**

Johnny: **Ciao Bella! Did you get the thumb drive? Is everything ok?**

Jessica: **Yes, I received it. We picked up packages yesterday after dropping off Courtney. Nothing happening right now. I'm watching Rufus poop. What's this thumb drive for?**

Johnny: **Just like last time, except this time it goes into Captain Ray's computer. It should be much easier than Chicago, with only you and him on the boat, no security guards, no cameras. Whenever you find your opportunity, take it. Oh, and in the future, please stick to the communication protocol.**

Jessica slid her phone back into her bag and watched Rufus squat with determination.

Much easier than Chicago, she repeated in her head. *No guards, no cameras. Just Ray.*

She already knew it would be easy. Ray barely touched his laptop password, left her alone on the boat all the time, and trusted her more than he should. She could plug the drive in any time he left the boat.

But still...

Her stomach tightened.

Why Ray?

Last time, Johnny said it was a mafia situation. A *family* thing, trying to monitor Campanelli. She didn't like it, but at least it had made a twisted kind of sense. But now Campanelli was calling the shots?

Ray, on the other hand, was the least threatening man she'd ever known. He drank silver tequila, avoided sunscreen like it was a government conspiracy, and listened to Kenny Chesney like the lyrics held the meaning of life. He laughed too easily, grilled lunch on the boat like it was his love language, and—if anything—seemed too transparent to be dangerous.

And yet...

Campanelli wants access to his laptop.

Jessica's mind narrowed in on one likely explanation: *Ray's bank account.*

She hadn't snooped, but she'd seen his account screen a few times. Charter captain or not, the man was sitting on a surprisingly healthy pile of money for someone who lived in board shorts.

So what's the angle?

Was Ray hiding something behind that laid-back smile, blue eyes, and golden tan? Was he laundering money? Ray had often joked about other charter companies in Red Hook being money laundering fronts - easy cash businesses with constant expenses, like boats. Or was he running guns between islands? Smuggling drugs?

Is Ray one of the bad guys?

That thought twisted deeper than she expected. She didn't *want* to believe it, but she also couldn't ignore what the thumb drive implied.

She took a long breath and gave Rufus a scratch behind the ears as he finished his morning mission.

"Come on, buddy," she muttered. "Let's go figure out if your captain's full of shit."

That evening, Ray and Jessica hit the town with a mission: drink, mingle, and avoid talking about anything real. The past few days with Courtney had been an intense ride of emotional waves for both of them, with her constant banter and teasing, poking at the unspoken edges of their relationship.

They bar-hopped through Red Hook with the ease of locals who had nothing left to prove. First stop: Tap & Still—greasy burgers downed with a round of shots. Then on to the Salty Siren, where Alli gave Jessica a once-over that landed more like a warning than a welcome. Ray's glass came heavy-poured without a word—standard treatment. Jessica caught a flicker in Alli's eyes, though whether it was respect or suspicion, she couldn't pin down.

As always, the night ended at Bernie's, the local dive bar where everybody ends up at the end of the night... because it's open. As servers and bartenders get off work, they all make their way to *Bernie's for One*, as the saying goes.

Trevor was already there, planted at the corner table, half-sunken into the bench and half-latched onto a stunning woman with sleek black hair and cheekbones that could cut glass. She was young, poised, and clearly bristled the moment Trevor's attention shifted to Jessica as she entered.

"JESSICA!" Trevor shouted, leaping up with the grace of a wounded walrus to hug her.

Ray caught the woman's side-eye and moved in quickly. He slipped an arm around Jessica's waist and laid it on thick. "Hi, I'm Ray, like a ray of sunshine. I'm a good friend of Trevor's. This beautiful woman is Jessica. Where are you from?"

She relaxed a little, raising her chin. "I'm from Hotlanta. Just here for a week."

"Ah," Ray said, nodding like a man who had heard that one before. "Welcome to the Virgin Islands." Ray knew she wasn't *from* Atlanta. People *from* Atlanta hated that nickname that would never seem to die.

Ray had seen a good share of first-time travelers the past few years. The locals called them 'stimulus check travelers'. Those folks who never traveled anywhere before, but suddenly figured out the US Virgin Islands were affordable and, actually, part of the United States - no passport required. They spent their COVID stimulus check on travel. They could have a decent vacation on $1,200 in the US Virgin Islands. Lots of travelers from Atlanta, Chicago, Washington, DC - all the places with direct flight access.

Jessica added, "Hi, I'm Jessica," directed toward the young lady. Jessica motioned to Ray to introduce them, but Ray just shrugged his shoulders. He leaned in to Jessica's ear and said, "She didn't say her name, and I don't think Trevor knows it either."

Jessica gave Trevor a displeased look, but Trevor was oblivious to her glare, his eyes glazed over with a whiskey haze. He seemed very pleased with himself. Jessica teased him regardless, "So, Trevor, how did you meet this young lady?"

"I don't remember. We just started talking. I think it was here." Trevor said in all drunken seriousness, "She seems to like my beard and dad bod."

Jessica snorted, "You gotta be a dad to have a dad bod, you asshole."

"I might.. I might.. " Trevor stuttered, "Might be."

"What, a dad, or an asshole?" Jessica deadpanned.

Trevor considered her question far too seriously, then spurted out, "Or maybe it's the coke... She really likes my cocaine."

Jessica's eyes rolled so hard they nearly fell out of her head. "I'm going to the ladies' room," she announced, which was a stretch of a definition for Bernie's disgusting single stall, with a sliding door that doesn't even close all the way. It was better than the men's lavatory, which had swinging saloon doors, a wall urinal, and a broken sit-down unit. It's the definition of a dive bar.

Ray seized the moment. "So, Trevor," he said, casually but deliberately, "Courtney mentioned a guy back in Chicago named Johnny while she was here. What's up with that?"

Trevor squinted like Ray had just asked him to do long division. "Johnny? You mean FBI John?"

Ray's eyebrow went up. "FBI?"

"Yeah. We hated him at Blackwater. Real square. Always got in the way. F*cking jackass."

Ray blinked. "Wait, Jessica dated an FBI guy?", skipping over Trevor's mention of Blackwater, the elite, questionable military contractor, widely rumored to be the corporate extension of certain three-letter government agencies.

Trevor frowned. "I dunno if she *knew* he was FBI. I don't think she did. I wasn't supposed to tell her. Don't think I told her. Definitely wasn't supposed to tell *you*." He sloppily pressed a finger to his lips and wobbled. "So...shhhh. I didn't say anything."

Ray's gears were turning, slowly from the tequila, but turning nonetheless. Trevor kept babbling. "Yeah, he got her into some deep shit. Really deep. Even I couldn't help her outta it."

Ray's voice lowered. "But you were in *Blackwater,* and you couldn't help? Must've been some big-time mess."

Trevor blinked again. "Who you calling *Black*? I'm Irish." Trying to backpedal from things he shouldn't have mentioned.

Ray was never really sure if Trevor worked for the elite private military company or not. So many people in the Caribbean have shady pasts and mind-blowing stories, but they also like to blow smoke up the asses of the willingly duped tourists. The islands were filled with misfits - people running from something, or hiding from someone, or trying to find themselves, or trying to lose themselves. Ray always thought Trevor knew way too much for a bar manager, and it seemed like a perfect cover for dubious activities.

When Jessica reappeared, Trevor immediately exclaimed, "Shots!"

Ray distracted him with a question directed toward his lady friend, and as the two discussed the answer, Ray nudged Jessica for an Irish exit of their own.

CHAPTER
FIFTEEN

August 2022 - St. Thomas
Hurricane Plan

Ray checked the weather every morning. Religiously. Especially during hurricane season.

Early on—June, July, maybe the first half of August—the storms were mostly mild, spinning up in the Gulf or off Florida, drifting toward the Carolinas or Louisiana. By late August, things changed. Sahara dust storms started sending heat waves across the Atlantic. These were the ones to watch. They rode the trade winds straight for the Caribbean, predictable but dangerous.

On August 18th, Ray pulled up the Five-Day Graphical Tropical Weather Outlook. Yesterday's chart was clear.

Today? Four systems on the map. Two yellow -- less than 40% chance to develop. Then an orange area, with a 60% chance of becoming a hurricane, with yet another yellow spot following closely. The orange area was only five days from St. Thomas.

Ray frowned. "That escalated quickly."

His original hurricane plan was to make the jump south to

Grenada—400 miles of open ocean. He'd done it before, back in 2020. That time, he had two experienced crew. No dog. No Jessica.

Now he had a novice sailor and a little Shih Tzu who got seasick every time a ferry wake smacked the hulls just right.

That wasn't the real problem, though. The real problem was the FBI.

Jessica didn't know it, but the feds were circling, waiting for her to steal Ray's money so they could pounce and arrest her. Ray had been working with them, reluctantly at first, trying to untangle what exactly she'd done, if anything at all. The whole operation was murky, full of half-truths and shifting loyalties. He was playing both sides now, trying to keep her close while also not blowing the operation.

The newest wrinkle was Johnny. Courtney had said he wasn't even really a boyfriend. Drunken intel from Trevor disclosed that he might be FBI. If Johnny *was* FBI, was he the agent assigned to get close to *The Siren*? Nothing was making sense. Ray knew that if Jessica executed the theft soon, the FBI would arrest her. He still couldn't bring himself to believe she'd do it.

Ray needed time to think, to figure out what the hell was going on. He needed to get them out of U.S. territory.

With the light wind conditions, St. Martin made sense. It was familiar, dog-friendly, and—most importantly—not under the immediate jurisdiction of the FBI. Any federal moves would take time, approvals, and coordination with Dutch or French authorities. It was the kind of bureaucratic red tape Ray could count on to buy himself a few precious days.

He could always blame it on the weather. That part was even true—they'd be in a much better position if they had to sail south to avoid a hurricane, sticking closer to the island chain to duck in for a dog break, or a hurricane hide-out if necessary.

Ray made a captain's call. "Hey Jessica?"

She looked up. "Yeah?"

"I was checking the weather. Hurricane season's kicking off early—and hard. Remember how we talked about sailing south to Grenada, like I did in 2020? I'm starting to think that might not be our best option."

He didn't say it outright, but the unspoken part was clear—Grenada was a long, exposed run, and Jessica was still new to all this.

"Oh yeah?" she asked. "So what are the options?"

"We could use this calm spell to motor east to St. Martin. It's about 100 miles—should take sixteen, maybe seventeen hours. I spent a few months there in 2021. Half French, half Dutch, super dog-friendly. If a storm does show up, we'd be in a better position to head south along the island chain—plenty of places to stop: Guadeloupe, Martinique..."

"Wait—wait," Jessica interrupted, eyes wide. "Are you asking if I want to go to St. Martin? Uh, hell yes! I've got friends from Chicago over there, Cass and Mike!"

Ray chuckled. "Of course you do."

He kept his tone casual, but the urgency was building. "We've got a solid weather window, so we should probably start prepping."

Jessica nodded. "When were you thinking of leaving?"

"In a couple of hours. If we head out around 4 p.m., we'll make landfall by morning. Smooth overnight motor."

"Wait, you're serious? Like... *today* today? No going-away party? No goodbye drinks with Trevor? No hugs? No Red Hook send-off?"

"Welcome to sailing, my love," Ray said gently. "The boat's ready, as she has to be this time of year. The weather, perfect. No wind, which never happens. Normally, this trip is an upwind battle, but we're in the quiet tail of that low-pressure system that just drifted north. When the weather says *go*, you *go*. That's the rule."

Jessica's smile faded. "I didn't think we'd just... leave. Not like this. No closure. No goodbyes."

Ray softened. "That's why I don't say *goodbye*. Just *see ya*."

She exhaled slowly. "How do you deal with this? I mean, emotionally? It's kinda jarring."

He studied her, then spoke slowly, choosing honesty over comfort.

"First—when you're with your people, *really* be with them. Laugh hard. Ask real questions. Be curious. Remember the ones who aren't there, and roast them properly. Only use your phone to take terrible selfies. Make it count."

Jessica blinked, surprised by the depth.

"Second..." he continued, "and this part kind of sucks: most people won't miss you as much as you think they will."

Jessica raised an eyebrow. "Wow. You just went from wise sailor to emotionally unavailable in two sentences."

Ray shrugged, "Sailing's like that."

He stood and stretched. "Come on. We've got to hit the store for some last-minute provisions. You might still bump into someone."

"You mean snacks?"

"Yes, I mean sailing snacks, but not much at all —the food is better and cheaper in St. Martin. Rufus could use a shore run for a little farewell trot. He deserves one."

Around 3:30 in the afternoon, Jessica returned from her snack run and dog walk. She ran into a few friends in Red Hook. To her surprise, no one seemed fazed that they were leaving so soon. But that's island life—friends come, friends go. Especially the sailing kind.

As she climbed back aboard *Purrfection*, her phone buzzed. A new message.

Johnny: **Emergency request. Text me immediately.**

She sighed, pausing in the shadow of the bimini before typing a quick reply.

Jessica: **Hola!**

Johnny: **Ciao Bella! What's going on? Anything interesting happening? Why haven't you inserted the thumb drive yet?**

She narrowed her eyes at the screen. He was fishing. It felt like he *knew* something, but she wasn't about to spill the part about sailing to St. Martin.

Jessica: **Not much, just a little grocery run earlier. I just gotta** find the exact right moment—he's been on the boat lately, and I've been the one running to shore.

Johnny: **The time is now. We need to get this done. As soon as you get the chance, insert the thumb drive into Ray's laptop, just like Chicago. It will do the rest.**

Jessica stared at the screen for a second longer, then deleted the messages and tucked the phone into her bag. Her gaze drifted back toward *Purrfection*, where Ray was already prepping for departure. Timing, as always, would be everything.

Ray fired up the engines to give them time to warm up. He secured the dinghy into the lift lines and began hoisting it—cranking up the stern with the heavy outboard engine using the winch, then pulling the bow lift line through the rollers using just his body weight, a few feet at a time, until it was fully raised. He tied off the painter around the davits and cleated the line to secure the bow. For the stern, a line from the U-brackets through the davits and down to a cleat was enough.

Good weather was expected—clear skies and winds light and variable. Normally, Ray would run jack lines across the deck—safety lines he could clip into while walking around the boat in rough seas. But tonight, the odds of that were so low it hardly seemed worth the effort.

Ray tapped the engines into forward gear, just to make sure the propellers engaged properly before disconnecting from the mooring. He signaled to Jessica to release the lines, starboard side first. She uncleated the line, dropped the bitter end into the water, and pulled it through the mooring loop. She repeated the process on the port side. They were free.

"I re-checked the weather before we left. It might even be calmer than I thought. There's been very little wind all day, and now absolutely no wind tonight. This is why we always keep thirty days of food on board. If we get halfway there and lose both engines, we'd have no wind to sail back for at least a week."

"Well, I do appreciate having food on board, but I know for certain we don't have enough *Jameson* to last that long," Jessica said with a smirk, then added more seriously, "How would we 'lose an engine,' anyway? Where's it gonna go?"

"We could run over a lobster pot and get a line tangled in the propeller. I might be able to cut it free, but maybe not. We could lose oil pressure any number of ways. Have a coolant leak. Break an engine mount. Clog a fuel filter. Shred an impeller or break an alternator belt."

"That all seems pretty unlikely. I think we'll be fine," Jessica said, trying to reassure herself. It was her first time out of sight of land, and her first night passage.

"Unlikely? I've owned this boat for six years. Every one of those things has happened—just never to both engines at once. The good thing about a catamaran? There are two of everything. The bad thing? There are two of everything."

"Wow. That's a helluva list. I'm not gonna pretend to understand it, but thanks for scaring the shit outta me before my first night sail," Jessica said, hiding her anxiety behind sarcasm.

"Yeah, sprung a leak in the starboard oil cooler going out the St. Augustine Bridge of Lions once. That triggered the low oil warning. I had to abort the bridge opening last minute with strong outgoing current, that was tricky on one engine. Then in the Bahamas, a coolant hose came loose—we lost all the coolant and got an overheat warning. Things just happen out on the water, and you deal with it," Ray said, calm and relaxed. "The things I've had to deal with on this boat... really took some reprogramming for my OCD engineer brain."

They motored around Cabrita Point and headed south out through the Pillsbury Sound inlet, pointing south-southeast to put some distance between them and the lobster pots off the south coast of St. John before turning east toward St. Martin.

"It's going to be a dark night, with no moon. It should be excellent stargazing. I bet we see the Milky Way and tons of shooting stars."

"What do you mean, 'No Moon'?" Jessica asked.

"It's a phase of the moon—the New Moon. It means no moonlight tonight," Ray explained, unsure what part she didn't understand.

"I'm from Chicago. We always have moonlight in Chicago," she said, completely serious.

"Uh... once a month, the moon goes through a full cycle. Waxing from zero to full, then waning from full to zero. Every month, there's a full moon and a new moon. This happens everywhere. Even in Chicago."

"Really? You aren't shitting me?"

"Nope. Just, you know... science," Ray said, once again questioning how this woman managed to hack into online bank accounts, but remembered she had been a city girl surrounded by skyscrapers almost her entire life.

"Well, I don't know shit about f*ck," Jessica said, quoting one of her favorite characters.

They made their turn to the east just as the sun dipped below the horizon. Ray was relieved to clear the lobster pots. The night stretched over the Caribbean like a velvet canopy, spattered with stars so bright they seemed close enough to touch. Ray sat at the helm, though the autopilot was doing all the work. The sea was calm—eerily so. The twin hulls of the catamaran slipped through the glassy surface at a steady six knots, engines humming softly beneath his seat.

Jessica perched at the bow on the edge of the trampoline netting, her knees tucked to her chest. The navigation lights bathed her in alternating green and red, her silhouette barely visible against the black sea and sky. She tilted her head back, eyes locked on the arc of the Milky Way.

"Feels like we're gliding through a dream," she called back to Ray, her voice carrying easily in the stillness.

Ray chuckled. "It's eerie, isn't it? Like the ocean's holding its breath. I've made this passage a few times. Even with light wind, waves usually build up on our bow. I've never seen it this calm." He glanced at the instruments out of habit, but there was little to monitor. The ocean was so flat it felt like they were cruising across a pond, not the open Caribbean.

A new moon gave the stars free rein to dominate the sky, but it was the water that held the real magic. As the boat pushed forward, the bow wake stirred up bursts of bioluminescence—a subtle glow that seemed to rise from the sea itself.

Jessica gasped and pointed. "Ray! Look! Jellyfish!"

Dozens of ghostly, pulsating orbs drifted just below the surface, their translucent bodies radiating soft, ethereal light. Their tendrils trailed like luminous ribbons, flaring brighter as the catamaran disturbed them—tiny underwater fireworks. Jessica's laughter broke the silence, a sound of pure wonder.

"They look like stars in the ocean," she said, her voice softer now, almost reverent. "What an amazing experience."

Ray joined her at the bow, resting a hand lightly on her shoulder as he peered into the water. Jellyfish glided in and out of the boat's path, their glow winking in rhythm with their gentle movements. It was mesmerizing.

For a moment, the enormity of the world shrank to just this—a boat, two people, and an ocean alive with light. The secrecy of the FBI operation, the logistics of the voyage, the looming consequences—all faded. In their place: peace.

Jessica broke the silence. "You think they know we're here?"

Ray smiled. "I think they're just doing what they do, same as us—moving forward, one slow step at a time."

The lights of St. Martin shimmered in the pre-dawn darkness, a necklace of golden pearls strung along the coastline. Ray stood at the helm of *Purrfection*, sipping lukewarm coffee from his Green Turtle Cay mug.

Jessica emerged from below deck, a steaming mug of coffee in hand, her hair frazzled from the night passage.

"Almost there," Ray said, his voice low in the stillness. "Well, 20 miles out, so four more hours, but Marigot Bay's straight ahead. We should be anchoring just as the sun comes up."

As the sky softened from black to indigo, the details of the shoreline began to emerge: the gentle curve of the bay, the dark smudges of palm trees, the buildings still in disrepair from Hurricane Irma. Ray throttled back the engines, guiding *Purrfection* into the calm waters. The first blush of dawn lit the horizon, painting the sky with streaks of orange and pink.

"This spot looks good," Ray said, glancing at the depth. "Twenty feet, just like the charts said. Your first time dropping the hook!"

Jessica moved to the bow, her bare feet silent against the deck. She coiled the windlass control loosely in her hand, ready to drop. But as she leaned over the side to check the water below, she froze.

"Ray!" she called back, her voice urgent but not panicked. "There's a starfish down there—right where we're about to drop the anchor!"

Ray leaned out of the cockpit to look at her, then shifted his gaze to the water. The light was growing stronger now, and he could just make out the sandy bottom beneath the clear, turquoise water. Sure enough, a large starfish lay nestled in the sand, its arms stretching wide like some celestial relic.

"We'll shift over a bit," he said, chuckling. "No need to ruin its morning."

Jessica grinned, her relief obvious. "Thanks. I don't want to be the reason it gets buried under this big ass anchor."

She glanced back toward the water and added under her breath, "You're welcome, little guy."

Ray nudged the wheel, maneuvering the boat a few yards to port. Jessica checked again and gave a thumbs-up. She released the anchor with the press of a button on the windlass control, letting the chain rattle out slowly until the anchor hit the bottom.

Ray put the engines in reverse to lay out 150 feet of chain. The anchor dug in as the boat gently pulled back on it. He came to the bow to attach the bridle—two lines that run from port and starboard hulls to the anchor chain—so the boat doesn't sway as much.

"All set," she said, brushing her hands on her shorts. Her gaze lingered on another starfish, this one safely out of harm's way. "We've got good neighbors down there. We'll have to go visit them."

The morning sun crested the hills of St. Martin, bathing Marigot Bay in golden light. The buildings along the waterfront glowed with soft, pastel hues, and the silhouette of Fort Louis stood watch from its perch above the town.

Ray cut the engines, letting the silence of the bay surround them. "I'll check in with Customs and Immigration after coffee," he suggested, "and maybe a snorkel later—check that starfish you saved."

Jessica nodded. "Great! I finally get another stamp in my passport!"

"Well, no. No stamp."

"Wait, what? Don't they have to stamp my passport?"

Ray smiled. "Welcome to the Caribbean. No, they don't. When I go to check in here, I'll go to a marine store—the same guys I'd go to for a fuel filter. I'll type in our info on their computer from 1986, but it isn't connected to the Internet. It'll take a few minutes because it's a French keyboard and the letter layout is different. It's just to get the forms to print. The guy will check that our passport numbers match what I typed in, and that's about it.

The best thing? They don't care about the dog either. Other islands are very strict, but French islands—there's not even a place on their forms to check 'dog.'"

They sipped coffee, looking out over the bay, the peaceful rhythm of the Friendly Island already settling over them.

CHAPTER SIXTEEN

August 2022 - St. Martin
Another Dinghy Dock

Once anchored in Marigot Bay, Ray and Jessica caught a quick nap after the long overnight sail. Refreshed, they snorkeled around the boat so Jessica could capture GoPro footage of her beloved starfish. After a few minutes in the water, their stomachs won out.

"I've never really anchored over here before, on the French side," Ray said as they climbed back aboard. "I'm more familiar with the Dutch side. I know the lunch spots there."

"Well, how far is that? Why didn't we just anchor over there?"

"Marigot Bay's shallow even a mile offshore, which makes it a good spot if you have to drop anchor in the dark. We happened to arrive in daylight, but still—twenty feet of water with a sandy bottom? Can't beat that. The French check-in process? They don't care where we came from, we don't need exit paperwork from our last port, and they don't care about the dog. It's much easier."

Jessica nodded. "Got it. Actually, I know a bar here owned by a guy from Chicago."

Ray raised an eyebrow. "Of course you do."

"I met this couple when I was bartending in Hilton Head. They said if I ever came to St. Maarten, *don't* go to The Dinghy Dock. Said the owner's an asshole."

"Wait—Seth? I mean, sure, he *can* come off that way, but most of us love it. It's like rudeness-as-performance-art. Who told you that?"

"His *mom*," Jessica said, laughing. "I'd like to think she was joking, but I couldn't tell."

"Well, that sounds like a woman who could be the mother of Seth," Ray said, grinning. "I used to go there all the time in 2021. My friends knew Seth, too. We were the reason he had to end 'Bottomless Mimosas' at Sunday brunch. We found the bottom. Let's go. It's almost Happy Hour, and his bar is dog-friendly. His dog might even be there."

Ray, Jessica, and Rufus piled into the dinghy and headed toward shore. Jessica scanned the waterfront.

"We're so close to land. How can the Dutch side be more than a mile away?"

"We have to go through the lagoon," Ray said, "wait till you see it. It's unique for the Caribbean."

He pointed the dinghy toward a jagged line of black rocks. As they got closer, Jessica saw the hidden channel, flanked by small red and green markers. Ray slowed to a no-wake speed as they entered.

"That's where I checked us in this morning," he said, nodding at a small marine shop behind a fuel dock. "Across the channel on the other side is Dock 46—solid place to eat. Shrimpy's is right there; he runs a laundry and a sailors' hostel. Coming up is the Sandy Ground Bridge."

Jessica tilted her head. "That's it? It looks tiny."

"Yeah, it's for smaller boats, not *Purrfection*."

They passed under the bridge and into the lagoon. Ray throttled up, getting the dinghy on plane as he turned south.

"It's *so* shallow!" Jessica said, clutching the seat, as she watched the rock and weed formations on the bottom zip past. "Are we gonna hit bottom?"

"It's just clear," Ray said, laughing. "We're fine in the dinghy. I've been through here a few times, but we mostly stayed on the Dutch side last year. I probably came over to Marigot twice."

The water opened up ahead as they rounded a point. A wide bridge spanned the lagoon.

"This is the Causeway Bridge," Ray said. "Technically, it's the Dutch side, but basically the dividing line. Dinghy Dock is just on the other side."

Ray pulled into the dinghy dock at the Dinghy Dock and tied up. The bar's clever name guaranteed it would catch the attention of sailors, all of whom eventually needed to find a place to come ashore. Much like the one in Culebra, this bar's name practically ensured it became a go-to spot. Calling it something generic like Seth's Place wouldn't have had the same pull.

Jessica hopped out of the dinghy, leash in hand, as Rufus eagerly sniffed the air. She led him down the dock to find a patch of grass, leaving Ray to secure the dinghy and head into the bar. Inside, the place was sparsely populated—just two young women chatting mid-bar and an older sailor at the far end, his grizzled demeanor making him look like he'd been planted there for authenticity. The picnic tables outside stood empty, their benches bleached by the Caribbean sun. As with most bars on the islands, the Dinghy Dock was open to Simpson Bay: no doors, no walls, no air conditioning—just an unobstructed view of the shimmering water of the lagoon.

"Ray, you want a Heineken?" a familiar voice called from behind the bar.

Ray looked up to see Rosie, the bartender, her hands busy with a dish towel. She greeted him with the knowing smile of someone who'd poured him many drinks last season.

"Hey, Rosie. Thanks, but I've switched to tequila and water with lime," Ray said, settling onto a stool. "Beer was starting to catch up with me."

Jessica returned and took the seat next to Ray, placing herself squarely between him and the two young women. Her body language was casual, but the message was clear. One of the women, a brunette with an easy smile, leaned forward to get a better look at Rufus, who had flopped at Jessica's feet.

"Your dog is adorable," the brunette said, her voice warm and friendly. Her accent carried a faint Midwestern cadence. "What's his name?"

"Rufus," Jessica replied, her tone polite but clipped. She glanced at Ray, then back at the woman. "He's not usually this well-behaved. He must be tired from the sail."

"Oh, like Rufus Du Sol! I love their music."

Jessica's eyes lit up for half a beat. Rufus Du Sol happened to be one of Jessica's favorites—she'd seen them live more than once—but she had no interest in discussing it with this stranger. She let the comment hang and said nothing.

The woman, undeterred, introduced herself as Tiffany. Her friend, Nicole, waved but didn't say much. Tiffany's confidence filled the space—her gestures precise, her smile practiced, and her gaze lingering just long enough to make her presence felt. "We're med students at AUC," Tiffany added brightly. "We just finished class, so we're just grabbing a drink before we go back to study."

Jessica nodded, a tight smile on her lips. "Sounds exciting," she said, but her eyes darted to Ray, silently warning him not to engage. He caught the look and focused on his drink, swirling the lime wedge around the rim of the glass.

"So, where are you guys from?" Tiffany pressed, clearly trying to keep the conversation going. Her gaze flicked between Jessica and Ray, lingering on him just a moment too long.

"St. Thomas," Jessica answered quickly. "We just anchored in Marigot after an overnight sail. It's been a long trip."

The subtle edge in her voice was enough to make Tiffany pause, though she didn't seem entirely put off. "Wow, sailing sounds amazing. You must have so many stories."

Jessica's smile didn't reach her eyes. "Plenty," she said, then turned to Ray. "Do you want to order some food?"

"Sure," he said, grateful for the shift. He raised a hand to get Rosie's attention. As they placed their order, Tiffany and Nicole exchanged a look and stood to leave. Tiffany lingered just a moment longer, adjusting her bag over her shoulder. She turned back toward Ray, her smile widening as her eyes met his.

"Maybe we'll see you around the island," she said, her tone light but unmistakably flirtatious. Her gaze held his for a beat longer than necessary before she turned and walked out, leaving Nicole to trail behind.

Jessica watched them leave, then sighed and picked up her Jameson, taking a long sip. "Med students," she muttered, more to herself than to Ray, "let's see if they'll flirt with sailors after graduation."

Ray hid a smirk behind his glass, letting the comment hang in the salty air. The tension eased as their food arrived. They shared a quiet meal, comfortable in each other's company, the weight of the overnight passage slowly giving way to the soothing rhythm of the bay.

Back aboard *Purrfection*, the warm hush of twilight settled around the boat, broken only by the gentle clink of halyards and the occasional splash of a fish in the bay. Jessica and Ray peeled off to their respective cabins without a word, the fatigue of the passage and the weight of subtle social combat at the Dinghy Dock clinging to their skin like salt.

Stretched out on her bunk, one hand absently resting on Rufus's warm back. She tapped out a message.

Jessica to Johnny: **Hola!**

The reply came fast.

Johnny: **Ciao Bella!**

She smiled, remembering the times when Johnny was just a friend —back when things felt simpler, before all the secrets and surveillance.

Before Campanelli. Before Ray. Wanting to share her day with someone who once felt safe, she let her thumb flick across the screen, slipping easily into the familiar rhythm of casual encryption.

Jessica: **With all those storms coming at us, Ray decided to sail us to St Martin! I love it here already! The big lagoon is so cool. We went to a bar owned by a guy from Chicago. The bar has no wall facing the bay. It's just wide open.**

She watched the typing indicator blink for a few seconds before the reply arrived.

Johnny: **That's not why you are there. I haven't told you this yet, but once we recover Campanelli's money from Captain De Soleil, he is giving us 10%. EACH! That's $100k, Jess. Keep your eye on the prize. You will get out of this with a nice payday without having to constantly look over your shoulder.**

Jessica's smile vanished, chased away by the sudden weight of numbers and consequence. She blinked at the message, reading it again, slower this time.

Recover the money. I knew this was about his damn bank account.

For a long moment, she just stared at the phone, her mind flipping through conflicting thoughts. Relief, confusion, temptation—and then the slow, creeping dread of what that payday meant. Campanelli wasn't the type to hand out rewards for clean endings. Once he had his money, Captain Ray De Soleil's usefulness might dry up. Jess had a sickening sense that when that happened, things would get ugly.

She turned the phone over, face down against the cushion, and lay back, staring at the dark night out the hatch above her head. Rufus shifted and tucked closer to her side.

"I didn't sign up for this," she whispered, more to herself than anyone else.

Even as she said it, part of her wondered if maybe she had.

Ray sat on the edge of his berth, the scent of musty clothes and a head that needed cleaning mixing with the night air sneaking in through the porthole. He pulled out his phone to finally fire off a message he should've sent hours ago; however, he had a message waiting.

Jake: **What are you doing Ray, sailing to Sint Maarten without even telling us!**

Ray: **Sint Maarten is the name of the Dutch territory. The island is called Saint Martin. But yeah, we just anchored.**

He scratched his new beard growth absently while waiting for the reply, already knowing the tone it would take.

Jake: **You were supposed to plan your departure with us, and we had hoped to catch Jessica red-handed in US waters. Nobody here is happy.**

Ray smirked. *Just anchored* was vague by design. Ray had a talent for parsing words. If Jake had asked for a time, he would've been honest. Ray took note *'nobody is happy'* was already the mood before he texted, so he knew the FBI was monitoring the boat or Jessica's phone location and was well aware of their trip.

Ray: **Sorry Jake, we had the perfect weather window. No time to get approval from the Feds. Who knows how long that would've taken? The most dangerous thing in sailing is a schedule. Sail when the weather says sail, and don't sail if it's questionable, but NEVER sail based on some date on a calendar.**

Jake didn't respond right away. When he did, the tone was clipped.

Jake: **We can't just fly into St Martin. We have to coordinate with their agencies. We have to call it a 'training' op. This will take at least 2 weeks, and that's supremely expedited. Can you just sail back here!**

Ray: **A tropical wave is coming off Africa, already. It's early in the year. I need to keep an eye on that, and we need to be East so we can run south if we have to along the islands. I'm not sitting through a hurricane if I can sail south for a day and be out of it. This was always part of the hurricane plan. I'm guessing a hurricane would screw up your operation, so let's avoid those.**

Jake: **We just weren't prepared for it.**

Ray: **Hurricane season starts June 1st for a reason. Sure, the big storms don't roll off Africa until later in the year, TYPICALLY.** No rules to this thing called weather.

Jake: **My bosses are pissed, but they are dealing with it. I'm going to fly to you soon, in an unofficial vacation capacity, until we get formal approval.**

Ray: **Great. See you in a few days. You'll love it here. French food and wine, the Dutch party.**

Jake started typing: **I'm NOT on a real vacation**. Then deleted it. Arguing further wouldn't help. Truth be told, he wouldn't mind seeing the island — finally, some tropical benefits of tracking '*The Siren*'.

Maxwell stood on the balcony of his St. Thomas hotel room and placed his nightly call to Director Beck. Beck answered without pleasantries. "Report."

Maxwell's voice was tight with frustration. "You're not gonna believe this shit. That asshole just *sailed off*. He headed for St. Martin."

Beck didn't even blink. "Is that so?"

"You don't sound surprised. Or concerned. This delays everything by at least two weeks!"

"It's not the worst thing," Beck said, calm as ever. "Remember—when this goes down, and we pin it on Jessica, we *don't* want to catch her. This gives her the perfect runway to disappear."

Beck continued, "Your tech guy, Kevin? He's stuck with a laptop and third-world Internet. We need his help shaping the narrative, but not enough access to start digging around with his nerd claws."

Maxwell scoffed. "It's like you planned it. Meanwhile, I'm racking up two more weeks of interest payments—so I guess it's all upside for you."

"I had a hunch," Beck said, smugly. "That's why I'm Director, and you're still playing stakeout in the back of a van."

Maxwell muttered, "No wonder you wanted to keep this guy away from Elana. Dang, he coulda sailed off with her like this?"

"For now, just keep acting pissed. Jake is in the loop. Kevin isn't. Let's keep it that way."

Click. Beck ended the call without saying goodbye.

CHAPTER
SEVENTEEN

July 2022 - St Martin
Agent Jake Lawrence, Pirate

As soon as Jake's plane touched down in St. Martin, he flipped off airplane mode and fired off a text to Ray.

Jake: **Just landed. Where are you?**

Ray: **Happy Hour at the yacht club.**

Jake: **Is Jessica with you?**

Ray: **No, she's back on the boat. She had to set up some trips for new clients—remember, she's a travel agent. She doesn't enjoy the Yacht Club scene anyway. Too many old guys hitting on her, even when I'm sitting right next to her. I guess they can tell we're not a couple. Or they just don't care.**

Jake: **Stay put. I'll find it. That's the one by the bridge?**

Ray: **Yep—Simpson Bay Bridge. The famous one where all the yachts parade into the lagoon. You sure know how to pick discreet meeting spots, don't you?**

Ray's follow-up text had a teasing edge, poking fun at Jake's choice of a bustling, open-air bar for a meeting that probably warranted more subtlety.

Jake: **My bosses are pissed, and I need a drink. Jessica's stuck on the boat without the dinghy, right? I think we're safe.**

Ray: **Relax, Jake. It's fine. I talk to strangers at bars every day. She's used to it. You ever heard the phrase 'never met a stranger'? That's me. Got it from my Gramps. The man could strike up a conversation with a rock. I'm just carrying the torch.**

Jake: **I just can't be seen. Can't be compromised. I'll be there in 15.**

Ray chuckled and flagged the bartender for another drink. It was a cruise ship day, and with island traffic, no way Jake was going to make the 4-mile trip in under an hour.

He settled deeper into his chair, letting the tropical breeze roll in over the water. He had time.

Jake marched into the Yacht Club with determined urgency, making a beeline for the bar where Ray sat, relaxed as ever with a half-empty glass of tequila in hand.

"Jake! Welcome to the Friendly Island, mate," Ray said, lifting his drink. "Got one on order for you already."

Jake stopped short, tension radiating off him. "Captain Ray De Soleil," he said with dry sarcasm. "You've put me in a tight spot. I had to burn my personal vacation time for this. Do you have any idea how much paperwork it takes to classify this as an official FBI trip?"

Ray barely flinched. "Why are you even here? You knew the main reason I needed Jessica was to move the boat for hurricane season."

Before Jake could respond, KoKo, the bartender, placed a tall orange drink in front of him.

"We didn't expect you to just vanish on a Friday afternoon," Jake said, eyeing the glass suspiciously. "What is this?"

"Did we leave on a Friday? Huh. Old saying—never leave port on a

Friday. Maybe it doesn't count if you don't know what day it is?" Ray grinned. "The weather window said go, so we went. That's called a Pain Killer, by the way. Traditional Caribbean rum drink. Figured you could use it."

Jake raised the glass, examining it like evidence, then shrugged and took a sip.

"Cheers," Ray said, looking toward Jake's eyes, not really expecting him to make eye contact, but suddenly Jake made direct, awkward eye contact, even leaning in a bit.

"Cheers," he echoed, before downing nearly half the drink. Ray watched with a barely noticeable smirk on his face.

"You've got me in deep shit, Ray. Once we realized you were leaving, it was too late to get the Coast Guard to stop you. Do you know the paperwork it's gonna take if she steals the money here, in foreign waters?" As Jake finished the sentence, he also finished his drink.

Ray shrugged. "If an American steals American money electronically from an American account, does it matter where they are? Seems like a big legal loophole. Buddy, the drinks down here are a bit stronger than you are used to, and KoKo makes a mean one. We don't call her KoKo the Killer for no reason. You drank that way too fast. Remember St. Thomas?" He gave a nod to KoKo, who was already mixing another.

"It's just a lot of red tape," Jake said. "It would be easier if you brought her back to U.S. waters so we can arrest her. Here, I'll have to get the Dutch police involved. It would be easier than dealing with the French."

"Ok, so maybe we move to the Dutch side? I can probably be back in US waters end of October, maybe. I'll need her to move the boat again anyway," Ray replied as the bartender returned with round two.

Jake lifted the fresh Pain Killer almost immediately. "Cheers," he said again, locking eyes once more. "To a successful venture."

Ray clinked his nearly empty glass. "Cheers... Is that a Chicago thing? The eye contact?"

Jake laughed, loosening up for the first time. "It's a Jessica thing for sure. Not sure about Chicago. Seven years bad sex is a hell of a penalty, so may as well just make eye contact." Jake blurted out. Realizing that his statement seemed too personal, Jake added, "You have to know your adversary, study them, know their habits and traits." Jake took another big swig of his drink and looked at Ray, "You say there's rum in here? I can't even taste it."

"Oh, there's rum. A lot of it," Ray said. "That's why it's called a Pain Killer. Watch out for the Rum Monster."

Jake finally leaned back, taking in the open-air view across Simpson Bay Lagoon. Anchored boats bobbed gently in the distance, with the causeway bridge to the north and the drawbridge just to the left. Mega yachts gleamed along the dock, a parade of polished fiberglass and shiny money.

"I get it now," Jake said, turning his back to the bar, Pain Killer in hand. "This life... I'm starting to feel like a pirate."

"You are starting to feel the rum! Calico Jake Rackham, you are not!" Ray chuckled. "Pirates know how to hold their rum—and plan for hurricane season."

"Rack... Rackham?" Jake slurred faintly.

"The pirate? His name was Calico Jack Rackham, said to be a pirate of great wits but small stature. Made his name by out-smarting and out-sailing his adversaries. That ain't you Jake, that ain't you." Ray smacked his back in friendly harassment. "His name was actually John Rackham. He became famous as Calico Jack, so he stopped correcting people. He sailed with Ann Bon...."

"YOU KNOW, MY NAME is John too... yeah... My dad's name was John, and I'm John, confusing as hell, so they started calling me Jake." Jake loudly and proudly interrupted Ray's rambling, drunk history lesson.

"Jake? How did they get Jake from John? I guess it's close..." Ray surmised.

Jake cut Ray off again, "From the John Wayne movie, 'Big Jake'. My grandpa always watched cowboy movies. So.... I was little Jake, growing up... and it just stuck. Jake is not a cool name, so for my friends I go by John. Gesh. Who the hell am I?" Jake pondered deeply into his rum.

"You're a drunk FBI agent, that's who, and you've just met the First Night Rum Monster. Welcome to the Caribbean, mate," as Ray smacked Jake on the back. "My grandpa used to watch cowboy movies all the time, too. I know that movie well. You realize this means your grandpa thought of himself as Big Jake, always looking out for you, doing whatever it takes, shooting whoever gets in his way... that kind of stuff." Ray wasn't immune to the tequila; he just had a better tolerance.

"I never... never ... never thought of it like that. That's really kinda endearing, isn't it? My grandpa was stoic like John Wayne, never really showed emotions, so it kinda makes sense." Jake recounted with a mist in his left eye.

Ray saw that Jake was tearing up. Not wanting to deal with a sentimental drunk, he tried to change the subject rapidly. "Hey, Jake, do you know the only movie where John Wayne actually robbed a bank?"

Jake sniffled a bit, recovering from that thought of his grandfather, and strained his brain. 'Well... in True Grit, Rooster Cogburn recounts robbing banks, but he is just recounting, remorsefully even. Never actually shows him robbing a bank. Hmmm.... Physically robs a bank? I dunno, I give up."

"The Godfathers," Ray stated factually.

"The Godfathers? I barely remember that one. Black and White, yeah? Isn't that almost a comedy? Don't they find a kid or baby or something?"

"Yep. Three nice guys decide to rob a bank. While the posse is in hot pursuit, they help a mother deliver a baby. When the mother dies, the three cowboys vow to take care of the newborn. It's the original *'Three Men and a Baby.'*"

"Huh.... I remember now. Didn't they say 'please' when they robbed the bank? Yeah, I think they did. If I ever robbed a bank, I'd say 'please'. Probably. I think I would. I need to rob a bank. I need to rob a bank to pay for my daughter's medical school. Girl is so smart and I can't afford it. Damn government salary. Damn ex-wife. Just a girl from a middle-class family, woulda ya gonna do, she won't get a scholarship." Jake rambled, taking yet another sip of his Pain Killer.

Ray interjected, "Robbing a bank like a cowboy seems a little old-fashioned and dangerous. Better to just do it electronically, like Jessica, eh? Maybe we should learn something from her."

"Yeah. But we pissed off the wrong person. Can't just take people's money and them not get pissed off, important people. If I robbed a bank, I'd say *Please*. But robbing the government, those bastards... I'd say f*ck you, that's what I'd say, Ray. F*ck you. That's who to rob, the f*cking government. Incompetent, nobody cares, sons a bitches... and nobody to get pissed, it's not their money... "

"Whose money? Who took what from who? ... Whom? ... Who?" Ray was confused, questioned Jake's statements, but realized he needed to get out of that bar. "Gesh, Jake, first time I've heard you curse. We need to tamper back this Pain Killer flow a little bit. It's your first night on the island, and that First Night Rum Monster is out to get you hard, AND a tropical storm is coming. Never know when that blows up into a Cat 1 hurricane. Don't want to be hungover for that."

Jake rambled on and on. "FBI's money. Nobody's money. Probably comes from drug cartels. Or China. Or the printer. I dunno, but they got lots of it. Nobody cares. Not like that guy in Chicago cared. He was so pissed at us. You know, at the end of the fiscal year, we have to make up travel trips, so we spend all our budget money. Otherwise, we don't get the same budget as last year. Nobody cares. Nobody."

Ray finished his tequila. "Okay, Jake. Got it. Step one: steal the FBI's money. Great plan. We'll work on the details tomorrow. For now, you need a taxi before I have to dinghy your drunk ass back to the boat."

"Oh no ... no, no way, nope, no. I can't go back to your boat. Jessica would be pissed. I'm not supposed to drink. I mean, she can't know I'm here. I mean, Jessica can't see me." Jake said defensively as he tried to put two feet under himself and stand from the bar stool. "Where's that taxi?"

"Ok, ok, yeah, Jake, John, Johnny Ol' Boy. I wasn't thinking. Or the tequila wasn't thinking. Jessica wouldn't know who you are, but I can't be bringing drunk dudes back to my boat. I have a reputation to protect, after all. Oh shoot, I need two bags of ice."

The cabin lay in stillness—only the creak of the salon windows and the occasional slap of water against the hull broke the silence. Ray had gone ashore for ice, the dinghy's outboard fading in the direction of the Yacht Club.

Jessica sat alone at the nav station, the flash drive a cold weight in her hand.

She turned it over, as if it might offer answers. Just plastic and metal. Harmless-looking. But it wasn't.

Ray's laptop sat closed on the counter, right where he always left it. She glanced back out the window, no sign of an approaching dinghy. Her fingers hovered.

She didn't know what the drive would do. She wasn't told. She was just told it had to be inserted, on this boat, into this machine. "It'll run automatically," Johnny had said. "You don't need to understand it."

She didn't.

A few seconds and it would be done. Whatever debt Ray owed Campanelli, this was the price. She was the courier. She was just the courier, she told herself.

Jessica hesitated.

Not because she feared getting caught—Ray trusted her now, trusted her enough to leave her alone on his boat. But because something about it felt wrong. Not illegal, *wrong*. Personal *wrong*. She liked Ray. Maybe more than she wanted to admit. Whatever this flash drive did, it wasn't going to help him.

She sighed and opened the laptop. The screen lit up with the familiar chartplotter software, a weather tab, a folder labeled "Boat Stuff." Nothing nefarious. Just Ray's world—winds, tides, routes, maintenance spreadsheets.

Her finger hovered over the USB port. One quick motion.

"I'm sorry," she whispered.

The flash drive clicked into place.

The screen blinked. A window opened, ran a command. Just a few lines of code, too fast for her to follow. Then—nothing. It closed itself. Like it had never been there.

Jessica pulled the drive out, slipped it back into her pocket, and closed the laptop.

It was done.

She stood there for a moment longer, staring at the closed computer. Whatever trouble was coming Ray's way, she couldn't stop it. She couldn't even warn him. She wasn't sure who was playing whom anymore. She felt sorry for him, quietly, deeply.

Then she poured herself a double Jameson, went topside, squinting into the sun, and forced herself to smile.

CHAPTER
EIGHTEEN

July 2022 - St Martin
Tropical Storm Tiffany

Jessica stretched in her bunk as the morning sun came glaring through her hatch. She reached for her phone to send her morning update.

Jessica to Johnny: **Hola!**

Jessica waited. And waited. After an unusually long delay, finally a reply.

Johnny: **Ciao Bella**

She noticed that Johnny forgot the exclamation point, a blatant breach of protocol. She hesitated sending a message. Was he testing her? Was it somebody else? Or did he just slip up? She decided to send something more cryptic than usual.

Jessica: **It's done. Installed without an issue.**

Johnny: **Good. That's step one.**

Jessica knew she shouldn't text anymore and wouldn't get a reply if she did, but 'step one' was concerning.

Jessica: **Step one? I installed it. It ran. That's all you said I'd have to do. You are so frustrating!**

She tossed her phone on the bed in disgust, hitting Rufus on his backside, stirring him from his slumber.

"Sorry, buddy", as she picked her phone up, ready to delete the messages, but then saw the text bubbles coming. *Johnny is breaking protocol? This must be big?*

Johnny: **Here's the thing, Jess. His bank account is locked to his computer only. I can't access his account like I did Campanelli's. You are going to have to log in and do the transfer yourself. Once the key logger does its job and gets his password, I'll walk you through it. With the software from the flash drive, I'll be able to monitor the screen and guide you through it.**

Jessica: **You have got to be kidding me? Me? You know how bad I am at computers. What if I screw something up? What happens to Ray after all this? He's a great guy, one of the good ones. I can't believe he is knowingly involved with Campanelli.**

Not expecting a response, her face became distorted when she saw the text bubbles coming again. *Johnny is really off his protocol this morning.*

Johnny: **Ray is going to be just fine. Campanelli parked some funds with him for a while, but can't contact him to get the funds back due to surveillance. He is not mad at Ray. He is grateful. It's not Ray's money to begin with, so don't feel bad about that either. He is just as broke as he looks. Ciao Bella**

She hadn't expected Ray to be safe, dealing with Campanelli—yet he was. The surprise brought a fleeting rush of relief, chased almost instantly by the weight of what she still had to do. Desperate for a distraction, she texted her friend Cass, who moved to St. Martin two years ago.

Ray sat in the cockpit, laptop open, mind firing on all cylinders as he dove into a stretch of software work. Jessica usually gave him space when he hit that zone, but this time she burst through the salon door, too excited to keep it in. "So, my friends that moved here from Chicago, Cassandra and Mike, they've invited me to Elevate tonight! I'm so excited."

Ray glanced up from his screen, irritation flickering for half a beat before the glow on her face disarmed him. His shoulders eased. "Okay, cool. Elevate? That's the Electronic Music festival thing up on the mountain at the zip line place?"

"Yep! I used to go all the time in Chicago, but Hilton Head was so lame, never had any shows."

"That sounds amazingly fun." Ray hinted at how much fun he might have there, but Jessica was in her own world.

"So we are going to have an early dinner with them at Dinghy Dock around 3 pm, if that's okay? I mean, Happy Hour for you, right?"

"3 pm is St. Thomas Happy Hour, that's early for here, but sure."

"I guess there are traffic issues, then we need to ride the ski lift to the top, and the party is up there. Oh, and I will stay at her house tonight, so you'll have the boat to yourself!"

"You mean, me and Rufus?"

"Oh no, I'm going to take Rufus over to their house. Mike is going to stay home with their dog, so Rufus gets a play date. Mike is driving us and picking us up, so we don't have to worry about driving."

With Mike not going either, Ray didn't really mind being left out —though it would've been easier if she'd just called it a girls' night from the start. Still, he felt a wave of relief knowing she wouldn't be climbing into a car with someone who might be driving under the influence.

Ray guided their dinghy into the well of the dock as Jessica cleated off the painter. She lifted Rufus onto the boards, then hopped out herself. As Ray climbed after her, Jessica spun, stepping in close enough that it looked like she might slip her arms around his neck.

Instead, she reached up and pinched the top button of his shirt closed with a faint smile.

"There," she said, neat and precise, as if tidying up a man who couldn't be trusted to do it himself.

Ray smirked. "You trying to make me look respectable?"

"Trying," she answered, turning back toward the open-air bar.

It was quiet for St. Martin—too early for Happy Hour—just a few sailors and the old man who never seemed to leave his post at the end of the bar. Cass and Mike were already at a lagoon-side picnic table, hands wrapped around sweating glasses, waving them over.

Before they could sit, Rosie leaned across the worn wood bar. "Ray! I don't know what the hell you're drinking these days... Heineken, rosé, Jameson, tequila? Make up your mind already—what's it gonna be tonight?"

Ray raised his eyebrows at Jessica, then back at Rosie. "Guess I'll keep you guessing, Rosie. Tequila, water, lime."

Rosie shook her head, laughing. "Hopeless."

They joined Cass and Mike, the table sticky with spilled Carib. Menus were scattered, though everyone already knew what they'd order.

Conversation drifted easily toward the day's adventures. Ray had managed a couple of unorthodox repairs that kept things moving, the kind only he could pull off. Jessica leaned in, eyes bright, her voice animated. "You know what's wild about Ray? He can fix anything. Boats, computers, engines—you name it. If something's broken, just hand it to him, and five minutes later—done."

Cass grinned. "That's a gift. Mike once spent two hours trying to fix a ceiling fan before I finally called an electrician."

Mike lifted his glass, muscles popping out of his shirt, unfazed. "Hey, I'm more of a jiu-jitsu guy."

Ray gave a modest shrug, eyes on his drink. "Half the time it's just improvising with what you've got. Duck tape, zip ties."

"Still counts," Jessica said quickly, a touch of pride in her tone.

The meal stretched, drinks drained, plates pushed aside. Ray was digging for cash when Jessica slipped her bag over her shoulder. "We're heading straight to Elevate, then Mike will take the dogs back, right?" she asked Cass and Mike.

That's when the noise from the street-side entrance swelled. A pack of sunburned, barefoot girls spilled in, hair damp from salt water, beach bags slung carelessly. Jessica knew before she even looked who was at the center—Tiffany, eyes bright, laughter too loud, gaze locking straight on Ray.

Jessica stiffened.

Cass noticed. "Do you know these girls?"

Jessica angled her answer toward the group. "Well, looks like no studying today, eh, ladies?"

Tiffany fired back without hesitation. "Can't drink all day if you don't start in the morning."

Cass leaned in, recognition dawning. "Oh, that's the AUC med student you were telling me about."

Ray chuckled low, sliding his receipt across the table. "Well," he murmured to Jessica, "looks like I've found friends for the night after all."

Jessica's jaw tightened. "Good for you," she said, and walked out with Cass and Mike, her voice clipped but steady.

Out in the parking lot, the heat of the day still clinging to the asphalt, she finally let it out. "Can you believe that? He's practically drooling at her."

Cass frowned. "What are you talking about? From where we sit, it always looks like you two are together."

Mike nodded. "Yeah, honestly—we thought you already were."

Jessica exhaled hard, the words catching in her throat. "Then maybe I'm the crazy one." She glanced back toward the laughter spilling out of the bar—Tiffany's laughter—and Ray leaning in, already caught in Tiffany's orbit.

"Ray! Captain Ray De Soleil!" Tiffany squealed, throwing herself onto his shoulder. "So damn glad you came to join the AUC girls! Rosie—get this man a Fireball!"

He barely made it to the bar before the shot glass was pressed into his hand.

"Fireball, huh?" Ray eyed it with a wry smile. "I've been on tequila all afternoon."

Tiffany wrapped him in a hug, kissed his cheek. Most of the girls barely noticed, though Nicole—who'd met Ray once before—watched with less enthusiasm.

"You know what they say," Tiffany announced. "Liquor before beer, everything clear. Beer before liquor... don't be a pussy."

Ray laughed. "Pretty sure that's not the quote. And it doesn't even apply—no beers tonight."

They clinked glasses. Ray held her gaze, the kind of steady eye contact Jessica always teased him about. Tiffany faltered for just a second under it, then tossed back the shot.

Turning to the group, Tiffany raised her voice. "Hey, ladies, Ray has a boat! Let's go swim! Where are you anchored, Marigot? Let's go!"

She didn't ask Ray—just assumed. But the other med students weren't buying it. They were in the Caribbean, yes, but still med students. Saturday night meant a couple drinks and then home by eleven to hydrate, swallow B12, and make sure tomorrow's study time wasn't ruined by a hangover.

Ray watched Tiffany's energy crash against the silence of her friends. He could sense that she was gearing up to come solo. He cut her off gently. "It's okay, maybe next time. I've got a pretty strict rule: you can get drunk on the boat, but you can't get on the boat drunk."

Tiffany tilted her head, trying to read him, then shot back in a mock-serious tone: "Aren't they more like... guidelines than actual rules?"

Ray chuckled. "Oh, some smartass has seen too many movies."

CHAPTER
NINETEEN

September 2022 - St. Martin
The Team Arrives

Maxwell and Kevin finally arrived in St. Martin, stepping into the heavy tropical air with the weight of bureaucracy finally—mostly—behind them. After weeks of diplomatic back-and-forth and late-night calls, their operation was officially sanctioned. Well, sort of.

To maintain appearances and stay within international protocol, their mission was designated as a "training exercise"—a favor to the Dutch police. A little show-and-tell on how to catch an electronic thief, Caribbean style. Of course, the real goal was to monitor a suspect vessel, but until they secured full cooperation, things like drones and surveillance cameras were off the table.

They walked across the sun-warmed tarmac toward the modest Customs building. Tourists in flip-flops and tank tops surged around them, eager to get to beaches and boat drinks.

A sign near the entrance caught Kevin's eye. Handwritten in block letters on whiteboard:

"Mr. Maxwell and Mr. Caldwell"

Maxwell walked right past it.

"Uh, Agent Maxwell?" Kevin said, tugging at his sleeve. "I think this is for us."

Maxwell stopped short, nearly causing a pileup behind him. A woman with a rolling suitcase huffed as she swerved around them, muttering something about government workers.

Maxwell turned. "Yes, I'm James Maxwell. This is Kevin Caldwell."

A wiry man in a linen shirt and mirrored sunglasses stepped forward with a wide, practiced smile. "Hello, I'm Jost. I'll be your attaché with the Dutch police force while you're here. We have a car waiting to take you to headquarters. Just a few more pieces of paper to sign."

Maxwell muttered to Kevin under his breath, "I thought Jake had all this nailed down ahead of time. He better have our van ready."

Kevin adjusted the strap of his messenger bag. "Uh, excuse me, Jost," he asked, a little hesitantly. "We pre-shipped two crates of gear—should be marked 'U.S. DOJ.' Are those at headquarters too?"

Jost nodded crisply. "Yes, most definitely. The surveillance van Mr. Lawrence requested is already on-site. Air-conditioned, tinted windows, very discreet. Looks like a taxi."

Kevin let out a small sigh of relief. Maxwell didn't relax.

As they walked toward a waiting government SUV, Maxwell leaned in and said, "We'll be lucky if this isn't another dance through red tape. You watch—they'll want us to train someone in phishing before we even get near the marina."

Kevin gave a half-smile. "At least we're here. That's something."

Maxwell nodded once, his eyes scanning the palm-lined horizon. "Yeah. Now let's find our thief."

The ride to the Dutch police headquarters wound through the narrow streets of Philipsburg, past pastel buildings, fruit stands, and mopeds weaving between compact cars. Jost drove with one hand and a near-constant commentary about the island's infrastructure challenges, especially how the power can go out at any moment. Maxwell tuned him out.

By the time they pulled into the modest two-story station tucked beside a marina access road, the late afternoon sun had settled into that hazy golden hour where everything looked prettier than it actually was.

Jake Lawrence was waiting out front in sunglasses and island casual: short sleeves, pressed khakis, and boat shoes. He looked tan, rested, and entirely too comfortable.

Maxwell stepped out of the SUV and walked straight toward him.

"Nice of you to join us," Jake said, arms slightly raised like he might go in for a hug, but thought better of it.

Maxwell didn't slow, instructing Kevin to go check the gear, so he could speak privately with Jake. "We're not here for vacation snapshots, Jake. It's time to wrap this up."

Jake nodded slowly. "I figured you'd say that. I've got eyes on Jessica, but she's not exactly cooperative. I think she realizes the implications this might have on her Captain. But good news, she seems to be pissed at him for something, so might make it easier."

Maxwell's expression didn't shift. "She doesn't need to be cooperative. She just needs to do what you tell her to do, when you tell her to do it — log in to Ray's account and move the funds. That was the whole damn point of embedding you down here. We had a window. You're letting it close."

Jake held up both hands. "Hey—I've been working her. But she's not stupid. She suspects Ray's involved in something shady, but she's not fully convinced yet. We couldn't have her transfer the funds until our team was in place anyway."

Maxwell turned toward the building. "Let's get inside. I want to see the van, confirm the crates, and review the last ten days of activity on Ray's boat. We'll be operational by nightfall."

Jake exhaled through his nose. "Alright. I'll text her tonight, make sure she's ready to transfer funds tomorrow."

Jake to Ray: **The rest of the team is on island and will be oper-**

ational tonight. Tomorrow, make sure you leave your laptop lying around, unlocked, if possible. It's time to see if Jessica will try to access it.

Ray: **You sure you've got the right girl? She doesn't seem tech-savvy. I seriously doubt she can pull this off.**

Jake stared at the screen for a moment before replying. They'd anticipated Ray might start to question the operation.

Jake: **We believe she's working with someone. Someone with technical skills.**

Ray put down the phone and leaned back, brow furrowed. The idea had crossed his mind—barely—but now it came crashing in with new weight. Maybe she *was* The Siren. Maybe she had an accomplice all along. Her constant tech fumbles, the way she'd played clueless... it hadn't seemed fake. But maybe that's exactly what made it work.

Jessica texted her nightly report.

Jessica: **Hola!**

Johnny: **Ciao Bella! It's time to get this transfer completed! Let's target tomorrow. Let me know when you have access to his computer.**

Jessica was still simmering over the Tiffany mess, her mood too sour to waste on worrying about Ray.

Jessica: **Fine. Let's do this so I can get out of here.**

The moment she hit send, regret pulsed through her. Did she really mean it? Was she ready to walk away from *Purrfection*—walk away from Ray?

Johnny: **Great. Normal texting protocol won't apply during the transfers; I'll need to send you detailed instructions. Talk tomorrow.**

Jessica sat cross-legged in the salon, Ray's laptop open in front of her like some ancient relic. The screen glowed faintly, humming with a low, judgmental buzz. She took a breath. Then another. Her fingertips hovered over the keyboard as if contact might trigger something irreversible.

It was quiet on *Purrfection*. Ray was still ashore, off doing something charmingly helpful or frustratingly oblivious, likely involving Tiffany, whose very existence had become a sore spot. Jessica didn't want to be jealous. She wasn't jealous. She was just... annoyed. That's what she told herself.

Her phone buzzed. A message from Johnny, disregarding messaging protocol for this delicate walk-through.

J: Open up the browser, navigate to www.troweprice.com. J: Username is just 'raykorte19'. Password is 'Sparkley0ct0pu$', but the O's are zeros, be careful! J: No secondary security. You should be in quickly.

When Jessica pulled up the website, the username was already filled in. On the next screen, the password was filled in. She bit her lip.

J: Just hit that 'view password' first. Make sure it's correct. You're doing great. Should take less than 3 minutes.

Jessica's jaw clenched. "Yeah," she muttered aloud. "Three minutes to betray someone who made me pancakes."

She clicked the icon and was instantly looking at Ray's bank account. Her stomach flipped. She didn't want to be here. Not on his digital turf. Not doing *this*.

Johnny's messages kept coming.

J: See the menu option that says 'Transfer', go ahead and click that.

She followed the steps like a robot. Each click louder than the last. Her hand trembled as she typed.

The transfer screen blinked at her, blank and waiting.

J: Enter the routing and account number that you wrote down earlier. J: Now check the box where it says to accept the charge for the immediate wire transfer.

She didn't.

Instead, she typed the first few characters correctly, fumbling the rest. Hit "Enter" without confirming.

The website threw an error for a bad routing number. She blinked at it, like it had spoken out loud.

"Oops, oh shit," she said flatly, and logged off with two rapid clicks. Her hands moved faster than her brain could talk her out of it.

Laptop closed. Done.

Her breath caught in her throat. That was it. She couldn't do it. Wouldn't.

Because Ray wasn't some lowlife degenerate. Yeah, he screwed up messing around with Tiffany, but he didn't deserve this. Johnny had said he wouldn't get hurt. That this wouldn't touch his accounts or assets. Just a temporary parking spot for Campanelli.

But even knowing that, maybe even believing it...

She couldn't shake the feeling that this—*lying to him*—was worse than whatever digital damage Johnny had in mind.

She stood up quickly, knocking her head against the low salon windows.

"Shit." She rubbed her head, then stared at the closed laptop.

She had done just enough to show Johnny she *tried*.

Jessica poured a glass of Jameson. A *pour* might've been generous—this was closer to a full-blown Irish baptism. She didn't bother with ice. Just grabbed the bottle, filled the glass to a point that would make most bartenders pause, and retreated to her cabin.

The door clicked shut behind her. She dropped onto the bed like a deflated sail, the drink sloshing but miraculously not spilling, pro that she was. The laptop had felt radioactive under her hands, but now her fingers were cold and twitchy, as if they'd missed a step on a high wire.

Her phone sat on the bed beside her, screen dark, daring her to look.

She didn't.

Not yet.

The first sip of whiskey burned like truth. The second settled in like denial. By the third, she was staring at the ceiling, replaying the whole sequence.

He won't get hurt, she reminded herself.

Johnny had said that.

So why did she feel like she'd just punched Ray in the ribs?

The phone buzzed.

She jumped, heart thudding, eyes locking on the screen like it might explode.

Johnny: **Ciao Bella! What the hell happened Jess? You were doing so well. We were so close.**

Jessica: **I heard a dinghy engine outside, then I panicked. It passed by, but by then I already screwed it up.**

Johnny: **Okay, no need to panic. He's not back yet. We can try again. Unless you've hit the Jameson already?**

Jessica: **Yep, too late.**

The room smelled like stale coffee, sweat, and stress. A clunky oscillating fan in the corner fought valiantly against the Caribbean heat, barely rustling the curtain. Cables tangled across the floor, connecting laptops, routers, and portable drives to power strips balanced precariously on the desk. It was a makeshift command center—improvised, but functional. No badges, no official signage. Just three men trying to orchestrate the takedown of a woman from a hotel room with a view.

Kevin leaned in close to the glowing screen, his eyes wide behind smudged glasses. "She's in! She's logged in!" he shouted, fingers flying over the keys. "She's accessing the account—finally."

Maxwell looked up from his seat at the round table, blinking slowly like a man who'd been woken from a dream—or a bad nap. He tried to sound surprised, "She's doing it? The transfer?"

"Yup. Just started the process," Kevin grinned, elated. "Once that wire hits staging, it'll trigger the alert tag. We'll have a full breadcrumb trail. This is it, Max. Game over."

Maxwell didn't share the enthusiasm. He nodded vaguely and rubbed at his temples with both hands. "Wonder where Jake is, he's missing it," he muttered.

Kevin swiveled his head toward the connecting door to the second room. "He's probably still texting his daughter," he said with a shrug, then turned his attention back to the glowing code waterfall on his screen.

Maxwell's expression darkened. He already *knew* where Jake was. Knew what he was doing.

The screen showed the cursor trembling. The bank interface blinked. A few numbers were entered, then deleted. Then nothing.

"She's... she's stalling," Kevin said, confused. "No, wait. That's—well, that's totally wrong. What is she doing now? She's backing out?"

Maxwell stood up abruptly, the chair legs scraping the tile floor with a squeal. "What the hell is this?"

Right on cue, Jake walked in from the other room, phone still in hand, mid-text. He froze in the doorway. Maxwell zeroed in.

"You wanna tell me what the hell just happened?" he snapped, voice low and venomous, directing his gaze firmly on Jake.

Kevin was still fixated on the screens and thought Maxwell was talking to him, so he tried to explain, "Well, sir, it looks like something spooked her. She had no technical reason not to keep going."

Jake added, "Yeah, she probably heard a boat nearby, thought Ray was coming back, or something like that. I'm sure she'll try again tomorrow."

"You don't think she'll take another shot? It's still Happy Hour. That half drunk sailor won't be back for another hour at least." Maxwell chirped.

"I don't think she'll try again tonight, no," Jake stated.

"Jake, we were *THIS* close. Better get your girl under control and get this done." Maxwell stormed out of the room, as Kevin looked on confused.

CHAPTER TWENTY

September 2022 - St. Martin
St Martin - The Friendly Island

The next morning broke with a hush, the kind of stillness that only happens when the wind forgets to blow. Ray had brewed coffee and scrambled eggs by the time Jessica emerged from her cabin, eyes still heavy with guilt.

She gave Ray a half-smile as she slid into the cockpit, the usual twinkle in his eye resurfacing, trying to distract herself from what she failed to do and whatever Johnny had planned next. "I was thinking... how about we play tourist today?"

Ray blinked, then tilted his head. "Tourist? Hmm... We could dinghy under the bridge, head to Buccaneer Beach Bar. Swim, day-drink, pretend we don't have a care in the world?"

She arched an eyebrow. "That sounds like just the distraction I need."

"Distraction? Your travel agent business is going that well, you need a distraction?"

By late morning, they were zipping through the lagoon in the dinghy, the engine sputtering contentedly as Ray navigated toward the bridge. Jessica sat sideways, her long legs stretched out, one hand trailing lazily in the warm Caribbean water. When the steel belly of the Simpson Bay Bridge loomed ahead, she turned to him.

"I love that we're doing this," she said. "Feels like... before."

"Yeah." Ray kept his eyes forward, but his voice softened. "Me too."

As they motored out of the lagoon, the timing turned out to be perfect—or depending on who you asked, an utter disaster. The Simpson Bay Bridge had just started its slow rise, warning horns blaring, red lights flashing, as the morning's scheduled opening began. A parade of boats had already gathered: sleek sailing yachts, charter cats lined with sunburned tourists, and a few clunky motor cruisers full of shouting Frenchmen holding cocktails way too early in the day.

Ray let out a quiet groan. "Of course. The boat parade."

Jessica looked at him sideways. "Aw... I love a parade."

"I hate *this* parade," he muttered, steering the dinghy closer to the edge of the line. "You know how many times I've taken *Purrfection* through here, doing everything right, and some jackass in a dinghy cuts across without even looking, like I can stop on a dime? I'm not doing that to anybody. We wait. We do it properly."

"Such a rule follower," she teased.

They hovered near the end of the line as the bridge reached its full upright position, allowing boats to pass out toward the open Caribbean. On the deck of the Sint Maarten Yacht Club, a crowd of locals, tourists, and camera-wielding onlookers had gathered, as they did most mornings, to wave at the boats like it was a coronation.

The captains didn't disappoint. A sun-hardened Dutchman on a 50-foot catamaran gave a dramatic two-handed wave, while a woman on a monohull in a red bikini danced to a steel drum track playing from her cockpit. Air horns blasted. Cheers erupted from the deck of a party cat loaded with college kids. The smell of bacon drifted from the Yacht Club kitchen.

Jessica leaned forward, amused. "Do they do this every day?"

"Twice a day," Ray said. "Bridge opens at 9:30 and 11:30 outbound. Reverse for inbound. Sometimes there's only a few watching, and sometimes they all act like it's Mardi Gras."

He throttled the dinghy forward slowly, matching the pace of the yachts. The little inflatable felt like a toy among the big boats, but Ray held his line. Jessica gave a mock-royal wave to the crowd. A tourist with a GoPro pointed it their way.

Ray deadpanned, "Careful. You're going to end up on someone's vacation video as the mysterious mermaid."

Buccaneer Beach Bar was already humming when they pulled their dinghy up to the pier, the reggae beat drifting lazily across the sand. They kicked off their sandals and strolled up to the bar, sun on their shoulders and the awkwardness of the past week melting with each barefoot step.

They ordered rum punches—Jessica insisted on the kind with the tiny paper umbrella, reminiscent of their time on St. Thomas at Duffy's Love Shack. They found loungers just feet from the shoreline. Between sips and splashes, they traded sarcastic jabs and sideways smiles. When Jessica accused Ray of checking out the bartender, he claimed he was actually admiring the bottle of Clase Azul behind her. She didn't believe him, not for a second, but she let it go with a teasing nudge to his ribs.

By the time the sun began its lazy dip into the sea, their laughter came quicker, the smiles lingered longer. Jessica forgot all about her upcoming task.

The sand still clung to their ankles when Jessica's phone buzzed with a new message. She shielded her screen from the sun and read it aloud.

"My friend Cass says, '*Unique Band tonight at Captain's Rib Shack. Bring Ray. You'll love it.*'"

"Hey, a unique band, now that sounds fun, doesn't it?"

Ray tipped his head with a grin. "I think the name of the band is *Unique Band*, but yes, sounds like we got ourselves a plan."

They turned back toward the dinghy, the late afternoon light stretching their shadows across the beach. Jessica gave one last glance at the golden horizon before stepping into the dink. "We've got about twenty minutes to look halfway presentable."

"Lady, this is about as good as I get," Ray said, easing the dinghy from the pier.

They made quick time to the boat, rinsing off the salt and sun. Jessica threw on a breezy sundress and slipped into sandals. Ray dug out a nice button-up shirt, fumbling to get it on over still-damp skin.

When they arrived at the Rib Shack, the place was already buzzing with music and the smell of smoked meat. String lights crisscrossed above picnic tables filled with both locals and sunburnt tourists. Cass and Mike were already seated at one, their drinks sweating in the humid air.

"There they are!" Cass waved.

Ray gave a quick wave back as Jessica leaned back against him, as if ready to say something seductive. She reached over and tugged at the collar of his shirt.

"Top button, mister," she whispered.

He blinked. "Really?"

Ray chuckled and obeyed, fumbling with the button as they approached the table.

"Sorry, we're late," he said. "She made me dress like a respectable human."

"You're lucky I didn't make you iron it," Jessica muttered, just loud enough for the others to hear. Cass raised an eyebrow and exchanged a grin with Mike.

Plastic cups of rum punch clinked as the band launched into their first set. *The Unique Band* didn't disappoint—tight rhythms, catchy hooks, and a lead singer with enough charisma to power a small island.

Halfway through the set, the lights dimmed briefly before a spotlight hit the stage. The lead singer re-emerged, now in a glittery dress, heels, wig, and full makeup. The crowd erupted with laughter and applause.

"This," Mike said, "is about to get good."

The singer sauntered into the crowd, sashaying with practiced flair. He zeroed in on Ray first, pointing dramatically.

"Ohhh my goodness. Look at this silver fox devil sittin' here like he runs the whole Caribbean!"

Ray nearly spit out his drink as the crowd hooted and clapped as the singer moved in closer.

"I bet you got a boat, a backstory, and a broken heart," the performer purred, twirling a finger at him. "Don't worry, baby, I'll be gentle with your secrets."

Jessica was doubled over with laughter, tears in her eyes.

"Okay, okay, who's this next to you?" the singer continued. "Ohhh yes. Mr. Tattoo Man over here." He gestured to Mike. "All these muscles and nowhere to run. What's that ink say? 'Born to flirt'? 'Too hot to handle'? Or just a whole lotta 'daddy issues'?" The singer sat down at the table, with his back resting against Mike, and broke into his next song.... Of course, *"It's Raining Men."*

Cass choked on her drink, slapping the table as Mike tried—and failed—to hold a straight face. Jessica captured most of the action on video, albeit shaky from the laughter.

By the end of the night, everyone's cheeks hurt from laughing. The music carried on long after the jokes, people dancing in the sand with bare feet and no shame. It was one of those island nights where the world felt smaller, and happiness felt simple.

As the group dispersed, Jessica followed Cass toward the parking area.

Cass slowed and gave her a sidelong look. "Are you sure you two aren't a couple?"

Jessica blinked. "What? No. I mean—we're just..."

Cass raised an eyebrow.

Jessica hesitated. "It's complicated."

Cass smirked. "Mmhmm. So is *every* good story."

Back on the boat, the silence of the cabin was deafening. Ray sat on the edge of his bunk, elbows on knees, head hanging low. His heart still pounded—not from the rum punch, but from *her*. From the way Jessica looked at him tonight, from the sparks that had danced between them.

He let out a slow breath, trying to shake it off.

His phone buzzed.

Jake: FBI has been watching all day. Man, she is falling for you. Hard.

Ray stared at the message, jaw tightening. He already knew that might be a problem.

Jake (continued): She is hesitating because of YOU. Maybe she has thoughts of running off with you. Don't get any ideas, Romeo. That account is locked to only transfer to her account. We're the FBI, we aren't stupid.

Ray wanted to argue, but let that one slide.

Jake (continued): If you want a payday, get the op back on track. She's either going to be arrested or on the run. There's no future with her. Wise up, and stop being so damn charming.

Ray tossed the phone onto the bed and leaned back, letting his head hit the wall with a soft *thud*. Charming. That wasn't a tactic—it was just *him*.

Part of him—the reckless, hopeless romantic part he usually kept hidden deep—wondered if she'd thought about running away with him. Not for the money, just *with* him. Living simply, scrounging for extra mahi scraps from the neighbors, doing odd jobs around the harbor, sleeping under stars if the cabin got too warm, barely getting by in the rhythm of the islands.

Could she love that life? *Could he?*

He lingered on the thought, foolish though it was, because it felt almost sweet. A life without stolen funds or federal shadows. Just sunsets, boat repairs, and maybe even a shared silence that didn't need fixing.

That dream belonged to some other world.

As far as Ray knew, Jessica still thought it was his money in that account. He thought that illusion was the only thing keeping her tethered to this mess. If she found out the truth, that it was FBI money, not his—and still wanted to stay—Ray didn't know if that made her a fool or something else entirely.

He sat up and reached for the phone again. No more dreaming. If this was going to work, he had to break the spell.

Ray: **I know how to snap her back into reality. I know just the person. I got this, Jake. Tiffany can wreck her salty dreams in two minutes tomorrow night.**

CHAPTER
TWENTY-ONE

September 2022 - St. Martin
Hurricane Tiffany

The Naked Pirate had its soft opening on a humid Friday night, with a makeshift banner barely clinging to the rafters and the bar still half-covered in sawdust. The smell of fresh varnish and cheap tequila mingled in the air, promising chaos. Tiffany had sent Ray a quick invite a few days back: **Naked Pirate Soft Opening Friday Night! Free drinks. Come.**

She hadn't invited Jessica. But Jessica came anyway.

Ray motored right up to the dock in front of the bar, waves slapping against the wood in lazy rhythm. He immediately noticed that the cleats were too small, making it difficult to tie up the dinghy. A barrel-chested man in a faded AUC t-shirt came to help Ray, apparently the first dinghy to tie up at the bar. With a cigarette dangling from his mouth, he grinned and said, "Hi, I'm Robert. Welcome to my new bar!"

Tiffany came running out of the bar, hair up in a high bun,

wearing a barely-there red tank top and a wide smile. She jumped on Ray, throwing her arms around him in a full-body hug.

"Sooo... you must know Tiffany?" Robert said with a grin and a shake of his head.

"You made it!" she said, her voice bright, almost giddy.

Ray hugged her back, friendly, but aware Jessica was just behind him. Tiffany saw her next. Her smile faltered for half a second, just long enough to be noticeable.

"Jessica," she said. Not warm. Not cold. Just... neutral.

"Hey," Jessica replied, brushing past without pause.

"Ray, this is Robert. He owns the place. Used to teach biochem at AUC before he went rogue."

Robert gave Ray a hearty handshake. "Come on in, drinks are free tonight. What can I get you?"

Ray couldn't help but mention, "You know, those cleats are a little small. If you want other sailors at this bar, might need bigger cleats."

"Really?" Robert asked. "I just thought those were good enough, and small enough that drunks won't trip over them when they go to look at the water."

Inside, the bar was packed with American University med students, island misfits, and curious locals. A thick energy vibrated through the open-air space. The stereo pumped out cheesy '80s bangers. Tiffany led Ray to the bar, practically ignoring Jessica, who lingered a step behind. Her jaw tightened, and she crossed her arms, eyes scanning the room but flicking back to Ray and Tiffany with barely concealed annoyance. She didn't say anything, but the tension in her shoulders said plenty.

Ray picked up the one-page menu and perused the drink specials. He noticed that Robert had dedicated a drink to Tiffany. "The Tiffany - shot of Fireball followed by another shot of Fireball." Ray smirked, *how appropriate.*

Nicole, who'd never quite warmed up to Ray before, suddenly appeared behind him like a storm, grabbing his wrist and yanking him off the barstool as if they'd been best friends all along.

"Dance with me, Captain!" she yelled over Cyndi Lauper.

Ray barely got a word out before she pulled him into the open space in front of the bar. Her hips moved with a silky motion, brushing against him without hesitation. Ray laughed and tried to keep up. But the whole thing felt awkward, like there was suddenly a competition for his attention.

When he finally escaped and flopped back into his seat, he turned to Tiffany.

"Is she actually flirting with me, or just drunk? I can't tell."

Tiffany leaned in, fast and intense. Her face hovered just two inches from his, her breath warm and eyes flickering with amusement.

"No," she said, her voice low and teasing. "You can't tell, can you?"

She didn't move—just stayed there like a dare, lips close enough to tempt but not touch.

For a moment, it felt like the whole bar fell away, and Ray wasn't sure if he'd just failed a test or passed one.

Then someone slammed a big red button on the stereo console. A siren blared.

"SHOTS!" shouted Robert.

Everyone groaned and laughed simultaneously as shot glasses were distributed. Tiffany and Ray had Fireball, while Jessica maintained her Jameson preference.

Jessica was across the bar, mid-conversation with a group of med students, but Ray caught her looking over. Not once. Not twice. Constantly.

The siren sounded again.

"Tiff!" Robert shouted. "Stop hitting the damn thing!"

"Make me!" she called back, hitting it again for good measure. More Fireball. More chaos.

By midnight, the bar had thinned out. People drifted off in pairs or disappeared into the night. Ray and Jessica climbed back into the dinghy together.

Tiffany stood at the edge of the dock, her arms crossed, almost pouting, watching. No goodbye hug this time. Ray had slipped into the dinghy before Tiffany could maneuver for a hug, knowing he had already sufficiently annoyed Jessica, yet still had to ride back with her. He was trying to break the spell, but still needed to sleep comfortably with the galley knives just outside his cabin door.

"You coming?" Ray asked, half-joking.

Tiffany looked him dead in the eye. "I'd love to, but ... crowded boat."

He nodded. Then he pulled away from the dock, the little engine buzzing softly as they slipped into the dark water.

Jessica didn't say anything for a while. Neither did Ray.

But both of them had noticed everything.

The night sky hung like a sheet of black velvet, pierced by the silver glow of the Caribbean moon. The gentle lapping of water against the dinghy's hull was the only sound, broken now and then by the sputter of the outboard motor.

Jessica sat at the bow, arms crossed tightly over her chest, eyes locked on the dark horizon. Her stomach churned—not from the rocking of the boat, but from the storm inside her. Every laugh Ray had shared with Tiffany replayed in her mind, each one a needle under her skin. She told herself it didn't matter, that she had no claim to him. But the tightening in her chest told a different story.

Ray sat at the stern, one hand gripping the tiller, the other holding a plastic cup from the bar. Frustration carved lines into his face.

"You were all over her at the bar," Jessica snapped, breaking the fragile silence.

Ray took a sip and scoffed. "Who? Tiffany?"

"You know exactly who I'm talking about," she shot back. "You spent the whole evening laughing at her jokes, hanging on her every word. What is a thirty-five-year-old even doing in med school? By the time she gets to be a doctor, she'll be like fifty. She's such a smart-ass."

Ray turned the tiller slightly, adjusting course back to *Purrfection*, avoiding obstacles by following the shimmering lights from shore. "So what? Since when do you care? We're not together. Are we?"

Jessica's jaw tightened, but she said nothing.

Ray pressed on, rare frustration creeping into his voice. "You act like we are a couple. You brag on me all the time, like you're proud of your *boyfriend*. You nag at me to button my shirt, and use a napkin, and clean my plate. We are together 24/7 and truly enjoy each other's company, but we aren't a couple. I don't know what we are."

Jessica snapped her head around, her eyes blazing. "I'm not jealous. Maybe a bit territorial. I don't like her in our space. I just—I don't know—just don't want this to end, and it scares me."

Ray gave her a hard look, eyes glassy but intense. "Right. Because you actually care about me? You sure seem to—sometimes. Or maybe I've just been fooled. Maybe you're just after the money!"

Jessica flinched, her face going pale. The words cut deeper than she had expected.

She looked down, blinking hard, trying to breathe through the drunken haze. Her fingers dug into the dinghy's strap like it was the only thing keeping her tethered. The buzz in her head made everything feel louder, heavier, messier.

Then, before she could second-guess herself—or sober up—she blurted it out.

"You're right, Ray. I *am* after your money."

Ray froze mid-sip. His hand dropped slightly, cup sloshing. "What?" he said, half-choked.

Jessica forced herself to meet his eyes, her voice wobbling but steady enough. "This is killing me inside. I can't take it anymore. It's not my idea. I have pressure on me. From Campanelli. From Johnny. They give me instructions. I don't have a choice."

Ray blinked, struggling to push through the Fireball fog in his head. The wind tugged at his hair. The dinghy drifted off course, but he didn't correct it.

She looked like a woman in too deep, drowning in something far bigger than either of them.

Jessica inhaled sharply, continuing before she lost her nerve. "Campanelli wants his money, Ray. He wants it *all*. Johnny, my ex from Chicago, has been texting me instructions on how to get it back. I don't ask questions, but... if you somehow owe Campanelli..."

"Campanelli? Campanelli, the yacht guy from Chicago?" Ray strained to recall the story, "I don't even know Campanelli."

Was Campanelli the driving force? Was Johnny the technical back-end? And Jessica, the face, the charm, the distraction?

"The Siren" wasn't a single person. It was a *team*. And the team was working for the mob.

At least, that's what Johnny has led her to believe.

The ocean stretched dark and infinite around them, the weight of her confession hanging between the waves and the silence. Ray's mind spun. The FBI had suspected Jessica from the start, but he had always defended her. Trusted her. Cared for her.

And now—confirmation. She *was* involved. But seemingly not by choice, unless that was another con she was pulling off flawlessly.

He needed to think. He needed to *understand*. The FBI had been investigating this for months. But what did they *really* know? Did they suspect the mafia involvement? How deep did this mafia connection go? Why did Jessica believe *he* owed Campanelli anything?

Suddenly, Ray felt expendable.

Ray met her eyes, his voice softer now, more sober than he felt. "We're getting out of this. Both of us. But first, I need to know everything."

Jessica swallowed hard and nodded. "Then you'd better listen carefully."

Ray eased the throttle back, letting the dinghy drift in the middle of the lagoon. The outboard fell quiet, replaced by soft waves and the occasional splash of water against fiberglass. Above them, the moon floated silently in the ink-black sky.

Jessica pulled her knees up slightly and wrapped her arms around them. She stared straight ahead.

"Remember when Courtney was visiting, and I told you about why I had to leave Chicago?"

"Of course I remember. You got caught messing with the laptop of a mafia boss and were asked to leave town. Kinda hard to forget."

"I didn't want to do it," she said, her voice quiet. "My friend Johnny—he was an accountant, apparently for the mob—he said some of Campanelli's people needed information about his other businesses. So he needed me to install something. Just plug in a thumb drive. That's all. He made it sound like nothing. I didn't want to, Ray. But... they knew my mom's address. She's a feisty lady, but not enough to hold off the mob. She's *not* leaving Chicago. I had to."

Ray's face stayed hard, unreadable. "So what happened when you did it?"

Jessica exhaled through her nose. "Nothing. That day, at least. It was a week later when all hell broke loose. I was bartending on the yacht, and Johnny told me something was going to happen, but he never said what. Just told me to watch."

"But *what* happened?" Ray pressed, his voice sharper now.

"I don't know. Tony got some text messages. Then he checked his laptop. Then he started calling people. He seemed kinda pissed, but he wasn't throwing things or yelling or anything. Just... tight. Serious. I was asked to leave almost immediately. I don't know shit about f*ck."

Ray let that one sit.

Jessica went on. "A few nights later, I got a text from Campanelli. It just said to leave town. I deleted it, but I took a screenshot first and emailed it to myself, then deleted the image."

Ray raised an eyebrow. "Wow, that was pretty tech-savvy of you."

"I know, right?" she said, cracking a small smile. "Surprised myself."

Ray smiled too—briefly.

"So you moved to Hilton Head, and then..."

"Then *what*?" she said. "I moved to Hilton Head because it was the fastest place I could drive to that was near the ocean. I took a job at that stupid pool bar. But then my lease got cut short—the owners were selling the condo. Then I met *you* online, and you flew in for our first date."

Her voice softened, the tension in her shoulders easing slightly. For a moment, she almost smiled.

"I still can't believe you didn't try to kiss me goodnight."

A warm feeling crept into Ray's chest—against his better judgment. Everything in him wanted to believe her. Maybe he finally did. But the moment passed.

He snapped back to the reality at hand.

"You moved to the boat. Then what?"

Jessica looked down. "After a few weeks, Campanelli texted me. Told me to unblock Johnny. So I did."

Ray's voice was calm but focused. "What is Johnny texting you?"

"He sends me instructions. He mailed me a flash drive. I already installed it on your laptop. I guess... so he can steal from your bank account for Campanelli?" She paused, frowning. "That doesn't even make sense. If you owe Campanelli, this is NOT how the mob usually gets its money back."

Ray's stomach turned. The FBI sting operation was supposed to trap *The Siren*. But now... the mafia? Campanelli? Jessica was clearly in deep, but this didn't match the playbook he'd expected.

She's not the Siren the FBI was looking for, he thought. Or... *was she?* And didn't even know it?

He tested the waters. "So... how many times have you done this?"

"Hacked?" she asked. "The Campanelli thing was the first time Johnny asked me to do anything like that. Before that, he just... asked about my day. Come to think of it, he always asked about the yacht. Who I made drinks for. Who I met. I thought he was just nosy. Huh."

Ray leaned back slightly, his brain clicking through the puzzle pieces. All the thefts. The multiple accounts. The timing. The tropical locations. The patterns. Jessica's role didn't line up—not with the Siren's history as told by the FBI.

She'd only done it once, under pressure. She hadn't profited. She hadn't planned. She didn't even understand what she was part of.

"Okay," Ray muttered, more to himself than to her. "As I thought. You aren't the Siren."

Jessica squinted at him, confused. "Siren? That's like a bad mermaid, right? F*ck you, I'm a good mermaid."

Ray smirked. "Yes, ma'am. That you are."

A long pause.

"We'll figure this thing out," he said.

Jessica nodded slowly, the moonlight reflecting off her suddenly pale face. Her eyes were wide. "We'd better. Now that I've told you everything, I'm gonna be in a *shit ton* of trouble."

Her expression hardened. The weight of what she'd just confessed hit her like a second wave. She looked at Ray, eyes full of fear, like she was realizing too late that the truth didn't set her free—it put a target on her back.

Ray saw it in her face: she thought she was doomed.

He knew in that moment that telling her about the FBI operation would only make things worse. It would destroy the fragile trust she'd just handed him—and maybe break her heart if she thought he'd only brought her on the boat for an FBI payday.

No. Not yet.

Until she could see that *he had no choice*—that everything he'd done was to *protect her*—his role had to stay his secret.

CHAPTER TWENTY-TWO

September 2022 - St. Martin
Collision Course

They'd been in the islands less than twenty-four hours, but the hotel room already looked like a war room—laptops, cables, and half-drunk coffee cups cluttering every surface. The blinds were shut tight to block the glare, the AC battled the humidity, and someone's shoes had started to smell.

Maxwell stretched his back, eyeing the door like it might lead to freedom.

He turned to Jake. "Let's grab some lunch. Maybe a beer. I mean, it's the islands, not Chicago. We finally made it to the Caribbean. Let's go over to that bar with the good beer, the owner is from Chicago."

Maxwell glanced over at Kevin. "Want anything?"

Jake added, "From Dinghy Dock?"

Kevin didn't look up from his laptop. "Yeah, kale Caesar with chicken."

Maxwell glared at him.

Kevin sighed. "Much appreciated, *sir*."

Maxwell gave a short nod. "They still out on the boat? Text me if that changes."

❖

Shortly after Jake and Maxwell settled into the bar chairs at Dinghy Dock, Tiffany sent Ray a message:

Hey, wanna meet at Dinghy Dock for lunch? Would be good to see you again.

Ray replied almost instantly:

Sure. Be there in 20.

He stowed his phone, pretending he hadn't been waiting for a message just like that all morning. Lowering the dinghy from the davits, he focused on unfastening the clips, trying not to grin.

The splash of the hull caught Jessica's attention. She appeared from below deck, brushing her hair from her eyes.

"Lunch run? I was about to scrounge something up, but we need a few things."

Ray hesitated. "I was heading to Dinghy Dock..." He trailed off, realizing she might insist on tagging along. The only excuse he could think of was the truth. "...Tiffany invited me."

Jessica raised an eyebrow. "Oh, a little lunch date? How cute. Shouldn't she be, I don't know, studying?"

Ray smirked. "She's a grown woman in med school. I assume she can manage her own schedule."

"Don't we have bigger problems to deal with? Do we really need THAT distraction?" Jessica queried.

"We gotta eat, absorb some more of this alcohol. We need some groceries from across the street, and I'm sure Rufus could use the walk."

From his monitoring station, Kevin saw the text messages between Ray and Tiffany. He thumbed a warning text to Maxwell, but the message turned up with a red exclamation —unable to send. Without WiFi, Maxwell wouldn't see it in time.

At Dinghy Dock, Maxwell and Jake slid onto bar stools, ordering beers. A few seats away, Tiffany sat alone, scrolling on her phone.

Not knowing who she was, Jake nudged Maxwell. "Damn, she's stunning."

Maxwell nodded, sipping his beer. "Oh hell yes, gotta love the islands."

Their quiet observation was interrupted by Maxwell's bladder. He pushed back his chair. "Gonna hit the head."

Outside, Ray tied up the dinghy. As usual, Rufus pulled Jessica down the dock toward his favorite patch of grass.

Ray entered first, casual but inwardly eager. He spotted Tiffany and leaned in to kiss her cheek.

"Hey there."

Tiffany smirked. "Hey. I've been waiting a whole five minutes. You're basically late."

Ray grinned. "Island time, I'm early. But yeah, had to bring Jessica and Rufus to shore—" But as he spoke, his gaze landed further down the bar.

Jake.

Ray froze.

"Shit."

He crossed the room fast. Jake, absorbed in his phone, looked up at the last second.

"Ray?" The color drained from his face. "What the hell are you doing here?"

"I could ask you the same. Jessica's right behind me. We come here all the time."

Jake flinched. "No service here—I didn't get Kevin's text."

Ray leaned in. "If you don't want to be seen, you need to leave. Right now."

Jake's eyes darted around. "We haven't paid—"

"We?"

Jake dropped a hundred under his mug and stood. Cutting toward the street-side exit, as he passed the restroom, he ducked his head in. "Jim! We gotta go. Now."

Too late.

Jessica walked in from the street-side entrance, leash in hand. Her steps slowed. Her eyes locked on Jake.

Then her mouth curled into a forced, too-wide smile. "Johnny? *Holy shit*! What are you doing here?"

Ray felt the floor tilt.

Johnny?

Jake—Johnny—stopped mid-step, his posture stiffening as if his body didn't know what to do next. His jaw tensed, and his eyes darted for the briefest second, searching for an escape, before he forced them back into place. Ray caught it—the unmistakable flicker of panic, quick but telling.

Jessica turned to Ray, trying to sound breezy. "This is... Johnny. We used to date back in Chicago. Didn't work out. Stayed friends."

Johnny forced a tight-lipped smile. "Yeah. Small world."

Ray's pulse pounded. Bits of conversation from the yacht club clicked into place. FBI Jake had been texting Jessica... as Johnny, the guy telling her to take the money.

The same guy who is supposedly trying to *catch* her stealing the money.

"Oh, really?" Ray said, his voice dry. "You've got a talent for friend-zoning all the tall ones."

Johnny laughed, a little too loudly.

Behind Jessica, Maxwell emerged from the bathroom, spotted the disaster unfolding, and *noped* right out, heading straight for the exit.

Jessica kept the conversation going with fake enthusiasm. "After my last job fell apart, I figured I'd finally move to the Caribbean. You too, huh?"

"Something like that," Johnny said. "Heard this bar was run by some jackass from Chicago. Had to check it out."

Jessica laughed. "Yeah, you'd think Chicago was a small town the way we all end up running into each other."

As if the situation wasn't tangled enough... The wind picked up, and in blew Hurricane Tiffany.

She stepped up behind Ray and Johnny, hands on her hips.

Jessica's tone flattened. "Oh, hey Tiffany."

Johnny whipped around, staring at Tiffany like she had just dropped out of the sky.

"You're Tiffany??" he blurted in disbelief.

Tiffany narrowed her eyes. "Uh, yeah. Who's asking?"

Ray stepped in fast, almost using the wrong name. "Uh—Ja-Johnny, this is Tiffany. Tiffany... Johnny."

Tiffany gave him a once-over. "Nice to meet you." Then to Ray: "We eating or what? I've got class at two."

Ray felt every thread fraying, stumbling for something to say, "Wanna join us?" he asked weakly, looking at no one in particular.

Tiffany shot him a *look*. Jake shot him a *look*.

Jessica smirked. "Aw, we wouldn't want to interrupt you lovebirds." But then she took a seat at the bar.

Tiffany muttered, "Interrupting is kinda her thing."

Ray sighed. "This is gonna be fun," he said to Jake, motioning for him to sit.

After lunch, Ray walked Tiffany to her car. Jake happened to be heading the same way, en route back to his hotel near the Yacht Club. Naturally, Jessica wasn't about to let Ray have even five minutes alone with Tiffany. She followed like it was her duty, pretending Rufus still had business left.

Ray gave Tiffany a polite goodbye and kissed her on the cheek. He could tell she was tempted to go for more—maybe even a big kiss in front of Jessica—but they were both hopeless romantics at heart. Not the right moment for a First Kiss. Instead, Tiffany wrapped him in an intimate, lingering hug, slipping her right knee behind his left in a subtle entanglement that screamed *notice me*.

Jessica noticed.

Jake gave a casual wave and strolled off down the road. Ray and Jessica turned back through the bar toward the dock in tense silence. Ray untied the dinghy without a word, helped Jessica in—Rufus tucked in her arm like a judgmental gremlin—then yanked the starter cord and motored them back to *Purrfection*.

The silence barely lasted five seconds before they both blurted out at the same time.

Ray: "So that's Johnny? *The* Johnny who told you to steal my money? What the f*ck is he doing here on island?"

Jessica: "I have no clue. He never told me he was coming."

Ray gripped the tiller tighter. Something was off—way off. But he wasn't ready to confess his role, not yet. He needed more pieces of the puzzle.

"Okay. This is weird. Just keep texting him like you haven't told me anything."

"No shit," Jessica muttered. "If he finds out I told you, I don't even want to guess what Campanelli would have him do."

Back aboard *Purrfection*, Jessica headed straight below deck to her cabin without another word.

Ray to Jake: **What the hell, man**?

Jake: **I can explain. Meet me at the Yacht Club.**

Ray: **When?**

Jake: **NOW.**

Ray: **I just got back to the boat. Now?**

Jake: **We know you just got back. We're watching, remember? See you in a few.**

Down below, Jessica fired off a message of her own.

Jessica to Johnny: **What the ACTUAL F*CK?**

Jake chuckled. When a woman typed it all out, no abbreviations, you knew she was pissed.

Johnny: **Ciao Bella! Where's your Hola??**

Jessica: **F*ck you and your Hola, Johnny, you know it's me. What the hell are you doing here? Why didn't you tell me? You think I can't handle this without you babysitting me? Did Campanelli send you? Wait—oh shit, is Campanelli upset with me??**

Johnny: **It's nothing like that. I'm here to protect you, that's all. Campanelli's research said Ray can get a little... belligerent when he drinks. We just need to make sure this transfer happens when he's calm. Sober. We don't want him turning on you. Stick to protocol, and everything will be fine.**

Jessica: **Are you serious right now? Ray and I have been blackout drunk together more than once. The guy won't even flirt with me when he's hammered. What research are you talking about?**

The silence that followed was as expected as it was infuriating.

Jessica: **F*ck you, Johnny boy.**

Up on deck, Ray called down, "Hey—you know we forgot to stop at the market across from Dinghy Dock. I'm heading back. Is the list the same? Coffee, butter, eggs, bananas, whatever else was on it?"

Jessica didn't miss the timing. "Oh, need to run back, huh? Did Tiffany's class get canceled?"

Ray winced. "No, Jessica. We all got distracted by your friend from Chicago. You didn't remember either."

He immediately regretted the words. They sounded like a bickering couple arguing over a grocery list.

Jessica's voice floated up, dry as ever. "Just what's on the list. It's on your damn phone. Don't forget to check for avocados."

"Yes, ma'am. This is all kinds of f*cked up, but we still gotta eat," he shouted back. "Let me know when he texts you."

She was about to yell that Johnny *had* already texted—but she wanted those bananas. So did Rufus.

CHAPTER
TWENTY-THREE

September 2022 - St. Martin
Assessing the Damage

Jake was already at the bar when Ray pulled up to the dock. He stood near the edge, arms thrown wide in theatrical confusion.

Ray climbed off the dinghy and approached, already mid-sentence. "What the f*ck, Jake—"

Jake cut him off with a sharp gesture: index finger to his lips, the other hand tapping his chest. Ray froze for half a second, then nodded. Wired. Of course.

He shifted tone without missing a beat. "—the f*ck are you up to today, Jake?" His voice was lighter now, casual, almost amused.

Inside a white panel van in the parking lot, Maxwell and Kevin leaned toward the static-laced speakers, listening closely.

Ray clapped Jake on the shoulder. "It's a great day for a dinghy ride, isn't it? Thought I might give you the five-minute tour. Show you that Naked Pirate bar in case anything interesting ever happens over there."

He motioned casually toward the dinghy, then turned to the bar just as the bartender slid a tequila and water in front of him.

"Aw, you're the best KoKo. Mind tossing that in a to-go cup for me? Throw it on my tab, please?"

She nodded with a smirk, already reaching for a plastic cup.

Ray turned back to Jake, eyes steady. "C'mon, Jake Rackham, a proper pirate. Let's go for a spin."

Ray and Jake walked down to the dock. Ray stooped to untie the line, balancing on the edge before hopping into the dinghy. He extended a hand to help Jake aboard—but Jake, in true landlubber fashion, stepped directly onto the air-filled side tube.

Jake bounced once, then twice—off one side and then the other —before launching himself into the lagoon with a splash loud enough to startle the tourists watching the Simpson Bay Bridge opening.

Ray shook his head in mock disapproval as he grabbed Jake by the collar and hauled him, soaked and sputtering, back into the dinghy.

Jake flopped over the side and sat blinking, checking the pocket of his cargo shorts. "Well... at least my phone is waterproof. Mostly."

"Oh yeah, you'll be fine," Ray said, cranking the outboard. "Hell, I dropped mine under the boat at night, dove for it the next morning, damn thing was still on. But I'm guessing your FBI listening gear isn't waterproof, now is it?"

Jake's eyes widened. Then narrowed. "You did that on purpose? You ass."

Ray grinned. "Just wanted a private chat."

Inside the FBI van, Maxwell and Kevin now heard only garbled echoes—like the microphone was still submerged.

"Good," Ray said, voice lower now. "Now we can talk, Johnny John Jake. What the f*ck are you up to? You're the one running Jessica? Does she even know you're FBI? How is that even legal, to arrest her for a crime YOU are directing her to commit? I've seen enough movies to know that's entrapment."

Jake raised his hands. "One thing at a time. No—she doesn't know. Yes—I've been instructing her. She couldn't do this on her own. You know that. But it's so much more complicated."

Ray's jaw tightened. "Start talking. I've got a few friends on speed dial that would love to hear this FBI corruption shit. So please, do tell. Not sure how this can get any more f*cked up, but I gotta feeling you are about to try…"

Jake exhaled. "We were originally monitoring some mob families in Chicago. One day, while tapping a known boss's phone, we hit the jackpot. He texted his bank login to his wife—full info, over unsecured SMS. Unbelievable. It wasn't his main account, just a side stash. Close to a million. Probably for her, or something off-books."

Ray stared ahead, steering casually toward the middle of the lagoon.

"Maxwell saw a golden opportunity to take it for ourselves. All we needed was someone to pin it on. Someone with access. Jessica had been bartending on his yacht. Boom. We fake a bank account in her name, stage some footage, and the heat's off us. Meanwhile, another FBI task force was tracking a hacker stealing from yacht owners—they called her '*The Siren.*' Maxwell figured, Why not create our own version?"

"So Jessica has never hacked anything. Not ever." Ray didn't phrase it as a question.

Jake shook his head. "Hell no. She can barely reset her own email. Ask her about her hacked Firestick sometime."

Ray grimaced.

"We just needed her on camera inserting a USB. Didn't even need it to work, we already had the password. I went undercover, got her to help me install a keylogger."

Ray's tone darkened. "So it went so well, you decided to do it again, but this time stealing FBI funds?"

Jake winced. "Well, no. The op was a complete cluster f*ck. We didn't know about the $100k limit per transfer. When that happened, Maxwell panicked and had Kevin keep going, even though Campanelli was getting security code texts. We had no way to pin it on Jessica after that. Maxwell only managed to get three transfers completed before somebody noticed and froze the account. But then the big problem hit."

Ray turned the motor down. "Let me guess. Somebody upstairs found out?"

"Worse," Jake said. "They didn't care we tried to skim mob money—but they did care we botched it. Maxwell was told to put it back. With interest. The kind the mob would expect."

Ray raised a brow. "So someone in the Bureau is tight with the mob?"

Jake gave him a tired look. "Surprised?"

Ray scoffed. "Not even a little."

Jake continued. "Maxwell didn't have the cash. So he came up with this—deposit Bureau funds in your charter account, frame Jessica as 'The Siren,' and steal it for himself. He figured by the time anyone untangled the truth, Jessica would be long gone."

Ray's voice was low now. Dangerous. "So she's the scapegoat. Again."

Jake nodded. "We do NOT want to catch her. That would make things ... uncomfortable."

"Oh, and Beck? He's pissed at you. You tried to sail off with his wife."

"Ex-wife," Ray snapped. "Well, well, so he is YOUR director? That makes sense, how I got involved in this shit show. Hell, I probably know who the real Siren is from my luxury yacht job in Miami, now that I think about it, but that's another story."

Jake chuckled. "We read *everything*. That 'just one dance' line? Maxwell almost choked on his coffee. You and Elana had a full romance novel in just your text messages. She was ready to sail the world with you."

Ray shook his head. "Glad the FBI has a front-row seat to my love life. No wonder Epstein was blatantly raising ceramic cows in the Virgin Islands to get his agricultural tax break—you guys are too busy tracking ex-wives."

Ray paused, then narrowed his eyes. "How the hell did a square like you end up in this shit? Maxwell got something on you?"

Jake looked away. "No. I was just desperate. He offered me a cut—$100k. I needed it for my daughter's medical school. Stealing money from bad guys almost seemed heroic, at least that's what I told myself."

"So what happens to Jessica in all this? She seems royally screwed either way." Ray asked.

"The only reason she is still alive is because the mob knows we need her for this repayment plan to work. She's the one we are supposedly trying to catch. They can't kill her yet. We need this to look at least halfway legit—for Kevin, for the auditors. For everyone."

"It's a million dollars?? Nobody at the FBI is going to miss that?"

"Oh, please, we have million-dollar accounting errors, let alone something like this, used in an operational account."

Ray frowned. "She's either getting arrested or hunted for life. No version of this ends well for her."

Jake sighed. "She won't be arrested by our team. We're not trying to catch her. But yeah... she'll be looking over her shoulder forever, running from either the FBI if it works or the mob if it doesn't."

Ray clenched the tiller. "And me?"

Jake met his eyes. "Depends. You blow this up, it won't end well for you either."

"Damn, Jake, was that a *threat*?" Ray asked, smirking. "From *you*, Mr. Square? I'm a little impressed."

Ray exhaled. "What the hell would I even tell her. None of this makes sense. I'm still getting paid, though, right? Charter money's still good?"

Jake nodded. "Contract's valid. Nobody wants to screw that up."

Ray's voice turned serious. "If she gets in danger... *actual* danger... I'm not standing by. You know that."

Jake gave a small smile. "Now, who is Big Jake? Big heart, bad plan."

Ray cracked a dry grin. "I know, that sounded a little John Wayne-ish when I said it.... But I couldn't just stand by."

"If things go the way we want, Jessica walks away."

Ray stared at the water, lost in thought. "Physically, maybe. But she'll be running forever."

Jake shrugged. "Good thing she likes to travel."

Ray gave him a look. "Cruel, Jake. Very cruel."

CHAPTER TWENTY-FOUR

Flashback - March 2022 - Chicago
Lightning Strike in Chicago

Kevin hunched over his workstation, a dim cubicle lit by the glow of multiple monitors. Three keyboards, a tangled mess of cables, and half-drunk coffee surrounded him like a cockpit. One of the side panels flashed red—an anomaly.

"Hey, boss?" Kevin called over the low divider toward Maxwell's slightly roomier cubicle. "Come check this out. I've never seen this account before. Look—he just texted the account number to his wife. Like, *texted* it."

Maxwell stood and ambled over, adjusting his glasses as he leaned in.

On screen:

Campanelli to his wife: **Here is the damn account number and login. You think I'm lying? Check it yourself. You'll see the money has been sitting there, doing nothing, for over two years, just like you asked. Account 99293882328, password is Danc-**

ingMonkey123! Tell me when you're going to check it. I'll have to send you the code they send me within 10 minutes.

Wife: **Ok, I'll check it now**.

Kevin's fingers hovered over his keyboard, frozen. "That's... real?"

A moment later, another series of texts popped up:

66987: **T. Rowe Price. Your security code is 81560799**

Campanelli to his wife: **81560799**

Wife: **Thank you, lover. This makes me feel so much better.**

The two agents stared at the screen, blinking in disbelief.

Campanelli never used plain texts for anything sensitive. He ran his business dealings through Telegram—fully encrypted, impossible for them to see. His regular texts were always innocuous: birthday messages, dad jokes, complaints about Chicago traffic. Harmless. Practiced.

"This is real," Kevin muttered. "He's giving her full access. To that account. In plain sight."

Maxwell rubbed his jaw, mind racing. "He knows we see his texts. He *knows*. Why would he do this out in the open?"

"Could be a trap."

"A trap? For who? His wife?" Maxwell said, already grabbing his folder and slipping on his jacket. "He probably forgot to switch apps. Got rattled. Maybe she caught him off guard. Or maybe he wanted it to look legit, like a 'trust me, honey' thing."

Kevin still stared at the screen. "But why now? Why *that* account?"

Maxwell didn't answer. He was already halfway to the elevator. "I'm telling Beck in person."

Flashback - March 2022
FBI Headquarters — Director Beck's Office

Director Beck didn't look up from his monitor when Maxwell entered. His voice boomed across the office like a warning shot.

"Now, what the *f*ck* is so important you gotta see me in person, no appointment, no notice? Just because we used to be on the same team back in the day?"

Maxwell stayed standing. "It's Campanelli. He just texted account info to his wife. Over regular text."

That got Beck's attention. He leaned back slowly in his leather chair, eyes narrowing. "You sure? Not Telegram?"

"Nope. Basic SMS. Kevin flagged it. It looks like a new account—maybe something he set up as her retirement stash."

Beck gave a long exhale, scratching at his jaw. "Sounds like a setup to me. Campanelli's too smart to text that kind of thing. He *knows* we monitor his lines. We don't even need a warrant anymore—we're basically God if it's national security adjacent. Why the hell would he serve it up on a platter?"

"I don't know," Maxwell admitted. "It's not one of his main accounts. Just over a million sitting there. Not in motion. Not even tucked in with the rest. It's almost... orphaned."

Beck's brow furrowed. "A million's couch-cushion change for Campanelli. He moves ten times that in a week. Could be some kind of backup plan, insurance policy for the wife in case he's iced."

Maxwell nodded. "That's my guess. But whatever it is, it's sitting there like low-hanging fruit."

Beck's fingers drummed on the desk. "This does seem like the opportunity we've been waiting for. We've talked about something like this for years, easy money. But we can't just log in and take it, he'll know it's us, we are the only ones who can monitor his texts. Do we have an asset in place, somebody close that can install a key logger, so it looks like that's how his password was compromised?"

"We might. Jake's been working an angle. He's got an asset—bartender. Works on Campanelli's boat sometimes."

Beck looked intrigued. "His yacht? In Lake Michigan? Jesus, that's perfect. We've got another team trying to nail this so-called *Siren*—stealing from rich yacht owners. Most of that's been coastal or tropical, but the first mark was a few years back in Lake Michigan, so one of our teams caught it. Maybe *'the Siren'* strikes again in, inland."

Maxwell smirked. "Jake is getting emotionally compromised. Can't really blame him—she's hot. Big mouth, sarcastic. You know the type. The kind of woman who'd throw your own drink in your face and make you thank her for it."

Beck raised a brow. "Jake always did like his women mean."

"He's already taken her out a few times," Maxwell said. "She thinks he's a low-level accountant for Campanelli's legit real estate ventures. Even went to his place for movie night. Met his daughter."

Beck winced. "Jesus. He's introducing assets to his *kid* now?"

"She didn't even kiss him goodnight," Maxwell added with a wicked grin. "The cringe. I swear, we were all watching the footage in the ops room with popcorn."

Beck laughed once, a sharp bark. "So is she in play or not?"

"Not yet. But I'll push her. Something like - Jake tells her he's been approached by a rival boss. That they want him to flip. And unless she helps him, harm will come to his daughter... blah blah."

Beck raised an eyebrow, impressed. "That old squeeze play."

Maxwell nodded. "It works. Always does. I've used it three times. She'll fold. Add in a veiled, unspecific threat to her mother... we got this."

Beck stood and crossed to the window, looking out over the city. "This could be the one, Jimmy. The Siren. The buried account. If this goes right, you're looking at retirement—and I'm looking at a bonus that finally lets me buy that place in the Keys."

He turned back to Maxwell, voice low and serious. "Don't f*ck it up."

❖

Flashback - March 2022
FBI Ops Room – Chicago Field Office

Maxwell stood just outside his cubicle, coffee in one hand, eyes scanning the team clustered in the beige maze of government-issue partitions. Kevin looked up from his screens. Jake leaned against the desk, arms crossed, sensing something was coming.

"Alright, team," Maxwell began, "we've got a change in direction."

Kevin swiveled his chair. Jake stayed silent.

"We found a new account tied to Campanelli," Maxwell continued. "Beck thinks it could be the tip of a larger operation. A whole business line we're not monitoring—off-books, off-radar, off-everything. That's not just inconvenient—it's unacceptable."

He sipped his coffee and nodded at Kevin. "Remote monitoring isn't cutting it. We need eyes *inside* the devices. Kevin, I need a thumb drive with a key logger. Something subtle, persistent. And fast."

Kevin blinked. "Done. You want remote exfil or just dump-to-device?"

"Remote, if you can pull it off. Minimal footprint. Nothing that lights up his IT guys."

Maxwell turned to Jake. "You, buddy—you need to prep your bartender friend to plant it."

Jake straightened. "Jessica? She's not an agent; she's not trained. She was only supposed to help us watch the traffic on and off the boat—who's visiting, when, where they dock. That was the deal."

"Well," Maxwell said, "deals change. We don't have time to insert a real undercover. Jessica already has access. She's practically family to Campanelli's crew at this point."

Jake shook his head. "She's not tech-savvy. She thinks RAM is a goat."

"Then tell her it's a Spotify update," Maxwell shrugged. "Just make her do it."

Jake frowned. "How, exactly, do you suggest I convince her to commit a felony for us?"

"Use a light squeeze. Veiled threat. Nothing overt," Maxwell said, too casually. "Tell her you work for a rival boss, and he thinks Campanelli is holding out. Use a vague threat on a close family member. You know the playbook."

Jake narrowed his eyes. "She's not stupid. She'll sniff that out."

"She's got street smarts, fine," Maxwell admitted. "But she's not going to connect every dot. Not when it's coming from you."

Jake let out a breath, frustrated. "I'm surprised she hasn't seen through my 'accountant' act already."

Maxwell smirked. "Jake, you couldn't be any more boring if you had a CPA certificate tattooed on your forehead. If I didn't know you, I'd ask you to do my taxes."

Kevin chuckled from his desk. "He's got a point."

"Just get her the thumb drive," Maxwell said, his tone turning cold. "We're sitting on a million-dollar breadcrumb. Who knows how many more are out there? If we miss this window, Beck won't care whose feelings got hurt."

Jake didn't answer. He just stared at the floor for a second, then nodded once.

❖

Flashback - March 2022

Jessica knocked twice, then a third time, already regretting whatever boring movie Johnny had lined up. The door creaked open slowly. Johnny, as she *knew* him, stood there already halfway into his accountant act, like a man putting on a beige trench coat one sleeve at a time.

She brushed past him into the apartment. "If you picked *Fool's Gold* again, I swear to God—"

"It's got boats, beautiful water, diving," he defended. "And treasure. And adventure."

"It's got *Matthew McConaughey* shirtless. Good enough for me. That's the only thing that makes it watchable. You think I'm watching that sober?"

She made a beeline for the Jameson bottle on his counter and poured herself a shot without asking. "You get Caribbean, I get McConaughey and whiskey. I guess that works. Or we spend 45 minutes browsing for something to watch like last time, and come back to this one again..." As she turned toward him. "You look like you ate a lemon after a tequila shot. What's going on?"

Johnny took a breath. "I've got something to explain, and something to ask. It's not going to be easy."

"Oh shit," Jessica said, pouring another shot. "That's not how movie night starts. You're making me nervous already. Do I *need* the Jameson?"

"Yeah," he said. "Probably."

She knocked the shot back and waited.

"It's not about us. Not exactly," Johnny said. "But it *is* about you and me. The people I work for found out you bartend for Mr. Campanelli. On his yacht."

Jessica blinked, already feeling the shift. "Okay... what about Campanelli?"

"You've noticed, right? He's young. Yacht, influence, friends in high places..."

"I just figured he was in the mob," she said matter-of-factly, pouring another shot.

"Well," Johnny admitted, "you're not wrong. He is. Small part, but part of the family. His uncle's the boss. Old-school—only daughters, so Antonio's being groomed to take over."

She rolled her eyes. "Of course. Chicago. So what's the big deal? He runs liquor. Has legit businesses. Mob guys need accountants, too."

"That's just it," Johnny said. "The people I work for want to know what else he's got going on. They think he might be hiding side ventures from the rest of the family."

"Your firm cares, why?"

"Because we work for... let's call them influential clients. Some of whom share blood with Campanelli. They don't like being cut out of the loop."

Jessica narrowed her eyes. "Okay. What does this have to do with *me*?"

"You're around him. On the yacht. Close enough to see things."

"I bartend," she said slowly. "I make drinks. I pour tequila. I hand out olives."

Johnny hesitated. "They want you to plant something. A thumb drive. Just insert it into his laptop for a few seconds. That's it. The software handles the rest."

Jessica stared at him. Then, at the bottle in her hand.

"Nope," she said flatly. "Not happening. That's a mobster's laptop. I like breathing."

"Jessica..." His voice dropped. "They've made threats. About my daughter."

Her face softened—briefly. But then hardened again. "I'm sorry, Johnny. I really am. But I can't. I'd love to help, and I care about Brittany, but this? This isn't bartending. This is criminal."

"They figured you'd say that," he said quietly. "They told me to tell you something. Just a message: 3927 North Lakeshore Drive."

Jessica froze. "That's my mom's address."

He nodded. "I think they wanted you to know they know it."

She stood, pacing now. "Johnny, this is f*cked up. How the hell did you get involved with these people? You are so... so... so damn boring and normal. What the f*ck, Johnny!"

"I didn't plan this. I got a job out of college, climbed the ladder, and found out I was already standing on the wrong floor."

"You *know* I don't know anything about computers. My mom had to hot-wire my Fire Stick."

Johnny winced. "It wasn't hot-wired. She gave you her password."

Jessica paused. "...Seriously? See..."

He held up the flash drive. "Look. This isn't hacking. You just plug it in. USB port. Regular or the smaller one—this has an adapter. See?" He flipped it back and forth.

She eyed it warily. "So... which one's the hole?"

He raised an eyebrow. "Let's not phrase it like that."

"I'm gonna die," she muttered. "You are going to get me f*cking killed."

"We'll practice," Johnny said quickly. "We'll do it over and over until it's easy."

"Okay, okay," she breathed, taking the flash drive. "Adapt, insert. Insert, then... pray."

"Exactly."

She shook her head. "When does this go down?"

"Tomorrow. You're scheduled to work on the yacht, right?"

Jessica choked on her whiskey. "Tomorrow?!"

"No time to waste. Or overthink. Tomorrow you walk onto that yacht like it's any other Saturday. The thumb drive and the earpiece will be in the vodka case — I'll be there with you. Wait for your opening before his screen locks, slip the drive in, fifteen seconds, tops. You've got this, Jessica. You've got this."

Jessica slumped onto the couch, drink in hand, flash drive in the other. "I guess shirtless McConaughey will have to wait."

CHAPTER
TWENTY-FIVE

Flashback - March 2022 - Chicago
Chicago Fire

Antonio Campanelli lounged on the leather couch in his high-rise suite, thirty floors above a shimmering Chicago skyline. The early sun cast a warm glow across the lake, gilding the water in gold. His espresso sat untouched on the side table, steam curling upward, while his laptop rested open on the glass coffee table in front of him.

Wife to Campanelli: **Shouldn't we put that money into a fund of some sort? It's just sitting there, not working for me. Like an index fund or something like that?**

Campanelli: **It hasn't been a big concern for me, love. So many other things to worry about.**

Wife: **If you say so.**

Antonio was a smart man, and he knew exactly what those words meant. With a sigh, he pulled the laptop onto his lap and logged into the account. He shifted 50% into an S&P 500 Index fund, and another 25% into a Russell 5000 Index fund—more than enough to quiet the storm he saw brewing.

Campanelli to his wife: **I moved 75% of it into general market funds.**

Wife: **Aw, thank you, love, I feel much better about it now. Much better. I'll show you how much better tonight after my spa day xoxo.**

❖

Maxwell stepped into the office carrying two cups of coffee, handing one to Kevin in his cubicle.

"Anything interesting overnight?" he asked, leaning against the partition.

Kevin nodded. "Yeah, good news. He finally logged into that side account. It's been almost a week since we installed the keylogger. Guy must be loaded—he hardly even checks it."

"That's interesting. Very interesting. Now we can execute this plan I've been contemplating."

Maxwell to Beck: **He finally logged in to the account.**

Beck didn't reply. He knew better.

Maxwell turned back to Kevin. "The plan is simple. We move the funds to an FBI holding account. Campanelli will think somebody in his organization stole it. We stir the pot and see who Campanelli blames, who he trusts, and who he throws under the bus. Beck signed off. We are gonna upend his entire organization."

Kevin furrowed his brow. "I need to do some prep. When do you want to execute the plan? Should we wait until he's distracted?"

"We're doing it today—before he changes his password, moves the money, or his wife steals it." Maxwell could see the payday in reach, and he wasn't about to let it slip.

"I should call Jake, see if he's available last-minute on a Saturday. We didn't plan for this," Kevin said.

"That guy's got nothing to do—he'll be home. Might help with monitoring the fallout when the shit hits the fan. Give him a call. He should tell Jessica to keep an eye on things and report anything we can't see." Maxwell didn't care what Jessica reported. He just wanted her to look nervous and guilty.

Kevin to Jake: **You are going to love this. Maxwell is going to confiscate Campanelli's side fund to see what it does to the organization. Tell Jessica to watch reactions and note the activity from the inside.**

Jake: **Wait, what? When is this happening?**

Kevin: **Later this afternoon. Maxwell doesn't want to miss this chance.**

Jake: **So Jessica's gonna be sitting in the hornet's nest when we poke it?**

Kevin: **Yep. I don't think Maxwell cares. Might be counting on it.**

Jake: **I'm coming in. See you in an hour.**

Jake burst into the office. "Have we thought this through? The technicalities? The implications?"

Maxwell gestured toward Kevin. "Kevin has this nailed."

Kevin leaned back nervously in his chair. "I did some quick research. The firm Campanelli uses has two-factor authentication for logging in, with both email and text message as options. We'll use the email method—since we've already got that password too."

Jake frowned. "Won't the email still go to his phone?"

"Probably, yeah. But the guy gets a flood of messages. His inbox has over a thousand unread. The odds he notices that specific one right away? Pretty low," Kevin explained.

Maxwell jumped in. "I don't think it'll matter. One transfer and the money's gone—nothing he can do about it. We execute today, while he's having lunch on his yacht. Jake's girl is working, so she can report the reaction. Let's get set up."

Kevin raised an eyebrow. "Got the FBI account number?"

Maxwell handed over a plain piece of paper with a handwritten account number on it.

Kevin glanced at it. "Shouldn't we have the official form for wire transfers?"

"Director Beck authorized this plan, and that's the number they gave me. You want me to go chase down the form on a Saturday?" Maxwell shot back.

"No, no, of course not. I'm sure Director Beck, or somebody, has one on file for the case," Kevin replied, his voice tight with nerves.

"Jake, text your girl and make sure she watches intently," Maxwell barked.

Jake hesitated. He knew the message would only make her more nervous—but maybe that was exactly what Maxwell wanted.

Johnny to Jessica: **Hey, we have word that Campanelli's organization might be in disarray today. Just try to remember what happens and who he connects with. We need to know what his process is for dealing with controversy.**

Jessica: **Good morning to you, too. What kind of disarray? This is my first time back since the hacking thing—are you sure they don't know anything?**

Johnny: **Positive. You'll be safe.**

Jake hit send, knowing full well he had no guarantee of that.

Kevin entered the login credentials with steady hands. When the system prompted him to choose a verification method, he selected **Email**, eyes flicking to a second monitor. The code had already arrived. He typed it in.

They were in.

He navigated directly to **Transfer Funds**. Everything about his movements was smooth, practiced—like this wasn't his first time compromising a high-net-worth account.

"Selecting 'Premature Withdraw,'" he said aloud, barely a murmur.

"I guess Campanelli will have some tax implications from this," Kevin muttered with a smirk.

"Just get it done," Maxwell snapped.

Next came the prompt: **Amount to transfer**. Kevin looked for the obvious choice—**All Funds**—but it was grayed out.

He turned to Maxwell. "What do we do?"

Maxwell leaned forward, barking, "Shit! Use 'Select Amount.' What does that give you?"

Kevin clicked. A field opened. Just a blank box. No guidance.

Maxwell didn't hesitate. "Try one million. Right now."

Kevin typed 1000000 and hit **Transfer**.

The screen shifted—but not to a confirmation.

Please enter the code sent via SMS.

Kevin's stomach dropped. "What the f*ck is that?" Maxwell shouted.

"It's a second layer of security," Kevin replied, eyes wide. "Campanelli set up text alerts. Probably didn't trust his wife."

Maxwell stood frozen. For a moment, the operation had seemed surgical. Clean. But now? Campanelli would see that code. He'd know someone was in his account.

They could still back out. Up to now, everything could be explained away by a keylogger virus—something Jessica could have plausibly planted.

But one transfer, one seven-figure score? That was real money. Retirement money. Only the FBI had legal access to real-time SMS intercepts.

Maxwell's jaw tightened. "Find the code. Enter it."

Jake looked like he'd seen a ghost, but said nothing. Kevin didn't argue. He just turned back to his screens, found the mirrored SMS log, and read the six-digit code aloud as he entered it.

But the system threw another surprise:

Transaction exceeds limit. Max withdrawal: $100,000.

Kevin exhaled, stunned. "This guy *really* didn't trust his wife."

Maxwell ran both hands down his face. Campanelli would know.

Not just that someone was in his system—but who. Only the FBI could've intercepted that text.

Still... even the mob couldn't pierce the bureaucracy fast enough to stop him from vanishing.

"Shit," he muttered. "He already knows we were in. Screw it—do the hundred grand. Get us something."

Kevin hesitated. "He'll get another SMS."

"No way to block it?" Maxwell asked casually. Too casually.

Kevin didn't even look up. "Well, yeah, I *could*, but that's a whole different part of the Patriot Act. Monitoring is easy—we can justify that six ways from Sunday. But intercepting or blocking an SMS? That requires a judge's approval."

Maxwell's jaw twitched. He'd been hoping Kevin's ego would get the better of him—that he'd block the message just to show he could. But now? Now Kevin had said it out loud. He *knew* the line. Maxwell couldn't ask him to knowingly cross it and commit a felony.

"Right," Maxwell muttered. "Just transfer the hundred grand."

Kevin initiated the transfer. Another code arrived. He entered it.

$100,000 transfer complete.

He leaned back in his chair, arms folded, letting the triumph sink in.

Maxwell slapped the back of his head. "Get back in there. Run another one. Let's see how many times it'll let us hit repeat."

Campanelli had invited a few attractive lady friends aboard for midday drinks—nothing extravagant, just enough to remind the harbor who was king of this particular yacht. Jessica handled the cocktails, gliding behind the bar with practiced charm. The women were flirty, the rosé was cold, and Campanelli was exactly where he liked to be: at the center of everything.

It was the perfect distraction.

At one point, as laughter bubbled from the upper deck, Campanelli glanced at his phone. Two messages. Both from his brokerage account.

Verification codes.

He paused just long enough to register the oddity—then shrugged. Calm as ever, he tapped out a message to his wife:

Campanelli: **Honey, you can't log in unless you get the code from me. What are you trying to do now? You want to day trade?**

He smirked at his own joke, dropped the phone face down on the table, and returned his attention to the women just as Jessica set a Manhattan in front of him with a crisp nod.

"Fresh Maine lobster coming up," she said.

"Perfect," Campanelli replied, raising his glass in a silent toast. No hint of worry in his eyes. Just good drinks, good company, and a quiet certainty that everything was under control.

Just as lunch was being served—steamed lobster tails, drawn butter, a chilled Sancerre—Jessica leaned in slightly toward Campanelli, tone casual but deliberate.

"Just a reminder, sir—your wife is expected around six. She texted earlier, said her spa day's wrapping up soon. I figured you'd want a little time before dinner service."

Campanelli's fork paused mid-air.

Right. His wife. Spa day. Her phone.

His expression didn't change, but something behind his eyes flickered. *She never touches her phone during a spa day.* His wife wasn't using the brokerage account.

Campanelli set his fork down with deliberate calm, wiped his mouth with his linen napkin, and pushed back his chair.

"Ladies, you'll have to excuse me a moment. Duty calls," he said with a smile, as if he were about to take a boring business call, not investigate a potential breach in his financial fortress.

He stepped below deck, made his way to the private office tucked in beside the master stateroom. His laptop waited, already powered on.

A few keystrokes. Fingerprint scan. Logged in.

His eyes locked on the number.

$500,000. Gone.

Gone clean—five separate withdrawals, each for $100,000. Before that, one failed attempt to take the full balance. Someone had tested the ceiling, found it, then bled the account dry beneath it.

He didn't swear. Didn't breathe differently. He just moved.

He placed an immediate hold on the account and changed the password.

He didn't go back upstairs.

Instead, Campanelli stayed in the cool hush of the cabin, letting the silence settle. Then, in one smooth motion, he stood and opened the hidden compartment behind the office bookshelf. A small, encrypted comms device sat inside. He powered it on and made a single call.

Moments later, footsteps echoed down the teak steps.

Little Gorgi appeared in the doorway, silent as ever, built like a freezer truck in designer linen.

Campanelli didn't look up as he spoke. "Tell the tech team I want a full sweep. Every inch of this boat. Anything electronic, anything wireless, even the kitchen blender if it has a plug."

Gorgi gave a single nod.

"Have them check my laptop for malware, keyloggers, remote access. I want a report in my hands in one hour."

Jessica, clearing cocktail glasses nearby, froze.

The words hadn't been meant for her—but they landed like a dagger anyway.

Check for malware. Keyloggers.

She stayed perfectly still, eyes on the stemware, fingers steady. But her breath caught in her throat.

That's me.

The realization hit with the clarity of a gunshot. They were going to find it. Not today, maybe. But soon. The tech team would sweep the system and find it. When Campanelli asked *who* had access to that laptop, who had been near his private office, who had touched his machine?

My name would be first on the list.

Somebody was going to check the video.

Behind her, Campanelli's voice shifted. Lighter. Smooth.

"Jessica, darling, you've done enough today. Once my guests finish their lobster, escort them out, no lingering. Then go home. Full pay, of course."

She turned to face him, her smile carefully neutral. "Of course, sir."

"Tell them I'm terribly sorry I had to step away," he added, already turning back to his screen. "Remind them I'll see them at the regatta luncheon."

Jessica nodded, retreating to the upper deck where the women were still picking at lobster tails and taking sun-dappled selfies. She played the perfect hostess—warm, attentive, unshaken on the outside.

Inside, her pulse thudded in her ears. She couldn't stop calculating. Campanelli might've dismissed her with full pay and a compliment, but it wasn't going to last. She was just hoping to make it off that yacht.

As the last guest stepped off the yacht with a wave and a kiss on the cheek, Jessica followed. She kept her head high, her pace steady.

As she reached the dock, heart hammering, she heard Campanelli's voice again—low and casual, like he was ordering dessert.

"Now... who's that guy at the FBI we know?"

A pause.

"Get him on the phone."

March 2022 - Monday Morning after the botched op
FBI Field Office – Director Beck's Office

"You really stepped in some shit this time, Jimmy," Director Beck said before the door even closed. "I can't believe you botched the plan that badly. How did we not know about the transfer limits?"

Maxwell lingered halfway to the chair, still clutching a to-go coffee like a life preserver. "It seemed easy," he muttered. "We had all the account info. We had a pigeon in place to take the blame. It was a side account Campanelli barely looked at. Took him a week to even log in. That gave us our window to blame the girl for the hack."

He sat down, eyes fixed on the knot of his brown, ugly tie like it held the answers. "We just didn't know the brokerage had those damn transfer limits."

Beck didn't sit. He paced behind his desk like a prosecutor preparing for trial.

"Well, Campanelli's calling it a *loan*."

Maxwell finally looked up. "He knows it was us already?"

Beck nodded once. "You panicked when the second authentication codes started coming through. Should've stopped at one transfer, maybe you could've pinned it on that bartender. But multiple requests? Campanelli's not stupid. He knows who has that kind of capability."

Maxwell exhaled slowly. "So... he wants it back."

"You'll repay the money. With interest."

"Me? Wasn't this *our* plan?"

Beck smiled faintly. "Nobody sees my fingerprints on any of this. I'm not the one desperate for cash after an ugly divorce. This whole thing screams 'Maxwell went rogue.' Well—*you*, and maybe a little bit of Jake."

Maxwell slumped. "F*ck me. Of course, your hands are clean."

"That's what happens when you plan ahead."

"So what's the interest on a mafia loan these days?" Maxwell asked, voice flat.

"He says you 'borrowed' half a million. You owe him that. Plus another ninety grand."

Maxwell let out a low whistle. "Ninety K... for five days of sitting in my account? Jesus. I don't *have* that kind of money."

Beck was already two steps ahead. "He's giving you time. Sort of. The interest goes up five grand a week. So I suggest you find it quickly."

Maxwell stared at the floor. "I'm screwed."

Beck's voice softened just enough to be dangerous. "You're *useful*, Jimmy. Your screw-up just gave me a new idea. One that gets us both some cash—and this time, not from the mafia. You might even come out ahead."

Maxwell raised an eyebrow. "Yeah? Almost like I was set up."

Beck didn't deny it. "You know about the thief who's been robbing wealthy yacht owners? The team's calling her 'The Siren.' Killer mermaid, hacker femme fatale, whatever."

"I've heard the gossip. Mostly from the Chicago team bragging about getting to winter in the Bahamas on the Bureau's dime."

"Let them brag. We're going to use her. Set a trap. You'll run point. If your hacker girl on Campanelli's yacht is involved, all the better."

Maxwell scratched his head. "Jessica? She could barely manage a thumb drive. She's a damn good bartender. We're not dealing with a tech genius."

Beck rolled his eyes. "Christ, Maxwell. You had the balls to steal from Campanelli, but you can't follow this? We'll use *an* FBI account. A real one. We *want* it to get stolen."

Maxwell blinked. "But if she steals the money—"

"She's not going to steal it. *You* are."

Beck leaned forward, lowering his voice.

"You steal it. We pin it on her. The Siren. Headlines write themselves. Then you split the take with me. You repay Campanelli, you get back on your feet, and maybe you even retire with something more than that sad pension."

Maxwell half-laughed. "Half a pension, actually. Ex-wife's got the other half."

Beck smiled coldly. "Even more reason to say yes."

Maxwell hesitated. "So, who do we use as *The Siren*?"

Beck stared in disbelief. "Jesus, Maxwell. Use the girl you already have in place. Jake's girl."

"But Campanelli's going to come after her. The footage—she's gonna get burned."

Beck shrugged. "Exactly. She'll have to disappear. Somewhere like, I dunno... the f*cking *Caribbean*?"

Maxwell scratched his temple. "Okay, I get it. She's already on the run, might as well give her a new role. But how do we get her *down* there?"

Beck had the answer ready. "I've got a captain in mind. Caribbean-based, cocky as hell, soft in the head. Already crossed paths with the real Siren once in Miami—too dumb to realize it. He's perfect for this."

"If she doesn't take the bait?"

"We have a fallback. I know of an asset on the island—semi-official. Used to be in Chicago. He's in place as a bar manager, knows everything about everybody. Perfect cover. If the captain doesn't work, he'll offer her a job. She'll go."

Maxwell sat back, calculating. "You really want this captain off the board, huh?"

Beck's eyes glittered. "Let's just say... I wouldn't mind watching him drown in the consequences."

April 2022 - Monday evening after the botched op

Courtney stood in the middle of the living room, arms crossed, watching Jessica yank clothes from drawers like she was racing a fire.

"I still don't get why you have to leave Chicago," Courtney said. "I know it's all COVID-y, but it's getting better, right?"

Jessica didn't look up. "You just don't understand—and that's okay. I can't tell you everything. I wish I could. But I can't. I just have to leave. I *have to*."

Courtney hovered near the edge of the couch, clearly not satisfied. "This is about Johnny, isn't it? But you didn't even care that much about him. You are *not* the type of girl to leave town over a guy. Chicago's your turf."

SUN, RUM, AND STOLEN FUNDS

Jessica ignored her, moving aimlessly from dresser to suitcase to closet, folding some things, crumpling others.

"Look," she said finally, "I got backed into a corner. I did something I shouldn't have, and now I'm paying for it. Believe me, it could be a lot worse than just being told to disappear. 'Leave town and don't come back, the farther the better,' was the *nice* option."

Courtney's expression changed in an instant. Her jaw dropped. "Oh shit. This is about *Campanelli*, isn't it?"

Jessica froze. She didn't confirm or deny—she didn't have to.

"Okay, nope, I don't wanna know *anything*. Do *not* tell me! I'm good. I get it. What can I do? We need Mr. Jameson, I think."

"Chinese food?" Jessica asked. "And of course, we need Mr. Jameson. Whiskey pairs beautifully with General Tso's."

Jessica managed a laugh as she shoved a handful of socks into the suitcase.

Courtney grabbed her phone to place the order. "Same as always. Twenty-five minutes. Guess they're not too busy."

She tried to change the subject, throwing Jessica a lifeline. "So... where are you going? You can tell me that much, can't you?"

"I'm thinking I need water. Ocean, preferably. I've got a lead on a bartending gig in Hilton Head. But I keep thinking about Puerto Rico. It's farther. Safer. I *loved* it when I went. I mean, Greece was great too, but let's be real—Hilton Head's drivable. I can bring Rufus and all my crap. Probably smarter."

Courtney tilted her head. "You kinda look Puerto Rican. Do Puerto Ricans have freckles?"

Jessica smirked.

"If it's islands you want, remember Trevor?"

"Trevor?" Jessica blinked. "Our old manager, Trevor?"

"He's opening a restaurant down in the Virgin Islands. Saint Thomas, I think."

Jessica paused mid-fold. "No kidding."

"Yeah, he was trying to get *me* to go. Said I could stay with him until I found a place. Apparently, finding housing there is all about timing and knowing someone who's moving out. Places go fast."

Jessica looked up from her suitcase just long enough to smirk. "He always had a thing for you."

Courtney rolled her eyes. "No, he didn't. Did he? I don't think so." She paused, then admitted, "I always had a thing for dad bods... but now he's got this island beard going on. It's a little too *untamed* for me."

Jessica snorted and went back to trying to fold something that didn't want to be folded.

"Huh," Jessica muttered. "Why didn't *you* go?"

Courtney hesitated. "I didn't wanna bring it up, with your whole... trauma drama. But I think I'm done with the service industry."

"What?" Jessica's head shot up. "You're the second-best bartender in Chicago, and one of the best managers I've ever worked with."

Courtney raised an eyebrow.

Jessica waited for a protest that never came.

"Yeah, COVID sucks," Courtney admitted. "But it's more than that. I've got a shot at doing sales. An online menu system. I'd be selling it to all the bars and restaurants I already know. I think I could make real money. I'm thirty-five, Jess. I know people. I think I could kill it."

Jessica held up a hand. "Hold up. Are we *waiting* on Chinese food before we bring out Mr. Jameson? Bitch, I'm packing for exile. *Serve. The. Shots.*"

With a laugh, Courtney disappeared into the kitchenette, rinsed two dusty glasses under the sink, and opened the bottle.

She handed one to Jessica. "Cheers, bitch. Here's to new futures— whatever they look like."

They locked eyes wide and awkward, holding the gaze a little too long.

CHAPTER
TWENTY-SIX

September 2022 - St. Martin
Sunday Funday at the Boon

Ray leaned against the wooden bar at Buccaneer Beach Bar, nursing a reposado tequila as the salt-tinged breeze ruffled his shirt. Simpson Bay Beach stretched before him, golden and lazy under the afternoon sun. His mind, however, was anything but relaxed. The pieces were coming together, but he needed more technical information—he needed Johnny to talk. Looking across the bay, he could make out the yellow umbrellas of Mary's Boon Beach Bar.

He turned to Jessica, who sat beside him, absently stirring her tequila. She was distracted, and Ray knew why. Her phone was face-down on the bar, but the way she kept glancing at it told him all he needed to know. Johnny was keeping her attention. Ray knew she was going to be upset until he could come up with a plan to free her from the mafia's grip.

"You should invite Johnny to Sunday Funday at Mary's Boon," Ray said casually, watching for her reaction.

Jessica looked up, her brows knitting together. "Sunday Funday? Why?"

Ray shrugged. "It's a good excuse to hang out. Get him comfortable, you know? A little booze, a little music, he'll loosen up." He took a slow sip of his drink. "We need him to loosen up."

Jessica hesitated, eyeing him. "Ray... I don't want to hang out with Johnny. I'm not sure I can stomach it."

Ray chuckled, shaking his head. "I have an idea. It's a crazy idea, but it just might work. It might free you from your mafia servitude. But I need some technical information from Johnny."

Jessica sighed, rubbing her temple. Deep down, she knew he was right. If Ray needed information from Johnny, Sunday Funday would be the perfect time to get it out of him.

"Fine," she said. "I'll invite him."

"Good." Ray swirled his drink, then added, "Oh, and I'll ask Tiffany."

Jessica's mouth tightened. "Why?"

Ray smirked. "Because Johnny needs to feel like he's in a safe, social situation. If it's just you and me, he might get suspicious. Plus, Tiffany's good at getting people talking."

Jessica clenched her jaw. She hated Tiffany—well, maybe hate was a strong word, but she didn't like the woman. She was NOT looking forward to seeing her in a bikini. Jessica wasn't happy about it, but she also wasn't stupid. If this was part of the plan, she'd go along with it. Reluctantly.

"Fine," she repeated, forcing the word out through her teeth. "But if she starts causing problems—"

"She won't," Ray assured her. "She's just there to fill the space. Lots of it."

Jessica sighed again and picked up her phone. A few taps later, a message was on its way to Johnny.

Ray watched her carefully. He knew what she didn't—Johnny was no regular guy. He was an undercover FBI agent, and that meant they were playing a dangerous game. Johnny had her in a corner, and Ray needed to get her out of it before she got caught in something neither of them could escape.

But Captain Ray De Soleil had a plan. Sunday Funday at Mary's Boon was going to be more than interesting—it was going to be the beginning of Ray's counterattack.

Jessica to Johnny: **Hola!**

Johnny: **Ciao Bella! What's up? We don't have a scheduled text.**

Jessica: **Hey, do you want to come to Sunday Funday with us? Ray is inviting Tiffany, so I thought having you would help me not to smack her.**

Johnny: **Text me back in 10 minutes.**

Jessica: **Text me back in 10 minutes, please.**

Jake chuckled to himself, remembering back to why he liked Jessica in the first place. He knew he wasn't supposed to send another text, but his playfulness took over.

Johnny: **Text me back in 10 minutes, please.**

Jake turned to Maxwell, "Hey, Jessica just invited me to Sunday beach day with Ray and Tiffany. I'm thinking I gotta maintain this 'we're in it together' thing with Jessica, now that she knows I'm on island."

Maxwell chirped, "You just want to see those two in bikinis. Dang. Both Jessica and Tiffany, one with tits for days and the other with an athlete's tight body."

"Glad you approve then, I'll say 'yes' when she texts me back".

"Now hold on a minute, this doesn't seem very useful in our overall plan, does it?" Maxwell snapped back to the operation and his need for it to succeed.

"I'm not sure what can go wrong. Maybe I can convince her to do it sooner in person so we can get out of here."

"Maybe you are right. She seems to be hesitating because she has a thing for Captain Ray. We can use Tiffany even more to drive a wedge between them, so she'll get off her ass and make the transfer."

❖

The sun hung high over Simpson Bay, casting a golden shimmer over the waves as they lazily lapped at the shore. Underneath the bright yellow umbrellas at Mary's Boon, Ray and Jessica lounged in their chairs, a chilled bucket of rosé between them, beads of condensation glistening on the glass bottle. Ray tilted his sunglasses down the bridge of his nose, scanning the beach for their guests, while Jessica swirled her wine absentmindedly, pretending not to be on edge.

"I still don't know about this," Jessica muttered, taking a slow sip. The cool wine slid down her throat, but it did little to ease her nerves.

"You'll be fine," Ray assured her, his voice relaxed but his mind already working several moves ahead. Attempting to ease her thoughts, "Let's play a game. See that couple in the water over there, make up a good story about them."

"What? I'm not in the mood for games."

"OK, I'll start. Those two just met yesterday. See how playful they are together. Just met, for sure. He was sailing from the Virgin Islands to St. Martin, and he needed crew, so he picked her up in Virgin Gorda, but mysteriously, she didn't want to officially check out of the BVIs. Turns out, she is traveling the Caribbean incognito, hiding from her evil ex-husband, who is a German spy. He smuggled her and her dog onto the island."

Jessica could not resist the creative competition: "Is that all you got?"

"What, that was a good one!" Ray replied, "OK, how about that old couple right there? They gotta be 80+"

Before Jessica could respond, Johnny appeared from the beach path, his pale skin practically glowing under the Caribbean sun. He looked like he had just stepped off a plane from Chicago, his shoulders already beginning to burn. He adjusted his sunglasses, a bottle of sunscreen clutched in his hand as he surveyed the scene.

Ray smirked. "Looks like someone needs SPF fifty—fast."

Johnny ignored the jab and dropped into the seat across from them. "I'm here," he said, his voice neutral, as if he were analyzing the situation like any good agent would.

"Relax, Johnny," Jessica said, forcing a smile as she poured him a glass. "It's just Sunday Funday."

Before he could respond, the wind rose, whipping sand across the beach as whitecaps rippled on the water — Hurricane Tiffany had made landfall.

Her sun-kissed skin glowed, accentuating the athletic curves of her body. As she moved, a few heads turned, appreciative glances following her path. Johnny, in particular, seemed momentarily distracted, shifting in his seat as he took her in. As she shimmied off her cover-up, the rose-colored bikini she wore seemed perfectly chosen for the occasion, clinging to her in all the right places. The men on the beach took notice, and Johnny was no exception.

Jessica's grip tightened around her wine glass. Not to be outdone, she slowly peeled off her own cover-up, revealing a deep, plunging swimsuit that accentuated every curve. If Tiffany wanted attention, Jessica would make sure she got competition.

Ray let out a low chuckle as he observed the silent battle unfolding between the women. "Well, this escalated quickly."

Tiffany slid into her seat, her eyes dancing between Johnny and Ray. "So," she said, reaching for the chilled wine, "who's ready to have some fun?"

Ray leaned back, a knowing smile playing at his lips. Sunday Funday had just begun, and if everything went according to plan, they were all in for a very interesting afternoon.

Ray took another sip of his wine before setting the glass down and stretching. He turned toward Johnny, who was already looking uncomfortable under the relentless Caribbean sun, struggling not to get caught looking in the direction of bikini tops.

"Hey, Johnny," Ray said, standing up and dusting the sand from his legs. "Why don't we hit the water? You look like you could use a cool-down."

Johnny hesitated for a moment, then took a final sip of his wine before nodding. "Yeah, probably a good idea. It's hot," he said, standing and following Ray toward the shoreline.

The water was cool and refreshing as they waded in, waves breaking at their waists. They swam through the break, a wave gently lifted the boys, and passed beneath them before crashing onto the beach. Ray ran a hand through his damp hair, glancing around before lowering his voice. "So, Jake, parabolic listening post?"

Jake frantically puts his index finger over his mouth to shush Ray.

As another wave came, Ray continued, "But it's at street level, yes?" Jake nervously turned to start to swim back to shore, not wanting to take part in a monitored conversation, but then realized what Ray was doing. He turned back.

"Yep. Street level. The guys are in that white van parked at the end of the street." Jake says. "I keep forgetting you're an engineer..."

Ray was timing his discussion as the waves passed by them, and blocked the parabolic dish reception, which required a line of sight. As the next wave passed and the two disappeared behind it, Ray said, "So about Jessica's situation, her running for the rest of her life... that just sucks for her, now don't it. Seems like we only have one logical choice."

"What's that?" Jake asked nervously.

Timing the wave, "We steal the money ourselves, for Jessica, so she can travel and have a life." Ray stated in a rogue, heroic fashion.

"Are you crazy? We can't do that." Jake answered quickly, knowing his portion of the conversation was more than likely picked up by the listening device on shore.

"Why not?" Ray pressed. "Jake, ten years ago—before I moved down here—I wouldn't have had the balls to even *think* about this. Back in Ohio, I was as straight-laced as you, just another cog in the corporate wheel, coaching my kids through whatever useless sport was in season. But then I sailed the Caribbean, and I learned the

Caribbean is the Wild West—rules exist, but no one's really enforcing them."

"You can't just go stealing money out of accounts? Can we?"

"Look at it this way, Jake...Maxwell was gonna do it. Why can't we? We just need to manage to our penalties, and what are the penalties, really? Nobody wants to catch Jessica; that would open up too many questions. So really, we just need to make sure the mob gets paid back, and we're good. Right? My motto is 'Just say yes.' So... why not?"

"I'm sure it's more complicated than just *'why not?'*" Jake replied.

"Is it? It's not really, if you think about it." Ray waited for the wave... "We have all the login info for both accounts, mine and Jessica's, and the account numbers. The two-factor authentication security codes come to our phones first, before the FBI reads them."

"Ok .... it might be easy to move the money, maybe, I guess. How do you not get caught? Or at least get away with it?" Jake asked, coming around just a bit, thinking of how this would totally screw Maxwell.

"I have a plan for that, I think. But it does involve Jessica. We need to transfer it to her account first, so she'll still look like she took the money on paper. She'll always be on the run, either from the mob or the FBI, but that's going to be the case regardless." Ray schemed.

"Why from your account to Jessica's? Why not just take it?" Jake asked.

"Because Kevin isn't an idiot. When I was using that account in the beginning, buying a few boat parts with it, I poked around and noticed it had several limitations. Obviously, the FBI didn't want me to just take the money myself, so they put an account lock on it after I used it. The money can only be transferred to one account - Jessica's. I know this because I tried to buy one little extra boat part. Unauthorized. I thought I could get away with it. I couldn't even get $1,200 more." Ray claimed.

"Wait, you tried to take more than you were supposed to?" Jake queried.

"Of course I did, Jake. What was the harm in trying? Absolutely no penalty. That's pushing the limits. It's what I do. That's why this plan will work!"

"Hell, this plan is risky AF, but sounds like it might be the only way Jessica stays alive. Tony's uncle is still out for blood, even though he knows Maxwell is the one who took the money. He's old-fashioned, and anybody who dares to cross the family…blah blah blah." Jake stated as Ray rolled his eyes at Jake verbalizing the abbreviation AF instead of cussing. "So what's your percentage take out of all of this, Captain Ray?"

"Shit, I've got enough problems with the FBI. I don't need to get on the mob's radar somehow. But I'll still get the remaining balance from the charter, right? What the FBI promised me, right? I ONLY want the charter money in my contract. I mean, I need that f*cking money, Jake."

"You should. I can't see why not. It's already been allocated." Jake replied. "Nobody in the government knows how to un-spend money once it's been allocated. I'm not even sure that's an option in the computer system."

"That didn't sound confident, but not sure I have a choice. How about you? What slice of the pie do you want THIS time? A few pieces of eight for your daughter's med school, maybe?"

"Oh, I can't be involved, AT ALL. I can't take any portion of it. Hell, I might be involved in the follow-up investigation." Jake surmised.

"So let's go over how all this is gonna work. Make sure I'm not missing anything in my plan." Ray halted Jake from speaking; he forgot about timing the waves.

Jake was startled, but on the next wave began detailing, "We can bulk transfer the entire million from your account to Jessica's. That's not a problem; no restrictions on your account to Jessica's; that's what we want her to do. But we can only transfer $100,000 at a time out of Jessica's account. Maxwell tried to get that limit removed, but the FBI learned from our Chicago mob friends. *Johnny'* will instruct Jessica to move $100k at a time into other accounts, all belonging to Maxwell.

When she starts a transaction to transfer, the system will text Jessica an 8-digit code for verification. Each transfer matches up with a specific 8-digit code."

"Ok, but there's no limit on how many transfers we can do, right? We can just do one after the other?"

"As far as I know, correct. No restrictions on how many or how quickly, just $100k at a time. Unless they lock down the account."

"F*ck Jake, 'as far as you know'"? Ray hated air quotes, but felt appropriate to use in that moment. "Then we just need to transfer the money out of Jessica's account to hide it."

Jake exhaled, dipping his hands into the water. "Well, there are ways. Secure VPNs, burner accounts, anonymous wallets, cryptocurrency." He gave Ray a pointed look. "But you already know all about that, don't you?"

"Doesn't hurt to have some confirmation, Jake." Ray hesitated, waiting for another wave. "But won't the FBI notice the transfer activity?"

"Yes, of course, alerts are in place. They'll see the text confirmation codes. Jessica is supposed to do all this under Johnny's supervision, but when they see the alerts firing off and the codes coming through text, they are gonna know she's doing it unsupervised."

"So we need a distraction. Something to confuse them, at least for a little bit, so we get a head start. Won't they lock the account as soon as they see Jessica make another transfer, like the mob did?" Ray asked, hoping he knew the answer already.

"No, I don't think so. Maxwell needs this money for his life, literally. If he locks it, he loses that opportunity. He will want to get as much of it as he can as fast as he can, and he knows Kevin is good enough. Kevin is clueless, but he's a superb tech guy."

"Ah ha! *THAT'S* what I was counting on! You just verified why I think this is gonna work. Maxwell can't let it *NOT* work. He needs that money. We'll be able to get some of it. So it's a race against Kevin?" Ray exclaimed.

"Yeah, it's a race against Kevin, one of the best tech guys the FBI has. You have to enter all the transaction information and wait for an authorization code for each one that matches your transaction. The next transaction cannot start until the previous one finishes. Once Kevin is on it, he's going to win most of the time. The key will be to get two or three transfers before they even know what is happening. You'd be lucky to get one more after Kevin gets activated."

"That's perfect. We want Maxwell's hands dirty in this anyway, and we want him to pay off the mob. We just need Jessica to get enough to travel on. Now, for the distraction. I keep watching this Tropical Storm coming at us. Would that be enough of a distraction?"

"More than likely, yes. We won't be able to fly the drone over the boat, and that could be an excuse to lose connectivity to the inside camera. The Dutch police will be occupied."

"More than likely? Sounds like I need to think of some extra drama. Don't cut the camera to the boat, I have a good idea to keep their eyes on the distraction." Ray paused, "And I thought this was going to be just another boring Tropical Storm to sit through. Let's get back to the ladies before they aren't friends anymore."

"They are friends now?" Jake quipped, with surprising comedic timing, that Ray laughed, spitting saltwater back into the ocean.

CHAPTER
TWENTY-SEVEN

September 2022 - St. Martin
Deception on the Horizon

The dinghy rocked gently as Ray and Jessica made their way back to *Purrfection*, the sleek catamaran bobbing in the calm waters just beyond the shoreline in Marigot Bay. The hum of the small motor filled the silence between them, though the tension needed no words to be felt. Jessica, legs stretched out over the side, watched the twinkling reflection of the moon on the waves, her mind a swirl of thoughts.

"So," she finally said, swirling the last bit of rosé in her plastic cup. "Do you have the plan yet?"

Ray exhaled, gripping the tiller with one hand. "Yeah," he said simply.

Jessica turned to look at him, eyebrows raised, her grip tightening slightly around her cup. A flicker of something in her eyes—curiosity, maybe suspicion. "And?"

Ray hesitated, then gave a small, mischievous grin. "You're going to steal the money."

Jessica blinked. "Wait—what?" She let out a short laugh, shaking her head. "Steal your money? Which is technically Campanelli's money... oh, this is brilliant. That's your big plan?"

Ray kept his gaze forward, his grip tightening on the tiller. "It's not my money, and it's not Campanelli's money," he admitted, his voice calm but firm.

Jessica's laughter faded. A slow dread crept up her spine. "What do you mean?"

Ray sighed, finally turning to meet her eyes. "It's FBI money. It's part of a sting operation to catch an electronic bank thief."

"No," she whispered, shaking her head. "No, that doesn't make sense. Johnny works for Campanelli, and he's the one..."

"Jess, Johnny is an undercover FBI agent from Chicago. I know him as Jake."

"Johnny?... Is FBI?" Jessica's stomach dropped. Her breath caught in her throat. "He's been having me spy on Campanelli.... I'm an informant?"

"For whatever it's worth, he seems like a decent guy. He is almost as caught up in this as you are; the team lead, Maxwell, is running the op. I've never met him."

"What am I caught up in? Who is this thief they are trying to catch?"

"Well, here is the funny part... It's you. You are the thief they are trying to catch."

"What me? I don't know shit about f*ck."

"That's why Johnny is guiding you, all the way. They are setting you up to steal this money, so that you'll be the person of interest in the investigation. Meanwhile, these corrupt agents use the funds to pay back Campanelli, and I'm guessing retire happily ever after on the remainder."

Jessica stared at him, her mind racing. "How did you get FBI money? None of this makes any sense."

"The FBI approached me to be part of this sting operation.

"Wait. You were part of this?" she whispered, her voice barely audible over the water. "From the beginning?"

The one man I can trust... The thought echoed in her head, but now it felt hollow, like a cruel joke. Her chest tightened as realization sank in, a mix of anger, hurt, and confusion swirling inside her. She had built her world around Ray's presence, his reliability, and now that foundation had crumbled in an instant. The words she had always believed, the certainty she had held onto, now shattered like a wine glass on a boat deck.

Ray nodded. "Not at the beginning, when we first met, it's complicated."

Jessica felt like she'd been punched in the gut. Her hands clenched into fists, her nails digging into her palms. The betrayal, the sheer audacity of it, was suffocating.

"All this time?" she asked, her voice laced with disbelief. "Every moment? Every move? You were working with them? Was any of it real?"

Ray swallowed hard. "I was protecting you."

Jessica let out a bitter laugh, her chest tight with emotion. "Protecting me? By lying to me? By pretending to be on my side while setting me up?"

"It wasn't like that," Ray said firmly. "It's not like that. I think you know that in your heart. The only way I could help you was to take the job the FBI was offering. If it wasn't me, it was going to be somebody else. Worst case, you really were a thief. Best case, I get to save the girl and sail off a hero."

Jessica fought back tears, an unfamiliar sensation tightening her throat. She never cried, but this—this was different.

"You had no choice? You expect me to believe that?"

"Oh, I had a choice. I could have chosen not to get involved, but this operation was going to happen with or without me. I chose to put my career, and maybe even my life, on the line to protect you."

Jessica tried to calm her emotions. She closed her eyes and imagined herself behind the bar, in total control, the chaos just a width of the bar away. She took a deep breath and tried to piece it together in her head.

"Johnny? FBI? Why is he telling me to take your money, which I thought was Campanelli's money, and now you say it's the FBI's money, but Johnny is the FBI? This is making no sense. Why is Campanelli in on this? He can't be FBI, he's mafia."

"Back in Chicago, the FBI agents tried to steal Campanelli's money. That's why they had you mess with his computer, so you'd take the blame."

"Johnny? Steal from the mob? No way, he's too boring."

"Not Johnny, his team leader. I think his name is Maxwell. They screwed it up badly. They didn't get much money, and Campanelli knew it was the FBI quickly. They had to pay him back, but with interest. Money they didn't have. So they hatched this little sting operation to catch an electronic bank thief, but instead they were going to take those FBI funds to pay Campanelli his interest, and once again, pin it on you."

"Me? I'm just a bartender from Chicago. Why is this happening to me? And you? How did YOU get involved in all this?"

"I stumbled into it, literally. When I came to visit you in Hilton Head, the FBI was already trying to tempt you with another Captain. I'm guessing they were behind some of your misfortune, also. So they recruited me instead of whatever Captain they had." Ray held back the full story; no sense worrying her with all the details.

"Captain Dillon...dammit. He makes sense now. And getting kicked out of my apartment. And somebody bought all my tequila bottle lamps at full price .... damn them."

"When the FBI approached me, I had to say yes. We had such a great vibe texting. What they were telling me wasn't making sense, so I had to find out for myself. I could've said no, stayed out of it. It sure seemed like you needed help, so I said yes." He leaned in, voice steady but low. "Do you trust me enough to listen to my plan?"

Jessica wanted to say NO, but in her gut, when she searched deep down, through all the chaos, she did trust him. "I'll listen, but I don't trust you." Jessica turned away from him, her gaze fixed on the dark horizon. Her mind spun, searching for solid ground in a world that had just collapsed beneath her feet.

Ray let the silence settle, his mind racing through everything that had led to this moment. He had known this day would come, but watching Jessica unravel in front of him was harder than he had anticipated. Nothing he could say would make it right, yet a part of him still hoped she would see the truth behind his choices.

CHAPTER
TWENTY-EIGHT

September, 2022 - St. Martin
The Sail Plan

The small dinghy bumped against the dock, and Ray tied it off as Jessica stepped onto the weathered wood. The neon glow from *The Dinghy Dock Bar* cast a warm haze over the waterfront, the sound of laughter and clinking glasses drifting toward them.

They pulled up two barstools and ordered Jameson, neat. Jessica wrapped her fingers around the glass but didn't take a sip.

"So what's this brilliant plan of yours, to steal the money ourselves?" Jessica asked before Ray could even take a sip.

Ray cleared his throat. "You're in a dangerous spot, Jess. You seem to have two choices. One, you could run now. That would ruin the FBI plan and greatly piss off Campanelli, since he wouldn't be getting his money back. A dangerous play, no matter how much he likes you. Or two..."

Jessica cut him off, "Well, that sounds better than being arrested by the FBI and serving time, doesn't it? But my mother... she'll never leave Chicago."

"Uh, the FBI does NOT want to catch you. That would leave way too much explaining to do. But after they collect evidence that you stole the money, you'll be on the FBI's Wanted list, and on the run. I'm not sure how they handle loose ends, but it could be similar to the mafia."

She exhaled sharply. "Go on."

Ray took a sip of whiskey, eyes locked on hers. "So either way, you are going to be on the run. I can't figure out a scenario where you aren't... uh... traveling the world. Why not be on the run with some money? Sounds better than broke, right?"

"So we just steal the money? It's that easy?"

"*YOU* steal the money. That's the tricky part. They have surveillance software on my laptop, so they record the keystrokes and the camera and the audio, even. I've researched it, and no way around it. They are going to have evidence of you stealing the funds."

"I saw your account before. A million dollars is a pretty good travel budget. I'm in."

"Another sticky point, you probably won't be able to steal it all. Once they see you starting the process, they might shut off the account or transfer money themselves. You can only transfer $100k at a time."

"$100k? That's not much to run for the rest of my life!"

"I have an idea to distract them, so hopefully you can get a few transactions before they notice, so maybe like $300k, minimum?"

"That would work, I think. I'd live cheap. What is your 'idea'?" Jessica pointlessly used air quotes around *idea*, making Ray smirk, bringing the hint of a smile to Jessica's face.

"Tropical Storm Fiona will be here in 2 days. We use the storm as the diversion."

"What if the storm gets worse than predicted?"

"Forecasts are pretty good these days, but that could always happen. I've sat through a Cat 2 before in St Augustine. If we tie *Purr-fection* up correctly in the marina, and we get the transfer in before we lose Internet connection, we should be fine.

"What if the storm gets weaker or turns?"

"Good catch... that part of the plan is going to involve Tiffany..."

Jessica opened Telegram on her phone, a secure messaging app the FBI couldn't monitor. Ray had installed it and set it up for her. Jessica needed some advice from Courtney, hoping she didn't have to explain too much.

[Messages not monitored by the FBI]

Jessica to Courtney: **Hey. I'm using the new Telegram app! Look at me!**

Courtney: **Ray installed that for you, did he? I know you didn't figure it out.**

Jessica: **Yes, he did. But I'm texting because I need some girl advice. I'm in a bit of a situation down here.**

Courtney: **What? You're pregnant already? That didn't take long.**

Ignoring Courtney's attempt at teasing her,

Jessica: **This is important. I need to decide to do something kinda crazy. So do NOT text this to anybody else, but turns out that Johnny is an FBI Agent. How about that bullshit?**

Courtney: **Johnny the Square? But wait, he had you spy on Campanelli? You were an informant?!**

Jessica: **Much worse. Those stupid agents tried to steal from Campanelli and blame it on me, but the idiots screwed it up and got caught.**

Courtney: **There was no JK after that.... Are you effing serious?**

Jessica: **AND now, they are down here in St Martin trying to get me to steal Ray's money, which is technically the FBI's money.**

Courtney: **OK, now I'm confused. Let me call you.**

Jessica: **Can't call, they might be listening. Ray is working with the FBI to help them catch a hacker who steals bank** account funds, but they were going to steal the money themselves and pin it on me!

Courtney: **That's alot of information. Ray is working with the FBI? How do you know all this?**

Jessica: **He told me.**

Courtney: **That doesn't seem very smart on his part.**

Jessica: **I'm going to be running from the FBI if I go through with it, and I'll be running from Campanelli if I don't. Ray has this new plan where I steal the money for myself! I'd still be on the run, but with some money.**

Courtney: **How much we talking? Why is Ray helping you? What's his cut?**

Jessica: **We are hoping to get at least $300k. But there's over $1 Mil in the account.**

Courtney: **Damn girl. Ray has this figured out, I'm sure.**

Jessica: **So I should do it, right? Follow Ray's plan? I mean, I trust him.**

Courtney: **Well, you do like to travel. You've got Ray wrapped around your finger. He loves you.**

Jessica: **What? No? I don't think so. He keeps flirting with this Tiffany bitch down here, some 35-year-old medical student, wanna be doctor.**

Courtney: **Uh... he's going up against the FBI and the Mafia... for you. Trust me, maybe in his own crazy pirate way, he loves you.**

Jessica had never really contemplated the risk Ray was taking, all on her behalf. Ray had asked for nothing.

CHAPTER
TWENTY-NINE

September 16, 2022 - St. Martin
Storm Prep

Tropical Storm Fiona wasn't due for another 24 hours, but the wind had already started to rise in gusty fits, kicking up ripples across the lagoon. Then it would die again, the calm before the storm. Ray stood at *Purrfection*'s helm, holding position with twenty other boats ready to come into the lagoon through the Simpson Bay Bridge.

"Alright," he muttered to himself, "time to thread the needle."

He throttled the engines into gear and guided *Purrfection* toward the bridge, falling into line behind a knotted trail of monohulls and motor yachts. A few tourists on the deck of the Sint Maarten Yacht Club waved, rum in hand, already tipsy and cheering like it was a parade. Ray gave a slight nod, eyes fixed on the narrowing passage between concrete pilings.

Purrfection passed through with a few feet to spare on either side, her twin hulls slicing the murky water. Once inside the lagoon, Ray turned toward the marina, where a long, empty double slip waited.

Jessica stood at the starboard bow, dock lines coiled at her feet, tension clear in the way she kept adjusting her stance.

Ray slipped *Purrfection* in with slow precision, easing her alongside the dock but not letting her touch. The water slapped gently between the hulls. With the engines holding her steady, Jessica tossed the bowline to the dock hand, then Ray tossed the stern line. The dock hand requested the midship spring line, but Ray yelled to him, "We are gonna spider tie in later, so no need for that yet."

Then came the storm prep. Not Ray's first time. He sat through Hurricane Irma in 2017, tied to an outside dock in St. Augustine.

Ray broke it down, "First thing, we gotta get all the dock lines out, and the extra lines. Old spare halyards, whatever is down in that locker. Then we will criss-cross them to the corners of the slip, creating a spider web, hopefully no one line taking the full force. We'll cleat them back on the boat, so we can adjust as needed. Once the storm starts to kick off, we want to be ten feet away from the dock, so no way to get on or off once we do that."

Ray and Jessica proceeded to run dock lines in every direction to the various cleats on the dock. Some lines ran across the double slip, 50 feet to the other side.

"We gotta stow anything that can fly or chafe," Ray said, already zipping up the sail bag and securing it tight with extra sail ties. "Double check all chafe gear—everywhere a line touches fiberglass or cleat. Once the winds pick up, it will come from every direction. When we are at anchor, the boat always points into the wind. Not this time, it's a wild ride as the wind shifts and diverts around these hills."

Jessica gathered up cockpit cushions, fenders, and the drying laundry that had been clipped to the lifelines. Anything loose got dragged below. The paddle boards were deflated, rolled up, and brought inside. Ray debated pulling the Bimini canvas off, but decided that with only a tropical storm, it would be fine.

They worked without much small talk, both aware of what a sloppy prep job could mean. The storm wasn't a hurricane—*not yet*—but storms in the lagoon had a way of funneling between buildings, bouncing off the hills, and slamming into boats at odd angles. A poorly placed dock line could saw through its own casing in a matter of hours.

By sunset, the sky had turned steel gray. The marina was nearly full now, every slip a temporary refuge. Lines groaned under pressure as the first serious gusts swept through. Ray stood at the edge of the dock, arms crossed, watching the motion of the boat.

Purrfection barely moved—suspended perfectly in her spiderweb.

"Alright," he said, mostly to himself. "Let's see what Fiona's got."

He looked toward Jessica, "Now we can start the real prep! You ready?"

With *Purrfection* secure in the marina like a cautious spider in a storm drain—lines leading from bow and stern to every available cleat—Ray finally felt the tension in his shoulders start to ease. Fenders were deployed. Everything movable was stowed. The grill was strapped down tight. Even Francine, the inflatable flamingo, had been deflated and folded like a war casualty stuffed into a cooler. The boat was ready for Fiona. Now came the hard part.

Jessica emerged from the cabin, still barefoot but armed with a fresh ponytail and a cold soda. "Storm prepped?"

Ray said, tugging at a line one last time. "Now it's your turn."

Her face dropped. "Ugh. The transfers."

Ray nodded. "Yup. Let's get your muscle memory in shape before the big show."

Inside, they sat at the salon table. The laptop was open. Two bank accounts already set up. One with five hundred bucks—play money to simulate the big heist. Jessica took her seat with the same enthusiasm she'd show for bartending back in Hilton Head.

Ray hovered behind her, leaning one hand on the backrest. "Remember, slow is smooth, and smooth is fast. Okay, go ahead and log in, like we did before. First transfer—go for a hundred bucks. I'll read you the code when it pops."

Jessica cracked her knuckles like she was about to whip up a batch of spicy margaritas. She typed, navigated, and clicked through the prompts. "Alright, it's asking for the confirmation code."

Ray glanced at his phone. "Okay, here it is: nine-seven-four-two-one-two."

The screen flashed:

$100 TRANSFERRED SUCCESSFULLY.

"Look at me," she grinned. "Hacking like a boss."

"Let's do it again. Second transfer."

She worked through it quicker this time, the hesitation already gone. "Code?"

"Six-two-zero-nine-eight-seven," Ray said.

Jessica typed it with confidence.

The screen flashed:

$100 TRANSFERRED SUCCESSFULLY.

"Boom. Another hundred. This is easy."

"Okay, okay. One more, make sure you've got this."

She prepped the third transfer. "Okay, I'm at the code screen."

Ray read off his phone—deliberately wrong. "Three-three-one-zero-seven-three."

Her screen flashed:

VERIFICATION CODE INCORRECT.

"There's no 'try again' button!" she snapped, scanning the screen. "It just canceled it! Did I lose the transfer?"

Ray let her fumble about. She clicked around, fuming. "It's gone. It didn't go through. I can't re-enter the code, I can't go back, it's just *gone*. Do I start another one? What do I do?"

She pushed back from the table, frustrated. "Why did you give me the wrong code?"

Ray let the silence hold for a moment. Then he spoke, quiet but steady. "You panic because you think the moment is bigger than you. But it's not. It's just a moment. It needs *you* to stay calm. Not perfect. Just focused."

Ray continued, "This is what is going to happen when their tech guy gets in the race. He is going to queue up a transfer. That code was for THEM. So you just need to calmly back out of this Confirmation screen, but NOT back to the beginning. We don't want to lose your place in the queue. You just need to wait for the next code to come through, and that one should be yours."

Jessica took a deep breath and nodded. "Okay. So... we go again?"

"Yes. But this time, we write it down. Step by step."

He grabbed a pad of neon sticky notes and a pen from the nav station. "Once you get a bad code, what's your step one?"

They walked through every screen, every step, every what-if. Each sticky note lined up in a row across the table like a neon breadcrumb trail.

By the time they finished, Jessica had a road map. And maybe—just maybe—a little more confidence.

Ray stood, stretching. "Storm's coming. But I think you're gonna be ready for the real one."

CHAPTER THIRTY

September 17, 2022 - St. Martin
Tropical Storm Fiona

Tropical Storm Fiona crept closer by the hour, its swirling bands already ruffling the palms along the marina and sending dark clouds racing overhead. But *Purrfection* was ready. Spider-webbed into the over-sized slip with lines fanning out to every available cleat, she bobbed gently in her cradle of rope. Fenders were set, chafe guards snug, and every loose item topside had either been stowed or lashed down.

Inside the salon, a different kind of storm was brewing.

Ray wiped his hands on a rag, gave the companionway a final glance, and exhaled with relief. "I think we've prepped as best we can. Everything looks tight. I just did one last check. Wind's picking up—and once it howls, that's it. Not much else we can do."

Jessica stood near the galley, arms crossed and barefoot, her eyes gleaming with mischief. "So... HURRICANE PARTY!" she shouted, raising both arms like a victorious maniac.

Before Ray could react, the Bluetooth speaker kicked on, blaring house beats from Rufus Du Sol. The bass reverberated off the fiberglass walls, and within seconds, Jessica was dancing barefoot on the salon floor, her hips swaying in rhythm, hair bouncing with each spin. She pulled Ray by the hand—half dare, half demand.

Ray laughed, already grabbing the Jameson. "We're drinking to good prep and bad decisions!"

They clinked shot glasses, making awkward eye contact, then knocking them back with synchronized head tilts. Then they were moving—wild, uncoordinated, free. Laughter rose with the wind outside, their bodies swaying not with fear, but celebration. *Purrfection* became their fortress, their nightclub, their momentary escape from the real world.

Ray's usual bravado softened in the glow of the salon lights. Jessica's sarcasm melted into genuine laughter. They danced, shouted lyrics over the music, took more shots, and clinked again, just for the hell of it.

In between beats and drinks, Jessica caught Ray's eye—really caught it—and held the gaze a second longer than necessary.

He held it back.

Somewhere beyond the lagoon, Fiona's winds howled into the night. But inside, time blurred with whiskey and rhythm. Two people, half-lost and half-found, dancing not because the storm was coming... but because they were still standing.

The dimly lit hotel room buzzed with tension as the outer bands rattled the windows and howled through the corridors outside. Inside, the FBI team hunched over their makeshift command center—three folding tables buried under laptops, routers, hard drives, and monitors glowing in the gloom.

"The drone is down," Kevin reported, eyes flicking across multiple feeds. "No visuals outside the boat anymore. Lost it when the first gusts came through."

"We still have the interior surveillance feed," added Jake, voice clipped. "And the marina gate camera. That's all."

"Turn the volume down," Agent Maxwell barked from his perch in the corner. He rubbed his temples. "I can't stand that techno garbage. It has no soul."

Kevin reached over and slid the volume control lower, though not off—he knew better than to mute the action entirely.

On the main monitor, *Purrfection's* salon looked like a surreal private club—lights low, shadows flickering across the interior as Ray and Jessica danced with wild abandon. The rising wind outside seemed a distant afterthought compared to the pulsing beat and the swirl of their movements.

"Dang, they are drinking," Jake muttered. "Hard."

"That doesn't seem safe, does it, with a storm coming?" Kevin asked, concern in his voice.

"With this idiot, nobody is safe. But this is not good," Maxwell said. "We need her to make the transfer as soon as this storm clears; we don't need her hungover."

Suddenly, Jessica broke from their spinning dance and slowed her sway, her movements languid now, deliberate. She stepped in close, until she and Ray stood nose to nose in the center of the salon.

Ray held still, a faint smile tugging at the corner of his mouth, letting her set the tone. The space between them pulsed with tension—whether playful or something more, it was impossible to tell.

Jessica's eyes sparkled as she tipped her head ever so slightly. Then, with a sudden giggle, she spun away from him, as she vanished down the companionway and out of the surveillance frame.

The agents leaned forward instinctively.

"Where's she going now?" Jake muttered.

Kevin kept his fingers poised above the keyboard. "Bathroom break?"

Maxwell just grunted. "If they only knew we were watching. Just need some popcorn."

Moments later, she re-emerged—wearing *that* costume.

The mermaid.

The flowing sequined tail shimmered with each step, the striking red wig cascading over bare shoulders. A white bikini top adorned with seashells barely concealed her curves. Hips swaying in perfect time with the deep bass, she strolled into the salon, the embodiment of temptation.

"Oh my," Jake said, louder than intended. "That was... unexpected."

The mermaid drifted closer to Ray, her movements slow, deliberate. Without a word, she extended a hand and coaxed him to his feet. Ray played along, eyes locked on her. The agents leaned closer to the screen.

She pressed her body to his, rising on her toes, her face inches from his. The boat rocked beneath them as another gust slammed into the marina, but they remained rooted in their dance. Nose to nose, breath mingling, the mermaid's lips parted into a sly smile—then she closed the gap.

Their first kiss unfolded in the flickering light, long and deliberate, as if neither cared about the storm battering the world outside. The hull shuddered with each crashing wave, but inside the cabin, they moved to their own rhythm.

Meanwhile, Jessica sat alone in her cramped cabin, the violent sway of the boat testing her every movement. Rain lashed the portlights in bursts, and the occasional wave hammered the hull, each impact rattling through the bones of *Purrfection*.

Ray's laptop rested on her knees, its glow painting the polished wood in cold light. Her own reflection stared back at her in the dark screen edges—face taut, eyes sharp. Determined.

She flexed her fingers once, twice, then hovered them above the keyboard. The storm wasn't the only thing howling tonight. Her pulse throbbed in her ears, the weight of what she was about to do pressing down like the eye of Fiona itself.

One wrong keystroke, one hesitation—she couldn't afford either.

Jessica took a steadying breath and leaned in, ready to pounce.

Here we go. I can do this. I can do this. She logged into Ray's account with minimal security and quickly transferred all the funds to her designated account. Now, she had to log in to her account, which triggered the login verification code texted to her phone.

"Oh, I hope those two have the FBI team distracted, or this is gonna suuuuckkkkk. " Jessica whispered to herself, knowing that her texts were being monitored. "First transfer queued up," she muttered under her breath. She typed furiously, her lack of formal training compensated by sheer audacity and the sharp lessons she'd learned from Captain Ray, his voice echoed in her mind: *Slow is smooth, smooth is fast.*

A text message came across her phone: Verification Code 806745. Jessica entered the code, and moments later her screen flashed:

$100,000 TRANSFERRED SUCCESSFULLY.

"Oh yeah, take that! I'm a damn computer sniper, or whatever, hacker?" Jessica muttered to herself as she continued her designated task. She queued up the next transfer to the next account number on the list. Another verification code, and another screen flash:

$100,000 TRANSFERRED SUCCESSFULLY.

Back in the hotel room command center, all eyes were on the monitor. Captain Ray was dancing, flirting, and kissing the mermaid—who, as far as the team believed, *was* Jessica. To their knowledge, the two had never crossed into anything romantic. This sudden display was unexpected, shocking even—and exactly as planned. It had them riveted, their focus locked on the swirling spectacle unfolding on screen.

Jessica's screen flashed again:

$100,000 TRANSFERRED SUCCESSFULLY.

"Yes!" Then again:

$100,000 TRANSFERRED SUCCESSFULLY.

Kevin's gaze flicked to a nearby monitor—then locked on it. "Holy shit," he blurted. "Someone's starting the transfers! Three hundred K... four hundred!"

"What?" Maxwell shot up. "That's only possible from Ray's laptop! But they're both—" he jabbed a finger toward the main feed "—right there. Drunk. A little teenage make-out session."

For a beat, no one moved. The contradiction hung in the air, thick with confusion.

Kevin leaned closer, eyes narrowing. "I—I don't get it. The system shows it's Ray's machine. Live session."

Jake frowned, trying to help the distraction play out just a little longer. "Maybe it's queued up? Automated somehow?"

"No," Kevin said flatly. "These are manual inputs. Real-time."

Maxwell's jaw tightened, a flicker of doubt creeping in. He looked at the screen again—Ray laughing, the mermaid twirling in his arms. He suddenly noticed the mermaid's bare shoulder -- bare, no tattoos.

Maxwell murmured in disbelief, "F*ck me..."

Kevin rechecked the feed from Ray's laptop camera, and sure enough, it was activated but showing a black screen. A chill ran down his spine as he realized what this meant. The black screen wasn't just a glitch; it was deliberate - someone blocked the camera. He leaned in closer, turning up the volume. Faint clicks of a keyboard filtered through, confirming his suspicion: someone was actively working on Ray's laptop. Kevin's jaw tightened as the gravity of the situation sank in. Jessica wasn't dancing drunk; she was executing a plan, and she was ahead. The stakes had just skyrocketed.

Maxwell panicked. He needed that money himself. His mind raced, calculating his dwindling options. If he didn't secure enough funds, the consequences would be catastrophic. Campanelli wasn't the kind of man to offer extensions on debt—he was the kind to collect by any means necessary. Maxwell's hands trembled as he realized just how much he was risking by betting everything on this operation. The weight of his desperation pressed down on him, making every second feel like a countdown to disaster. "Well, don't just sit there, Kevin, start transferring."

"Shouldn't we shut down the account?" Kevin quipped.

"No, no. Just transfer it back to the FBI account I gave you earlier." Maxwell had given Kevin an account number, alright, his account number.

"But, she's still going to be able to..." Kevin stuttered.

"Just F*CKING do it!" Maxwell screamed.

Kevin smirked and turned to the glow of his computer screen. "She's a bartender, I got this," he said, his tone dismissive. His fingers danced over the keyboard, confident that Jessica's unorthodox methods would soon falter under pressure. "This isn't like mixing drinks, Jess," he muttered to himself.

But Jessica had no intention of slowing down. Her phone pinged, and she clutched it, her heart racing. The text verification code had arrived. She entered it with practiced speed and hit Enter. The screen flashed:

$100,000 TRANSFERRED SUCCESSFULLY.

Jessica allowed herself a small grin. "Boom," she said under her breath, but loud enough to come through the FBI speakers, already moving to queue up the next transfer.

Back in the hotel room, Kevin's focus was firmly on the transfers. He queued up a transfer and waited for the computer screen to flash the verification text. He expeditiously entered the verification code. His screen flashed:

$100,000 TRANSFERRED SUCCESSFULLY.

When Jessica received the verification text, she entered it quickly. Her screen flashed:

VERIFICATION CODE INCORRECT.

Her transfer failed, and she felt a wave of panic coming over her. She knew that Kevin was in the game, and it was the code for his transfer. The race was on. She took a deep breath, snapped her friendship bracelets twice, and looked at her cheat notes on the side of the laptop screen. She knew she had entered a failed code, and had to follow a very specific procedure and complete it before Kevin completed another transfer, or the verification code texts would be out of order and confusing.

"Ok Jess, just follow the sequence... You can do this. Live in the now." As she carefully navigated back to re-enter the code for her transaction, she knew one misstep and she'd have to start the transaction over. Another verification code came into her phone. If this were for her transfer, all is well. If Kevin had managed to get another one queued up, her transfer would fail again. She quickly entered the code...... in just a few seconds that felt like an eternity, her screen flashed:

$100,000 TRANSFERRED SUCCESSFULLY!

"Yes, I'm back in the game!" Jessica shouted proudly, booming over the FBI speakers in the command center. She didn't let herself get caught up in her triumph, rapidly entering her next transfer, knowing Kevin was doing the same. The storm outside intensified, the boat rocking violently, but she didn't flinch. Her fingers danced over the keyboard, her determination unshakable.

Kevin saw the verification code and knew it wasn't his. "One for one from here on," he said aloud, his voice cocky. "We will see about that. Better keep up, Jess."

Kevin's focus was his usual surgical precision, not dulled by the distractions of the audio feed from Ray's laptop. He quickly queued up another transfer and hit the button to wait for a transfer code. The code arrived, a triumphant gleam in his eye as he entered the code and completed his third transfer:

$100,000 TRANSFERRED SUCCESSFULLY.

Jessica was entering her next transaction as quickly as she could, but just before she hit the 'Submit' button, another Verification code came in. Jess knew it wasn't hers. Even though Kevin won another transfer, she smirked at herself, proud that she didn't enter an invalid code again.

"Damn, he got two in a row," Jessica muttered." But I'm way ahead, and I've got this last one, her grin widening. She imagined

SUN, RUM, AND STOLEN FUNDS

Kevin's frustration and reveled in it. "Not bad for a bartender." A verification code came in, she typed it in, and her screen flashed:

$100,000 TRANSFERRED SUCCESSFULLY.

Jessica removed the tape covering the laptop's web camera and proudly gave a middle finger. "You can have the scraps. I don't even have another account number to transfer it to." As she gently closed the case, the team could see her big smile and confident nod of success as the video from the camera shrank smaller and smaller and finally went black.

Kevin looked at the account screen. It only had some $36k remaining. Maxwell was looking over his shoulder. "What the hell did you stop for?" Maxwell screamed at Kevin.

Kevin glared at his superior for the first time in his career, and hesitantly and slowly entered the final transfer to move the remaining funds. The money was gone, scattered across untraceable accounts. The race was over, but the consequences were just beginning.

On the computer screen, monitoring Jessica's text messages, a message flashed:

Jessica to Antonio Campanelli: **Hey Tony, Jessica here. Hope you are well. Tell your uncle that Agent Maxwell should have his interest payment ready. Tell Eva I said hello.**

Antonio Campanelli: **Will do, Jessica. Eva sure misses your margaritas. I wish you could come visit, but my uncle is still not happy about your involvement. He is very old-school and strict. You were technically an informant. DON'T tell me where you go. Safe travels.**

Jessica to Johnny: **Ciao Bello, you son of a bitch! You won't find me. You won't want to find me. I know what you're team has done... and so does my friend in Chicago. Goodbye.**

Maxwell slumped in his chair in disbelief. "I'm going out for a smoke," he said, and he stormed out the door.

Kevin looked at Jake, "But he doesn't smoke. Does he? What does she mean, Maxwell owes Campanelli? I'm so confused."

"It's gusting to 60, so I doubt anything would light." Jake replied,

"I'll give him a few minutes, then go talk with him. This hit him hard. All I can say, Kevin is 'stay confused'."

"I don't understand. Why don't we storm down to the marina and arrest her ass? We have all the video proof we need. Yeah, the funds are gone to who knows where, but we have her digital footprint, video, audio - all of it."

"We need the Dutch police with us, and they aren't coming out in this weather, not for us, meaning the USA. Now remember, stay confused."

"Did we know that? With this storm? That seems like an important detail, being able to arrest her whenever we need to." Kevin surmised.

"Mistakes were made, Kevin, all I can say. It's best to stay confused."

Outside the hotel room, Maxwell leaned against the concrete wall in the covered corridor, shielded from the worst of the wind. The storm howled around him, but the chaos outside couldn't compare to the turmoil within. His mind raced, replaying every decision that had led him here.

With a trembling hand, he pulled out his phone and opened his bank app. The brief thrill of seeing the money in his balance was already fading, replaced by the cold realization of how little it actually solved. By the time he paid off Campanelli and split with Beck, he'd be under six figures.

Or I could just take it all. No better place to disappear than the Caribbean, he thought, as he pushed hard against the door, the wind fighting him every inch.

Maxwell stepped into the storm—never to be seen again.

Jake paced in the hotel room, phone pressed tightly to his ear as he spoke to Director Beck. His voice was steady, but the weight of uncertainty sat heavy in his gut.

"We don't have the full picture yet," Jake admitted. "Still running diagnostics, trying to piece everything together."

Director Beck's voice came through sharp and clear. "You're telling me you lost Maxwell?"

Jake exhaled slowly, glancing at Kevin, who stood at the console, nervously checking and rechecking the transaction logs. "Maxwell vanished right after the transfer completed, mid-storm."

Beck was silent for a moment. "And the money?"

Jake ran a hand through his hair. "Kevin transferred it where he was told. But the account—it belonged to Maxwell. It wasn't an FBI account. We don't even know if Jessica had her own account, or if this was Maxwell's play all along. Could have been an elaborate misdirection to keep us chasing shadows."

"So you're telling me Maxwell could have taken it all?" Beck asked, voice unreadable.

Jake hesitated, then nodded, even though Beck couldn't see him. "Yeah. Right now, we just don't know."

Kevin looked up from the console, eyes filled with doubt. "Do you think he played us? Was he controlling Jessica, or maybe…"

Jake held up his open hand to get Kevin to shut up. "Yes, sir, we will keep you informed."

"Kevin, please, please, please! Stay confused!"

CHAPTER
THIRTY-ONE

September 17, 2022 - St. Martin
Race Results Posted

Jessica stretched luxuriously across the Egyptian cotton sheets of the king-sized bed, the gentle rocking of the yacht lulling her into a sense of absolute triumph. The cool night air filtered through the slightly open porthole, carrying the scent of salt and freedom. She had done it. She had outwitted the FBI, outmaneuvered their agents, and disappeared with the money. Every risk, every careful calculation had paid off, and now she was here, in the lap of luxury, far from their reach.

The sailing yacht, a sleek, multi-million-dollar 81-foot Swan, with gleaming teak decks and polished brass fixtures, rocked gently as the winds began to calm. Somewhere above her, the hum of quiet voices and the occasional clink of glasses hinted at the others on board, but for now, she was alone in the master suite, wrapped in the spoils of her daring success.

A soft knock at the door pulled her from her thoughts.

Jessica sat up, tucking a stray strand of dark hair behind her ear as the door cracked open. Flora stepped inside, her face half-lit by the warm glow from the hallway.

"Are you okay down here?" Flora asked, her voice calm but laced with a knowing edge. "The worst of the storm is over, barely raining anymore. Sleep well."

Jessica grinned. "Thank you so much for helping me out. I truly appreciate it."

Flora gave a half-shrug. "David and I would do anything for Ray."

At that, Jessica's smile faded slightly. Ray. The only reason she was safe, in luxury sheets on a luxury yacht. He had set everything in motion, had planned the impossible, and made her believe it could work. And now, they were both safe—because of him.

Flora lingered in the doorway for a moment longer before giving a small nod and slipping out, leaving Jessica alone again.

Jessica exhaled slowly, rolling onto her side to grab her phone from the nightstand. The screen lit up in the dim room, illuminating an unread message from Johnny. But there was only one person she needed to text.

Campanelli.

Jessica to Antonio Campanelli: **Hey Tony, Jess here. Hope you are well. I'm guessing you know about Maxwell's plan to repay you. I kinda messed that up tonight. I just want to keep my mom safe, so tell me any amount Maxwell doesn't pay back, and I'll pay it.**

Campanelli: **That's well over $150k. It's not yours to pay.**

Jessica: **If he can't repay it, it's my fault, and you'll find out about it eventually, so I just want to be upfront.**

Campanelli could not help but grin as he responded.

Campanelli: **Sounds interesting, whatever happened down there. You found your edge again, like that spunky, sarcastic smartass bartender who talked back to me in Chicago.**

Jessica: **I guess I have Tony. I've grown, but I AM back! I'll text you from my new number in a few days, see how much I owe you.**

She typed her reply, shoulders softening as it dawned on her just how much she had changed — and how Ray had made it possible.

Jessica transferred $100,000 to an account specified by Captain Ray. He said it was a worthwhile charity, and she trusted him. No questions asked.

Then, she let the phone slip from her fingers, sinking back into the pillows. As the gentle sway of the yacht rocked her, her eyelids grew heavier, and soon, she drifted off to sleep.

❖

September 18, 2022

The next day, Jake and his team of Dutch police arrived at the marina, the tropical morning already thick with heat after the storm, fallen branches almost fully removed by the efficient marina staff. They moved toward *Purrfection*, its pristine hull gleaming under the rising sun. Jake stepped onto the dock, scanning the deck where Ray moved sluggishly, rubbing his temples as if nursing a hangover.

"Hell of a storm, wasn't it," Jake stated more than asked.

"I don't remember much of it, but I had fun." Ray barely looked up as he loosened a dock line, mumbling under his breath. His disheveled appearance was convincing, but Jake knew it was an act. An act for nobody, because he knew the truth, and the Dutch police did not care.

"Is Jessica around?"

"I haven't seen her yet this morning, had a little rough night in more ways than one. She ended up sleeping on her side, not that I didn't try. But her gear is gone, and so is her dog. Maybe out for a walk? Dunno." Ray claimed dispassionately.

"Kevin says her phone is still close by," Jake said.

"Is it now? Well, there are 100 little places on board she coulda stashed it, if you wanna look? Got anything more specific than 'close by'?" Ray replied.

"Where's your dinghy? Lost in the storm, maybe?" Jake asked, staring at the empty space off the stern where the dinghy should be.

Ray glanced aft, watching the lift lines sway from the davits, no dinghy in sight. Ray noticed that even during the storm, she remembered to connect the bow and stern lift lines, so they didn't sway violently; he had to use his hand to cover the millisecond smile.

"Huh....", moving his hand to rub his chin.

As Ray continued to stare blankly at his missing dinghy, a sleek, 81-foot sailing yacht passed by, leaving the marina to catch the 9 o'clock outbound bridge. Ray raised two fingers to his forehead, in a hungover salute to his friend Captain David at the helm.

"You haven't seen Agent Maxwell around, have you?" Jake knew he wasn't going to get an answer.

"You lost your team lead? I'm not even sure what Maxwell looks like." Ray replied.

"What's the plan, Ray?" Jake asked, voice casual but firm.

Ray let out an exaggerated sigh, wiping Jameson sweat from his brow. "I gotta get out of this marina. I can't afford another night at double slip rates. Gotta watch my funds until my FBI charter check comes in. I'll sail back to St. Thomas for some charters and try to find a cheap used dinghy, I guess. She musta borrowed mine."

The hint of a smirk tugged at Ray's lips, barely concealed. The Dutch officers standing behind Jake didn't seem to notice—or care. They weren't here for subtext. But Jake caught it. He didn't know what Ray knew, but he was sure of one thing: Jessica had pulled it off and made her escape.

Jake held his gaze a beat longer. "We're not done. Talk soon."

Ray shrugged. "It's never 'goodbye', Jake, always 'see ya later'."

Morning light filtered through the porthole, casting soft golden rays across the cabin. The yacht hummed with quiet activity as preparations were underway. A knock at the door brought Jessica out of her slumber.

Flora's voice was steady as she called from the hallway. "Jessica, we're departing. We'll be through the bridge in a few minutes. You can come out on deck after we are through if you'd like."

Jessica stretched, savoring the peaceful moment before pulling herself out of bed. She took her time getting ready, knowing that this was the beginning of something new.

Above deck, Captain David stood at the helm, guiding the yacht toward the Simpson Bay Bridge. As they approached, he waved toward the Yacht Club, catching the attention of a beautiful young woman with long dark hair, who raised a shot of Fireball to cheers their safe journey. Then she raised her phone and snapped a photo, the moment captured and preserved.

The yacht slipped through the bridge, its path clear and unencumbered toward Antigua. Flora turned toward Jessica with a small nod. "We're through."

Jessica stepped onto the deck, her bare feet meeting the warm wood. She closed her eyes, inhaling the salt air, letting the morning sun soak into her skin. This was it. A fresh start, new adventures waiting just beyond the horizon. With a deep breath, she tossed her cell phone into the clear blue water as a sacrifice to Poseidon.

With a satisfied smile, she watched the coastline fade in the distance. No regrets. No fear.

Only open waters and endless possibilities ahead.

CHAPTER
THIRTY-TWO

October 2022 - St. Martin
Back in Da Hook

The sun slanted west over Simpson Bay, casting a warm glow across the water as Ray De Soleil crouched to rig the last dock line for departure. The twin engines of *Purrfection* purred at idle, sending a soft vibration through the dock as a splash of exhaust water pulsed rhythmically beneath the stern. Ray and Tiffany stood near the transom, caught in the familiar mix of sea salt, diesel fumes, and the lazy drift of music from across the lagoon. St. Martin had been good to him—but it was time to move on. St. Thomas—and a few scheduled charters—beckoned.

Tiffany stood on the dock, arms crossed over her tank top, looking every bit the med student she was—except for the rum punch in her hand. Her dark hair was wind-tossed, and her sun-kissed face lingered between a smirk and something softer. Something that looked a lot like regret.

"Well... thanks for securing my dinghy over at the Yacht Club. Can't let the FBI catch me with it just yet; they might figure something out. Doubt it, but maybe." Ray said, trying to lighten the mood. "I'll be back in a few months to pick it up. Maybe pick you up too."

"So this is it? Goodbye?" she asked.

"Our story isn't over yet, so I don't say goodbye—just 'See ya.' Besides, we've got one of the best First Kiss stories anyone's ever gonna have, my little mermaid. I wonder if the FBI would give us a copy of that video? I'll ask Jake." He paused, more serious for a beat. "I still can't believe you agreed to help Jessica. Thank you."

"Well, you did say it would help get her off your boat," Tiffany teased.

"Ah, so it was selfish motivation to eliminate the competition. Damn, that's sexy." Ray gave her a lopsided grin— the kind that had a way of leading to unplanned detours, unforgettable nights, and stories best told on a barstool. "You could still come with me, you know. Ditch the textbooks. Trade them in for sunsets and strong drinks."

She scoffed and rolled her eyes. "Ray, I've got four years of student debt already controlling my life—and two more years of med school to go. This isn't exactly something you just 'give up.'"

Ray considered leaning in, but the weight of her words grounded him. The idea of what might have been hovered just out of reach, tangled in the reality of her path—and his. He wondered, fleetingly, if she ever thought about it too. If she ever imagined another version of life, one that didn't involve fluorescent lights and hospital rotations.

But the moment passed, slipping away like a wave retreating from shore.

"Fair. But if you ever dream of a life less ordinary, I'll swoop in pirate-style to steal you away. We'll stock up on Tequila and Fireball and sail off into the sunset. You can be my ship's surgeon, patching me up after too much sun, too much rum, and too many bad ideas."

Tiffany laughed, shaking her head. "Great. Nothing like knowing my backup plan involves high-seas kidnapping and excessive drinking."

Ray placed one foot on the transom of *Purrfection*, gripping the rail for balance. "Hey, ship's surgeon is a noble title. On pirate ships, they were rarely formally trained. I'm sure your med school skills will help someone down island. We'll start a new charity. Call it 'Doctors Without Degrees.'"

She took a sip of her drink, the cool sweetness cutting through the ache that had crept into her chest. A part of her still wondered—what if she did go? But responsibility reeled her back in. She looked up at him, more serious now.

"You sure you'll be okay sailing alone? At night?"

"I don't *like* sailing solo," he admitted. "But I don't really have a choice, do I, Doc? Gotta time the bridge opening, sail all night, and pick up my mooring in Red Hook in the morning light."

Tiffany stepped closer and reached up to squeeze his hand. "Take care, Ray."

He looked down at her and gave a lazy salute, tapping his temple. "You too, Doc. Study hard so you can go save lives someday—and don't let the Caribbean, the Fireball, or some drunken sailor like me knock you off course. See ya."

With that, he stepped aboard and pulled the last dock line onto the deck. The engines hummed to life as he guided *Purrfection* away from the dock, her bow slowly turning toward the bridge.

Tiffany just waved, shielding her eyes from the sun as he motored away.

Ray exhaled, letting the wind and salt air settle over him like an old friend. The rhythmic slap of the waves against the hull, the distant thump of music from the bar, the familiar hum of departure—it all wrapped around him as he moved toward open water. A pang of loneliness stirred in his chest, then slipped away, replaced by the steady anticipation of the sea.

One long horn blast from the car ferry echoed across the bay—the navigational sound for "*getting underway.*" Ray stirred from his nap after the overnight passage from St. Martin.

The ferry raised its gate, then let out three short blasts, indicating

"*Operating astern propulsion, engines in reverse.*" As the ferry backed out and turned toward St. John, Ray stretched his arms and arched his back.

It was 3 o'clock on a Saturday. Happy Hour.

Ray found a white linen button-down shirt and a pair of shorts, gave them the sniff test, then stuffed them into a dry bag and sealed it. He pulled on clean board shorts and a not-so-clean Purrfection rash guard, slung the dry bag around his back, and dropped a paddle board in the water. Kneeling, he began paddling toward shore, already dreading the wet, upwind slog on the return trip.

Halfway across, he dipped a hand in the Vessup Bay water and splashed his face and the back of his neck. Then he kept paddling.

He tied up under the mangrove tree—close to shore, where dinghies dare not go—and made his way up to Tap & Still, pulling up a stool beside Bud Light Bob.

"Is she gone?" Bob asked, opening the conversation like they'd just spoken yesterday, even though weeks had passed.

"Yep, Bob. She's gone. Somewhere, dunno where. She took my dinghy with her. I had to paddle board in."

"What? She stole your dinghy? What the hell happened in St. Martin?"

A tequila and water appeared in front of Ray, accompanied by a familiar giggle. He raised the glass, nodded to Izzy, took a sip—and choked.

Then, turning to Bob with a wink and a hint of an Irish smirk:

"I never said she *stole* it... It's such a long story, Bob, I could write a book."

He leaned back with a half-grin.

"But at least I made enough to get *Purrfection's* rigging replaced. Should be able to stay afloat another year. Just gotta find more charters... and maybe new crew. Let me get changed into dry clothes, and we'll head over to the Salty Siren and I'll tell ya all about it."

EPILOGUE

November 2022 - Chicago

Jake Lawrence stood at the kitchen counter, absently stirring his coffee as the late afternoon sun filtered through the blinds. The mail sat untouched by the door, a modest pile of bills and junk that had accumulated over the past few days.

He heard the front door swing open.

"Dad!" Brittany's voice cracked through the silence. "Dad, *oh my God*, look at this!"

She came bounding into the room, waving a letter like it was a winning lottery ticket. Her face was flushed with excitement, the way it had been when she got into undergrad, or when she found out she'd aced her MCATs. But this was different—more disbelief than pride.

"I got it. I *finally* got it. A full scholarship. To med school." Jake set down his mug as she shoved the paper into his hands. "In St. Martin!"

His eyes scanned the letter slowly, absorbing each word with growing unease. *The Dr. John Rackham Foundation is pleased to award you a FULL scholarship to attend the American University of the Caribbean...*

Rackham.

Jake didn't even need a second guess. That was Ray's pirate story about Captain John Rackham— Calico Jack.

He blinked at the paper, then looked up at Brittany. She was practically glowing.

"This is... incredible," he managed. "You earned it, kiddo. I'm proud of you."

"I don't even remember applying to this one," she said. "But I must have. Right?" She laughed nervously. "Who cares? I'm going to the Caribbean!"

"Uh, you're going to Med school!" Jake smiled and nodded, pulling her into a hug, but his mind was already elsewhere.

Once she left the room—off to call her mom and her friends—Jake pulled out his phone, using Telegram for messaging.

Jake: **Brittany just got the scholarship letter... You shouldn't have.**

The reply came almost instantly.

Ray: **Aw, you figured it out? You are quick there, Pirate John Lawrence. You might be related to Calico Jake after all.**

Jake: **No, I was serious. You really shouldn't have. This implicates me.**

Ray: **Huh. Does it? Interesting...**

Jake set his phone down and leaned back against the counter, arms crossed. Of course, Ray did this. Sweet and reckless, like always. A Robin Hood with a boat and a conscience, distributing stolen fortune with just enough flair to make it feel like a prank.

He wasn't mad. Not really. He knew the FBI would never figure out what happened, especially with Maxwell in the wind.

He looked back at the letter one more time, thinking about how far the ripples had gone. A failed sting operation, stolen funds, a disappearing agent, and now... a second chance for his daughter. Maybe this wasn't justice. But it was something.

Jake chuckled to himself. "Damn it, Ray."

He folded the letter, tucked it into a drawer, and poured himself another cup of coffee, dutifully preparing for another night surveillance op.

Thank you for reading *Sun, Rum, and Stolen Funds*. If you enjoyed this book, write a review or mention it to a friend. Thanks!

ABOUT THE AUTHOR

Raymond Patrick Kremer was born and raised in Dayton, Ohio, where he graduated from the University of Dayton with a degree in Electrical Engineering. After a brief stint as a U.S. Air Force pilot—cut short when the first Gulf War ended almost as soon as it began—he settled into civilian life, raising a family and building a career as a software engineer.

Once his kids left the house, Ray traded cubicles for catamarans. He sold nearly everything, moved aboard his sailing catamaran *Purrfection* in St. Augustine, Florida, and never looked back. In January 2020, he set course for St. Thomas in the U.S. Virgin Islands to run day charters—just as the world decided to shut down. After a few years of running charters with mixed results, he chose to explore farther afield, sailing deeper into the Caribbean – St. Kitts, St. Barths, Guadeloupe, Dominica, Martinique, St. Lucia, St. Vincent and the Grenadines, Grenada, and Trinidad.

These days, Ray still lives aboard *Purrfection*, sailing between islands, diving reefs, exploring beaches, and raising a glass at sunset. His stories draw from a life lived on the water, where every port hides a new tale and every happy hour has its own kind of wisdom.

ALSO BY RAYMOND PATRICK

The Misadventures of Ray De Soleil

Sun, Rum, and Stolen Funds [Book 1]

Sun, Rum, and Hidden Treasure [Book 2]

www.ingramcontent.com/pod-product-compliance
Lightning Source LLC
LaVergne TN
LVHW091715070526
838199LV00050B/2408